UNTIL

the

WHEELS FALL OFF

Natasha,
Congratulations!
I hope you enjoy!
Sorry for the delay!
Happy Reading!
Kay Shanee

Until the Wheels Fall Off

Kay Shanee

AboutFace Media AFM, LLC

Georgia

AboutFace Media AFM

www.AboutFaceMediaAFM.com

This book is a work of fiction. Names, characters, places, and incidents either are products of the author's imagination or are used fictitiously. Any resemblance to actual events or locales or persons, living or dead, is entirely coincidental.

First Edition

10 9 8 7 6 5 4 3 2 1

Manufactured in the United States of America.

DEDICATION

This book is dedicated to my college sweetheart. When I started writing this story, it was supposed to be about how our love story began. Then I realized that our relationship didn't have enough drama to keep the readers interested. We had our share of drama but I allowed my imagination to take the character's relationships to places that I'm grateful ours never went. But I'm still riding with you until the wheels fall off baby.

ACKNOWLEDGMENTS

I would like to thank my husband for going down memory lane with me, as I tried to remember our college days and update them to current times. Thank you to my college roommate and teammate, and our son's Godmother, for being a good sport about a character kinda, sorta being based off of her but not completely and totally. Thank you to my husband's college roommate, our daughter's Godfather, and our brother from another mother and father, for allowing me to base a character off of him and giving me the liberty to falsify some actual events. To anyone else that I may have loosely given you a part in this imaginary life that I created in my head, remember, this is a true story based on false events that happened but never really happened.

ABOUT THE AUTHOR

Kay Shanee is a forty something wife and mother, born and raised in the Midwest. During the day she is a high school teacher. In her free time, she enjoys spending her time with her family and friends. Her favorite pastime is reading romance novels by authors that look like her. She enjoys it so much that she decided to become one of them.

SYNOPSIS

Track star, Karizma "Rizzy" Davis is ready to lose the dead weight that is her boyfriend, Marcus, and start her freshman year of college single and free. However, when Marcus doesn't want to let go, Taylen comes along and saves her, eager for a place in her heart. But does Taylen really want to deal with all of the drama that seems to follow Rizzy?

Football star, Taylen Andrews is what every girl dreams of. Tall, dark, handsome, and smart. Being that he can pull any girl on campus, he has no desire to be tied down to just one. Until Karizma catches his eye.

Chapter 1

Karizma Davis

I stood in the room that my younger sister Kayla and I shared in our two-bedroom apartment, looking over my luggage. My excitement is almost uncontrollable. I can't believe the day is finally here. I'm leaving for college in a matter of hours and I couldn't be more excited. I've been dreaming of the day that I could leave my mother's house and my hometown. Don't get me wrong, I love my mom, I just don't love all of her rules. Growing up in Waukegan, IL wasn't horrible, but it wasn't the greatest. By the time I got to high school, my mom divorced her first husband, Joseph, who is my sister's dad, and we moved to the neighboring town of Gurnee. It was cool, but none of the friends that I grew up with lived near me and initially, I didn't like it. Eventually, I became close with a few people so overall, it wasn't so bad.

Being in a new environment and not knowing anyone, caused me to be rebellious. I got into numerous fights and was suspended several times. Running track was my saving grace. It was the only thing that kept me out of trouble and motivated. Then my mom had the nerve to remarry and her new husband, Wade, is an ass. Hell, if she would get rid of him, I wouldn't be so anxious to leave. They've been married for two miserable years. I swear that man thinks he's God's gift to women. He is often unemployed, so my mom pretty much carries us financially most of the time. Her marrying him put more of a strain on our relationship. I was looking forward to it just being me, her and my sister. But I suppose my mom didn't feel like she could make it on her own.

Her first husband, Joseph, was physically abusive towards her from the time they started dating. It's beyond me how they made it to the altar, but they were married for seven years. I hated his ass more than I do her current husband, Wade. Joseph would beat the shit out of my mom, right in front of me. I called myself jumping on him several times when he was beating her, even pulled a butcher knife on him once. But nothing stopped him when he got in that "zone".

My mom, Jacinda, got pregnant with me her senior year of high school and her and my dad haven't been together since she gave him the news. They never married, which is a good thing because he ain't about shit anyway. I'm the oldest of my dad's seven kids with three other baby mamas. Need I say more! It's clear to me that my mother has a poor choice in men. I feel like she is afraid to be alone.

As beautiful as she is, her self-esteem leaves a lot to be desired. Her skin is the same color as caramel and it's always so smooth and soft. Whenever I'm out with my mom, she turned the heads of many men. I've seen her stop traffic. Why she chose the most good for nothing ass men all time was beyond me. Maybe one day she'll get it together.

But anyway, my boyfriend, Marcus, and his dad will be coming to our apartment to pick me up in a couple of hours to make this six-hour drive to Carbondale, IL. He lives in another neighboring town, North Chicago, which is about twenty minutes from my house. Speaking of my boyfriend...UGH! I was hoping he would be my ex-boyfriend by now. However, back in February, when I told him that I was accepting the scholarship offer to run track from Southern Illinois University at Carbondale (yes, ya girl is fast), his ass decided that he wanted to go there as well. I wanted to punch him in his mouth when he told me that shit! But instead, I pretended like I was excited and I don't know how in the hell I'm going to end this shit.

We've been dating for about ten months and it started off cool. But after about three months of dating, he became overbearing. Then he started talking about marriage and that's when I knew that I this needed to be over. Shit, I'm eighteen years old and marriage is the furthest thing from my mind. Even if I was thinking about it, I wouldn't marry his ass! I just don't know how to break it off, so I pretend everything is all good.

"Rizzzyyy!" I heard my mom yelling for the second time as I opened the door.

"Yeah Ma?" I replied.

"Didn't you hear me calling you? I packed some snacks for you to take with you on the road. Make sure you have everything because we don't have the money to be mailing large packages."

"That's what I was doing before I was interrupted," I mumbled under my breath as I rolled my eyes.

"I know you ain't gettin' smart! Are you tryin' to get your ass beat before you leave?" she fussed at me with her hand on her hip, frowning.

"Naw, ma, but I was just checking my stuff to make sure I have everything," I said, trying to fix that up real quick.

I shook my head, once I rounded the corner and was back in my room. As you can see, my mom don't play and she will still beat my ass. Me being eighteen means absolutely nothing to her. Hell, I just got my ass beat a couple of months ago for going to the movies with my lame ass boyfriend after she told me I couldn't go. You see why I'm excited to leave! Let me finish all of my packing and put my shit by the damn door!

*****

A few hours passed, and Marcus and his dad arrived to pick me up. My mom and his dad knew each other from back in the day so they were catching up. Yeah, I know, small world. As they were talking, my boyfriend took my stuff to the car to load into the trailer that they had rented.

I said goodbye to my sister, who is eleven years old. She drove me crazy most of the time, but I'm going to miss her annoying ass. My mom always thought I was a handful, but my sister is making me look like an angel. I hope my mom can handle her without my assistance. For some reason, Kayla seems to listen to me more than she listens to my mom.

I hugged my sister, who was already crying. "Kay, I'll be back to visit. Stop all this crying sis."

"I know, I'm just going to miss you. And who's gonna listen to my side of the story when I get in trouble," she cried, with her head in my chest. Kayla is tiny for her age because she has Sickle Cell Anemia.

"Kayla, how are you already planning to get in trouble? If you just act right, you and Mommy will get along just fine. Stop fuckin' up," I whispered in her ear. "You gotta try to do better."

I think Kayla uses her illness as an excuse to why she misbehaves. She was held back in first grade because she was sick so much that she missed half the school year. Even now, she misses a lot of school and falls behind in her school work a lot. Instead of trying to get caught up she acts out in class.

"I know, Rizzy, I will." She hugged me one last time.

I walked over to my mom, who stood off to the side, watching the exchange between Kayla and I, waiting her turn. As much as we argued, the love I have for my mom is unconditional. My issue with her has always been about the men that she has allowed into her life and let break her spirit. I pray that she will soon learn to love herself.

"I'm gonna miss you Rizzy. Don't get to that school and lose your damn mind. I know we have our issues, but you know I love you and I'm very proud of you. Just keep making me proud." She hugged me and kissed my cheek.

"I'm gonna miss you to Ma. I'll do my best to keep making you proud. I love you!" Then the tears were flowing from all three of us while Marcus and his dad looked on.

"You guys drive safe and make sure you call me when you get there," my mom told me.

"Okay, I will. Love you!

"Love you more baby!" She gave me one more kiss and hug.

Marcus got in the front passenger seat while I got in the back. His dad spoke a few more words to my mom before he got behind the wheel and we hit the road. I had six hours to figure out how I'm gonna break up with his ass. Let the planning begin.

As you can see, I didn't mention saying goodbye to my mom's husband. People always ask me why I don't refer to him as my stepdad. He's an asshole and I don't like him so I refuse to acknowledge him as anything other than her husband. I was happy to not have to see his face before I hit the road. He knows how I feel about him so I wasn't surprised that he didn't show up to say goodbye to me.

Chapter 2

Taylen Andrews

Two weeks have passed and it's time for the rest of the student population to start arriving. I'm on the football team at Southern Illinois University at Carbondale and we had to arrive on campus at the beginning of August for football practice and camp. There haven't been very many people on campus because summer classes ended before we arrived and the fall semester has yet to begin. That means that the number of women that we had to choose from around here these past couple of weeks was very slim. I suppose since I got a girl back home in Chicago, I shouldn't be thinking about other women anyway. But that's never stopped me before so it definitely won't now. I've managed to stay out of trouble since football has taken up most of my time anyway and I've been exhausted from practicing in this hot ass sun all damn day.

Growing up on the Southside of Chicago wasn't as bad as the media portrays, but it could be a challenge at times. I'm the oldest of three and my parents expect me to be the example for my fourteen-year-old sister and nine-year-old brother. There is some gang activity in the neighborhoods and I've had my share of involvement. Some of my friends are still involved, unless they are dead or in jail. What saved me was when I was recruited to go to Leo Catholic High School to play basketball during my 8th grade year. Although, I received a football scholarship to SIUC, back then, basketball was my thing. The neighborhood gang bangers saw my talent, along with the talent of a few other neighborhood kids, and started placing bets on us when we played at the neighborhood park. Word got around that I was being recruited by Leo and instead of allowing me to get more caught up in the gang life, the gangbangers encouraged me to play ball. They even came to my high school basketball and football games, even though I'm sure it was because they were making bets. But because they wouldn't let me gang bang anymore, I just began to focus on school, football and basketball.

I haven't had much free time since I've been on campus, it was either practicing, watching film, eating, or sleeping. I'm glad that the season is about to officially start because I almost feel like it will be easier than camp. Not to mention that I'm tired of looking at these dusty ass niggas. I'm ready to slide up in something warm and wet so I'm glad classes are starting next week. Being on the football team, I should have no problems finding some pussy to get into. I'm sure they will be throwing it at me. I ain't a conceited nigga but I know I look good. I'm a starting freshman on the football team, playing outside linebacker, so my body is solid and all muscle. The ladies seem to love it so that's all that matters. I guess I'd better get my ass to practice.

Chapter 3

Karizma

This had to be the longest six-hour drive known to man. I sat in the backseat alone for the entire ride, even though Marcus tried to sit back there with me after we stopped for gas the first time. I told him that I was tired and wanted to be able to stretch out. If we didn't get there soon, I was contemplating jumping out of the window. Marcus and his dad are so much alike that it's sickening. The whole ride, they've been going back and forth about the dumbest shit. I mean shit that don't even have a right or wrong answer. Who does that? These two idiots, that's who! Don't get me wrong, I appreciate the ride but being in a car with the two of them got me thinking suicidal thoughts. Thankfully, we got off at an exit and the GPS says that we will be there in 20 mins. Finally! I let out a huge sigh of relief.

The only good thing about the ride is that I was able to think about how I was going to break up with this nigga. Marcus is a nice guy and extremely smart. But his personality is overwhelming and obnoxious most of the time. This is my first long-term relationship so I didn't know what to expect. However, as the weeks and months passed, he just got more and more annoying and I felt smothered. He tried to clock all my moves, didn't want me to hang out with my friends, and wanted us to spend every free moment together. He even tried checking my phone on a few occasions. We argue all the time because there is no way I'm about to let him run my life like that. It's been time for this to be over.

When we pulled on campus, it was pure chaos. Families unloading cars, luggage everywhere, not to mention when we arrived at the dorm, the line for the elevators was ridiculous. My soon-to-be ex wasn't living in the same building even though dorms were co-ed. Thankfully, we came to my dorm first because my nerves were getting bad. It was so crowded that we had to wait about thirty minutes before we were able to get on the elevator. But we made it to Room 817 and I unlocked the door.

"Oh my God! Finally! I thought I'd never get here!" I dropped the bag that I was carrying and fell on the bed that I assumed was mine because my roommate was already settled in on the other.

"Yeah, that was a long ride. Do you need us to do anything else before I go find my room?" Marcus asked as he sat the bags that he was carrying next to my bed and glanced around the room.

"No, I think I'm good. I'm gonna just get unpacked a bit and see what's up with my roomy. I have her number already because we spoke over the summer. Do you wanna hook up in a few hours? Maybe walk around campus?" I rambled as I began moving things around.

"Yeah, that's cool. Just hit me up when you're ready." He leaned in to kiss me and I turned so that he pecked my cheek. He looked at me sideways but I guess he didn't feel like arguing so he let it slide.

"Thank you, Mr. Briggs. I appreciate the ride and you getting me here safely." I hugged him before they turned to leave.

"No problem, young lady. Don't forget to let your mom know that you're here safely," Mr. Briggs replied, hugging me back.

Once they were on the other side of the door, I closed and locked it, releasing a deep breath as I leaned against it. "I've got to break up with his ass. Lord don't let me punk out! "

*****

About two hours later, my clothes were put away and the bed made. I was just about to jump in the shower and the sound of the key turning in the door caught my attention.

"Ahhhhhhh! You're here!" Hazel screamed as she pushed open the door. Her long legs allowed her to cross the room quickly.

We hugged each other. You would think that we've known each other our entire lives but this is our first time seeing each other in person. Over the summer, we face-timed each other all the time and texted each other every day. We were both excited about starting this new journey together.

Hazel is on the track team as well, but her specialty is the 800-meter run, whereas I run the 100, 200, and 400-meter races, with the 400-meter being my specialty.

"Yes girl! I've been here for about two hours. Marcus and his dad dropped me off and went to his dorm. The whole ride down I was trying to figure out how I'm gonna dump his ass. I plan to do it tonight. I wanna start this year off free and clear of all the bullshit," I told Hazel as I continued gathering my things for the shower.

"I can't believe you didn't do it this summer. I was sure you'd be ready to kick it tonight since we only have a few days before classes start." When she laughed, her hazel eyes sparkled.

"I know! I swear I planned to, but I just couldn't. It didn't make it easier that he has a car and I don't. I needed to be able to get around this summer and he always let me use his car while he was at work. It was just too convenient for me." I shrugged.

Hazel just shook her head and her medium-sized afro swayed from side-to-side as she laughed. The little patch of hair that was dyed bronze complemented her caramel complexion.

Hazel plugged in her iPhone 7 as she told me, "Well, good luck! I just came to charge my phone. I see you were about to shower so you go ahead and finish. I met some others from the track team and I'm gonna go hang with them. I'll be back in about 30 minutes."

Hazel left and I showered and got dressed. I decided to wear some denim shorts, that were pretty short and exposed my muscular legs, and a black tank, with no bra because I hate them. My boobs aren't the biggest anyway, but they are a nice handful and perky. I complemented the look with some black flat sandals. Just as I finished touching up my hair with my flat irons, Hazel came back into the room.

"Look at you! You better not chicken out!" Hazel exclaimed while smiling and giving me the once over.

"He just sent me a text to meet him in the lobby. The next time you see me, I will be a single woman," I said as I grabbed my purse and headed for the door.

*****

As I rode the elevator down to the lobby, my thoughts were on how this breakup would turn out. The elevator doors opened and Marcus sat on a couch directly across from the doors, focused on his phone. I stepped off of the elevator just as he happened to look up. He smiled and got up to meet me halfway. Marcus is fine and I'm gonna miss seeing his handsome face. His good looks aren't worth me staying in this relationship, though.

"Hey!" he greeted me and leaned in to kiss me. Since this was the last time that was going to be happen, I let him have that.

"Hey yourself! How's your room? Is your roommate here yet?" I asked as I led him towards the doors.

"My room is cool. But my roommate won't get here until Saturday. I have the room all to myself tonight and tomorrow night. You should come and stay with me." He cheesed, showing all thirty-two teeth. I knew that me spending the night with him would have made his entire life.

"I don't know about that. Let's just take a walk and maybe grab a bite to eat somewhere on campus for now." I gave him a tight smile.

"Okay." He placed his hand on the small of my back as we walked towards the doors.

We maneuvered our way around the students and relatives helping them move in and made our exit . We walked, silently for a bit.

"Are you excited about track and classes starting?" Marcus asked, breaking the silence.

"Yeah! I'm a little nervous about track. Not sure what to expect," I replied.

"I'm sure you'll be fine. You know you're a beast!" He paused and stopped walking to face me. "What's up with you? You've been acting funny since we left home. Something wrong?"

"Nothing's wrong, exactly."

"Are you sure?"

Now is as good a time as any. "Well, I'm not sure how to say this." I paused nervously, turning away from him and walking again.

"Say what?" he asked, following me.

"I just think it's time for us to---"

"To what? Make love? That's why I want you to spend the night with me. You don't have to be nervous about it if that's what's worrying you. I'll be gentle," he cut me off.

"Marcus, what I was going to say is that I think we need to take a break." I stopped walking again and turned to face him.

"What do you mean, take a break? As in breakup?" Looking confused, he grabbed my wrists.

He held my wrists so tightly that it made me nervous. I know I need to choose my words carefully but I don't know how to break this to him gently.

"Yes. I don't think that now is a good time to be in a relationship . Things with us have been rocky for awhile and I don't want the stress of being in a relationship right now. I want to focus on school and track." I yanked away from him.

"Not a good time! Are you saying that I stress you out? What the fuck is that supposed to mean Karizma?" he yelled, causing a few people looked in our direction.

"How the fuck are you gonna breakup with me now?" he continued. "I chose this school because of you, to be close to you, so we could be together!" The look of rage in his eyes scared me.

"I didn't make you choose this school, Marcus. I don't want to be in a serious relationship right now." My heartrate picked up and I backed away.

Marcus paced back and forth in front of me and the crowd of people grew around us. God, I hope no one is recording this.

"So you think you can just break it off with me, just like that? Do you think I'm gonna let you go that easily? Naw fuck that! We ain't breaking up!" He leaned in and I could feel the heat from his breath.

"I wasn't giving you an option. I'm telling you that it's over. I don't want to be with you anymore. You can't make me stay in a relationship with you!" I tried to push him away from me and move around him. He grabbed my arms and pulled me into his chest. His eyes were dark and filled with anger. I've never seen this side of him before. He looked crazed.

"You can't just fuckin' end us like this. We ain't over. I'm not letting you go. You can forget that shit right now!" he screamed in my face and shook me by my shoulders. The crowd got thicker but no one came to my assistance.

"Let me go! You can't make me stay with you if I don't want to. That's not how this works. Let - me - the - fuck - go!" I tried to wiggle my way out of his grasp. He was too strong and I wasn't doing anything but tiring myself out. The hold he had on me was too tight.

He backed me up against the wall and pushed his hand into my chest, all while shouting in my face. I don't even know what he was saying anymore because I was trying to figure out why in the hell nobody was helping me.

Chapter 4

Taylen

Another long football practice is over and I'm freshly showered and on my way back to my dorm room. As I neared my building, I saw some commotion off to the side. I walked in the direction of the crowd and heard a female voice.

"Let me go! You can't make me stay with you if I don't want to. That's not how this works. Let - me - the - fuck - go!" the female screamed, as I worked my way to the front of the crowd.

"What's going on here?" I asked no one in particular.

"It sounds like ole girl just broke up with him but he ain't havin' it," some random dude answered.

"I'm not letting you go! You coming to my room so we can talk this shit out. We not breaking up Karizma!" the guy screamed in her face while pulling her by the arm.

"I'm not going with you. Let me go, you're hurting me!" the girl spat back and struggled to get her arm out of his grasp. I could see the fear in her eyes and hearing those words set off my alarm. I moved in close to them and tapped the guy on the shoulder. He turned and looked at me, while still holding her arm.

"Aye homie, she asked you to let her go," I stated very calmly. There is no way I'm gonna knowingly allow him to put his hands on her and walk away.

"Mind your fuckin' business and get the fuck on. This has nothing to do with you," he stated.

"I realize that, but she clearly said she didn't want to go with you and asked you to let her go!" I raised my voice an octave.

"Look," he let her go and turned his full body towards me, "this ain't your fuckin' business so I suggest you get the fuck on."

She rubbed her wrist as she moved away from him. I took a quick look at shorty and she was fine as fuck. I probably wouldn't want to let her go either.

"I'm not about to stand here and watch you put your hands on her. If she said she's done, just let it be homie. Don't force the situation." I turned to walk toward the girl to see if she was okay.

This nigga grabbed me by my shoulder, attempted to turn me around, and swung. Luckily I'm quick on my feet. I ducked and tackled him to the ground. I was able to get off a few punches before I felt some arms pulling me away. It didn't take long for me to realize that it was a couple of my teammates. I'm glad they stopped me because the last thing I need is to get in trouble with my coaches.

Once they calmed me down, I looked around and saw the girl walking fast as hell back towards the dorms. I jogged to catch up with her to see if she was okay. Damn, she's fine!

"Aye, you good?" I touched her shoulder and felt a spark. I moved my hand away quickly, as she did the same with her shoulder. She must have felt that too.

"Umm, yeah. Thanks for your help. I can't believe people were standing around watching and you were the first to do something." She gave an uncomfortable smile, while still rubbing her wrist, as she slowed her pace a bit.

"Well, you know how people are these days. They'd rather record it for the 'gram than help. Can I walk you somewhere? I see you're rubbing your wrist. Are you sure you're good?" I asked.

From a distance, we heard someone yelling and looked back to see that it was her guy, or rather, ex guy. "This is not fuckin' over Rizzy! This shit ain't over until I say it's over. Do you fuckin' hear me? I'm glad I was fuckin' other bitches since your ass act like you couldn't give a nigga no pussy. Fuck that! I've been way too patient with your ass for you to come at me with this bullshit. We ain't fuckin' over!" I guess he finally picked himself up off of the ground.

She looked completely embarrassed by the whole situation and picked up her pace, without saying a word.

"Hey!" I jogged to catch up with her again. "Let me walk with you and make sure you get to your destination safely. I'm Taylen, by the way. My friends call me Tay." I stuck my hand out for her to shake but she ignored it.

"I'm good, I don't need an escort." She brushed by me and continued walking. I'm not sure why she felt she could outpace me, but she gave it a shot.

"So, I risked my scholarship trying to save your cute ass and you won't even let a nigga walk with you? That's cold!"

"Look, I'm sorry. I just want to get away from this entire scene." She stopped walking and covered her face with her hands briefly, shaking her head, before she continued. "I do appreciate you, Taylen. I'm just trying to get back to my room. I'm embarrassed enough as it is. Thank you again." She turned to start walking again.

"Wait a sec. Hold up! You're not gonna get rid of me that easily. What building do you stay in? Let me just walk you to your building," I persisted. I hate to admit it, but I was feeling shorty and I wanted to make sure that she was okay. Not just physically but emotionally as well.

"I stay in Neely. It's just right there so I'm good." No matter what I said to her, she insisted on brushing me off. However, I wasn't about to let that happen.

"Well, aren't you lucky? I stay in Neely too. Let's go." I turned and walked towards Neely Hall with her right next to me. "So, I'm gathering your name is Rizzy?"

She sighed before answering and rolled her eyes. "No, it's actually Karizma. But my friends and family call me Rizzy."

"What do you want me to call you?" I asked, looking to the left a little bit and caught of glimpse of her legs. *Damn!*

"Karizma is fine." The tone of her voice let me know that I was annoying her. *Why was I unbothered by that?*

"Oh, so it's like that. I'm not your friend?" I questioned her.

"I don't even know you so...I would say no." Her mouth said no but I finally got a smile out of her.

"I'd like to be your friend Karizma, if that's okay. I mean, I did just kinda help you out of a crazy situation," I said whatever I could so that she wouldn't kick a me to the curb already.

"It's the least you can do," I persisted.

When she smiled again, those cute ass dimples were on display. "I suppose we could work towards being friends. Are you sure you wanna be associated with me after this mess?" she hesitated before asking while looking down at her feet.

We made it to Neely Hall and I held the door open for her as we entered the building. "It's gonna take a little more than that to scare me away, pretty girl." I winked at her when she looked up at me and she gave me another smile.

I let her walk in front of me as we went towards the elevators so that I could see what that ass was looking like. *It's perfect!* We stood in front of the elevators in quietly. When the doors opened, we got on and I pressed four and she pressed eight as the doors closed.

"I guess you can put your number in my phone," she hesitated, as she handed me her phone and our hands touched in the process. *There goes that spark again!* I think she felt it too. I shook the feeling off and called myself from her phone so that I could have her number as well.

The doors opened to the fourth floor and I said, "Use my number, anytime, pretty girl." I walked off backwards as the doors closed.

As soon as I walked into my room, my roommate, Bishop, grilled me about what happened. Hell, I didn't have much to say because I only knew what I saw, which was pretty much the same thing that everyone else saw .

"Man dawg, I don't know what the deal is with shorty and ole boy but it looks to me like she dumped his ass and he wasn't trying to be dumped," I told Bishop as I flopped down on my bed.

"I saw you walking with her. She ain't say nothing?" Bishop asked.

"Not about him or that situation. I got her number though. I plan on hittin' her up. Shorty bad!"

"Nigga, don't you got a whole girlfriend at home?"

"So the fuck what! You know that shit is 'bout dead! I'm trying to see wassup with Miss Karizma." I laughed.

Bishop looked at me sideways and shook his head. He and I been boys since eighth grade so he knows my girl. He also knew how I got down so I don't even know why he mentioned her at all.

"Man, she gon' fuck you up if she come down here and find out you fuckin' around," Bishop warned.

Her name is Imani and she's a junior in high school. We've been dating for a little more than a year but if I'm honest with myself, I ain't been feeling her for a minute. I'm hoping that the long distance causes us to grow apart. Well, more so causes her to lose interest in me because she's never had my heart. She's just been someone I could get pussy from on the regular. I've never been faithful and I've had a few other girls in rotation during our entire relationship and that's not even mentioning the ones I've gotten head from. I've never been fully committed to her. She was a sophomore and I was a senior when we started dating and she let me hit it after a week and I wasn't her first. I've never taken our relationship serious.

Imani is what many would call a typical hood girl. She is a brown-skinned beauty that has had the body of a grown woman since she hit puberty. Her hair is always in a weave down the middle of her back and I don't know what her real hair even looks like. She can be real messy when she wants to be. The whole time I've been dating her, every other week she was involved in some kind of drama with her friends. I just chalked it up to her being a couple of years younger than me and less mature. She has no desire to do anything with her life. Anytime we talk about the future, she has no idea what she wants to do after high school, except not go to college. She said school ain't her thing and she just wants to graduate from high school. I have a feeling that her plan is to get knocked up by a nigga that's paid so she can be taken care of for the rest of her life. I should have broken up with her before leaving for college but I didn't want to seem like an asshole because I'm not about to be her meal ticket.

"She'll be alright. I'm gon' always do me and she knows that shit."

"Yeah, if you say so. Aye, you ready to go to dinner? I'm hungry as hell," he announced, changing the subject.

"I was working so hard trying to get Karizma's number that I forgot all about eating," I joked. "Let's go!"

"Damn she got you like that already! Let me find out you in love and ain't even hit it yet!" Bishop joked back.

"I ain't gon' say all that. But umm, I do wanna see wassup with shorty. Did you see her? She fine as fuck!"

"Yeah, I'd hit that fa sho!" Bishop raised his hand up for a fist bump and I looked at him like he was crazy. For some reason, I already feel like she's mine.

"Nigga she off limits to you and anybody else for that matter!" I threw my pillow at him for even thinking about her like that.

We locked up our room and made our way to the dining hall across from our dorm building. The lobby of our building was swarming with people. Seems like parents have been dropping off kids all damn day. I guess it'll be this way for the next few days since classes start Monday.

We admired the view as we walked through the line. There were some fine ass females walking around here and it just made me happy. This campus has been a ghost town for the last two weeks and just seeing all of the ladies put a smile on my face.

"It's gon' be hard just choosing one," Bishop stated while he marveled at the beautiful ladies.

"I feel you on that. I'm in need of some pussy or some head. Both would be ideal! I'm sure one of these lovely ladies would be happy to oblige. But how you gon' talk about me having a girl at home and you know your baby mama is crazy as fuck. Are ya'll together or are you just co-parenting?" I asked as we sat a table with some of our teammates.

"Man, don't even mention her right now. We just co-parenting. Everything was cool before I left for camp. My mom and sister are helping her out, picking up my slack because I'm here. I know it's not the same as me being there but what the fuck does she want me to do? Her ass been trippin' the last few times I talked to her so I don't know what's up with her."

Karizma and her friend caught my attention as they got up from their table with their trays. She looked my way and I gave her a wink. She smiled, showing off those sexy dimples. Damn Karizma is beautiful, with the most perfect legs I've ever seen. I wonder if she works out a lot. Her friend is fine too, Karizma is just more my type, a dark-skinned beauty. She has shoulder length hair, deep dimples on both cheeks, and long eyelashes.

"Damn, she fine as fuck! That's you Tay?" one of my teammates, Keith commented.

"Naw, not yet. But she will be!" I had to stake my claim early.

"Who the fuck is ole girl with her? She bad!" Bishop expressed.

"Man, I barely know Karizma so how the fuck am I supposed to know her friend?" I looked at him, confused.

"My bad! I need you to get to know her so she can introduce me to her friend."

"What the hell do I look like? A matchmaker? Go talk to her yourself if you want to know who she is," I teased Bishop.

"I'm just gon' wait a lil bit. School ain't even started and she don't look like the type to just hand out the pussy and pussy is what I'm trying to get into," Bishop said, high-fiving me.

"Karizma don't strike me as one that's gon' just give up the pussy real quick either. But she's gon' be mine, regardless."

Damn near every male and female in the cafeteria watched them as they walked to the front to put away their trays. I may have to lock her down sooner rather than later, before one of these other niggas snatches her up.

Chapter 5

Karizma

I cannot believe my first day on campus has been this eventful. Marcus showed his entire ass today and honestly, I'm glad Taylen came along when he did. I have never seen Marcus act that way and it scared me.

Even though I ended my relationship barely hour ago, this Taylen guy has peaked my interest. He seems to be genuinely nice and it says a lot that he helped me when he could have just kept it moving. Especially considering all the people that just stood by and watched or recorded on their phones.

As I walked to our room, I received a text from Hazel saying to meet her by the dining hall. I continued on to our room to drop my purse off and went to meet Hazel. As soon as she saw me walking up, she ran over to me and hugged me.

"Girl, please tell me that this is not you and that nigga Marcus all in my Snap," she whispered loudly.

"Ummm, what do you mean?" I questioned, playing clueless.

"You know exactly what I mean. People are posting this shit like crazy," she went to her Snapchat and showed me a few stories. "I would ask what happened but I figured that shit out from all these stories. I've seen at least one from every angle. I guess he didn't take the breakup too well. And, you got a knight in shining armor coming to your rescue too! Who is he?"

"It's not that serious, Hazel. Taylen is his name and that's all I know about him. I'm glad that he stepped in when he did, cause nobody else did shit. But let's not think more into it," I told her.

We walked into the dining hall as we talked and proceeded through the line, making our food selections.

"Did you get his number?" Hazel inquired.

"I just broke up with Marcus. Why would I get his number ?" I turned to give her the side-eye.

"So you gave him your number?" Hazel was persistent.

"I gave him my phone and he called himself." I smirked.

"Yes, bitch! That's what I call moving on! Now let's find somewhere to sit."

While we ate, I filled Hazel in on what happened with Marcus. I noticed Taylen walk by our table with another guy but he didn't look my way so I didn't say anything. When we finished eating, we got up and walked towards the front of the dining hall to put our trays away.

As we walked past Taylen's table, he and I made eye contact and he winked. I couldn't help but smile. I overheard one of the guys at the table say to him, "Damn, she fine as fuck! That's you Tay?"

"Naw, not yet. But she will be!" He never broke eye contact with me and my stomach had butterflies. I had to end our staring contest before I ran into a wall.

"Earth to Rizzy!!! What the heck are you daydreaming about?" she asked, following my gaze. "Oh my! He is fine as hell. I couldn't see much on the video but yeah, you should definitely bust it wide open for that nigga!"

"Shut up! I am not trying to jump from one relationship to another. I am not busting shit open for nobody." I shoved her lightly on her shoulder.

"I'm just saying. That nigga can surely get it. But umm, who is his friend?"

"Hell if I know!"

"Shit! He can certainly be Zaddy," Hazel expressed.

"You're on your own. It looks like they both must be on the football team since they sat at that table with all of those other big, greedy niggas. I also remember Taylen saying that he risked losing his scholarship trying to save me." I laughed.

"That's even better! I guess I'll to keep an eye on him!" Hazel said, looking at Taylen's friend like he was a whole damn meal.

"So what's poppin' tonight?" I asked Hazel, changing the subject. Her ass knew everything for some reason.

"There are a couple of clubs on the strip that we can go to. A few of the frats are throwing something at their houses too. But I think we should go to the party at the Student Center."

"Whatever you wanna do, I'm down!"

We went back to our room to get ready for some fun tonight. I sat on my bed and I grabbed my phone, turning it back on. I had turned it off before we went to dinner because Marcus kept calling. Once it powered back on, I immediately went to his number and blocked his ass. I'm done thinking about his crazy ass. It's time to enjoy my first night as a college student!

Chapter 6

Taylen

We finished up dinner and went back to the room. Technically, the football team is still on restriction and have a curfew of ten pm. However, Bishop and I plan on sneaking out once the coaches do bed check.

"What's good tonight? Have you heard about any parties?" I asked Bishop as we walked back to our room.

"There are a few parties going on but I think we should stay close to campus and go to the one at the Student Center. It'll be more low-key since we ain't supposed to have our asses out anyway."

I laughed. "True! Yeah that sounds like a plan. I'm about to take a quick nap then until they come by for bed check. Whatchu 'bout to get into?"

"I ain't tired so I'm about to go kick it with Steve and Jay. Play some 2K or something." We dapped each other up and he left.

Just as I was about to lay down, there was a knock at the door. I figured Bishop forgot his key and opened it without asking who it was or looking through the peephole. To my surprise, it was a girl that I think worked somewhere on campus because I've seen her around these last two weeks.

"Oh, uhh, hey! I thought you were my roommate coming back for something. How can I help you?" I asked her.

"Hey...hi, I'm Faryn." She stuck out her hand for me to shake and I did.

"I'm Tay...can I help you with something?" I asked again. She's a cute girl but nothing about her stood out for me.

"Uhh, yeah. Well, umm, no. Not really. I live across the hall so I thought I'd come by and introduce myself."

"Oh, okay cool! I'm on the football team and I've been here a couple of weeks. I've seen you around. Do you work on campus or something?"

"Yes, I work in the Bursar's Office. This is my second year here. Umm, are you busy?"

I realized we were still standing at the door. I guess I can wait a few minutes before I take my nap.

"No, no, you can come in if you like. I'm just chillin'. Was actually gon' try to take a nap." I stepped to the side, giving her some room to come in.

I took a quick peek at her ass and I must say, shorty had a nice one. She wore some short dark denim shorts, a white tank top, with some white converse sneakers. She ain't have nothing on Karizma in the looks or body department. *Wait, did I just compare her to Karizma?*

She sat in the chair at my desk, while I sat on my bed. "So, what are you getting into tonight?"

"Nothing. We still have curfew so we have to be in by ten," I told her, not wanting to make myself seem available.

"And you're actually going to abide by the rules?" She smirked like she knew that wasn't the case. "That's new. Most of the players skip out after bed check."

"Really?" I said, acting surprised. I don't know this chick or who she reports to so I'm not giving her any information that she doesn't need.

"Yeah, it's pretty much tradition the last two nights of curfew. I think the coaches even know it but they pretend not to and don't say anything."

"That's interesting."

Then there was this weird silence as we just sat there. Suddenly, Faryn stood and walked the two steps it took to stand in between my legs.

"You've been on this empty campus for a couple of weeks, puttin' in work, around nothing but guys," she paused. "I bet you could use a release huh?" She grabbed the waistband of my basketball shorts.

"Uhhh, yeah, it's been a minute since I've been able to have one of those," I agreed, leaning back on my elbows.

My dick was already semi-hard at the thought of her mouth being wrapped around it. She stuck her hand into my shorts and boxers, grabbed it and slowly started sliding her hand up and down. Before I knew it, this bitch was licking up and down all of my ten inches, spitting on the head to give it more lubrication, before she took the whole thing in her mouth. I don't know this girl and I probably should stop her. *But why would I do that?*

I lay flat on the bed and enjoyed the hell out of this amazing head. Faryn had absolutely no gag reflex as my dick kept disappearing into the deepest part of her throat. I swear I could feel her tonsils. She focused on her craft and let out a moan. My dick throbbed as my nut made its way to the top. I wondered if she was going to let me cum in her mouth but the thought left quickly as my nut shot out and she swallowed every last drop! I don't know how she managed because I know I was backed the hell up.

"Shit!" I let out as I released.

She stood up, wiped the sides of her mouth and sat back in the desk chair like nothing had happened. I shoved my dick back into my shorts and we stared at each other awkwardly, saying nothing. Faryn has a slight smile on her face and I'm not sure what my expression is because I'm still a bit shocked at what had just occurred.

"So, I guess I'll let you get back to your nap. You should sleep well now. Sorry to interrupt." She walked over to the door and placed her hand on the knob and turned the handle. Before she opened the door, she said, "Maybe we can do this again sometime?"

"Uhh, yeah, sure," I responded as she opened the door and walked across the hall to her room. I closed the door and leaned against it for a minute.

"What the fuck just happened?" I asked myself as I went to grab my phone to call Bishop and just my luck, he walked into the room.

"Bruh, you will not believe what the fuck just happened?" I whispered.

"What? Why are you whispering? I thought you were taking a nap?" Bishop said, confused.

"Ssshhh! Let me turn this on T.V. for some background noise. Man, wait 'til you hear this shit!"

"Damn! Just tell me, shit," Bishop whispered back.

"You know ole girl that we saw a few times on campus the last couple of weeks. The one with the short hair, kinda slim thick with the big ass?" I asked Bishop.

"Yeah."

"Well she lives across the hall. Right after you left, she knocked on the door. She introduced herself, her name is Faryn, by the way, and I ended up inviting her in."

"Aww shit nigga! I can see where this is going. You forgot about Imani and Karizma that damn quick," Bishop joked.

"Naw nigga, shut the fuck up and listen. So, I invited her in and we were making small talk. She asked what I was getting into tonight and shit like that. For a second, neither of us said anything and the next thing I know, she asked me if I needed a "release" and was sucking my dick."

"What? You lyin' bruh. You are fuckin' lyin'! You mean to tell me that bitch just found out your name and she already sucked your dick?" Bishop yelled, but in a whisper. "Why can't shit like this happen to me?"

"Dawg, I'm still in shock. But that bitch can suck the hell outta some dick. She has no gag reflex whatsoever and guess what?"

"Shit, there's more?"

"The bitch let me nut in her mouth and swallowed every drop!"

"Damn! How the fuck? What's really going on? Are you shittin' me right now?" Bishop quizzed, shocked by the whole story.

"I swear to God! That shit just happened. I can't believe this shit myself. Fucked up my whole nap and everything." I leaned back on my elbows on my bed.

"Nigga, you just got some bomb ass head and you talking about a fuckin' nap! Get the fuck outta here. That's some crazy shit. Not to mention her ass lives across the hall. That could be good and bad!" He looked at me in disbelief.

"Bad? How can it be bad?" I sat up.

"I mean, shit, that whole story is kinda crazy if you think about it. She might be a little crazy and her ass lives across the hall. Do you plan on ever bringing anyone here?" He stood with his arms folded giving me a minute to think about what he had said.

"She ain't my girl so me bringing someone here shouldn't be a problem. She wanted to suck my dick and I let her. Simple as that!" I answered very matter of factly.

"Yeah okay. You better hope it's that simple. I mean, she lives across the hall! This could get pretty tricky." Bishop shook his head.

"Naw, I ain't worried 'bout no shit like that. But that head though, anytime she's thirsty, I can help her out with that." I grabbed my nut sack.

"As much as that sounds like a dream come true, you better hope her ass ain't a nightmare!" Bishop warned.

I shook my head as I thought about what he said. I sure hope this bitch ain't crazy. But what's done is done and that was some good ass head. It's nine o'clock already so I decided to jump in the shower and get ready for bed check. As I was bathing my thoughts went back to Karizma, wondering if she would be out tonight. I was low-key hoping I'd run into her.

Chapter 7

Karizma

Hazel and I were finished getting dressed for our night out and snapped pictures of each other to put on Instagram and Snapchat. She decided to wear some short, high-waist black shorts with a red crop top, and red platform heels. She put a leopard printed flower in her hair and wore large gold hoop earrings, gold bangle bracelets and a leopard print choker necklace. Hazel was killin' it!

I decided to wear a short, black fit and flare dress, with leopard platform heels. My jewelry was simple dangling black earrings, a thick black bracelet and no necklace because I didn't need one with the way the dress was made. My hair was flat-ironed with a part down the middle. No makeup was necessary for either of us but Hazel did wear a light layer. I just wore mascara, eyeliner and my favorite shade of lip gloss. I was killin' it too.

We grabbed our purses, locked up our room and headed for the elevators.

"You should have called Taylen. Do you think him and his buddy will be out tonight?" Hazel asked as we waited for an elevator.

"Why would I call him? I'm not trying to seem thirsty," I told her with a slight frown.

"I'm just saying! They are both fine as fuck and I told you his friend might be Zaddy."

"Oh my God Hazel! Just stop!" I said laughing as the elevator opened and we got on.

We rode in silence, with our faces in our phones until the elevator stopped on the fourth floor. I looked at Hazel and I could tell she was thinking the same thing that I was. We didn't have time to express our thoughts before the doors opened and Taylen and the guy he was with at dinner, walked on.

"Hey Pretty Girl! So, we meet again?" Taylen said as he walked into my personal space.

"Uhh, yeah. Where you guys headed?" I replied, nervously, attempting to take a few steps back, but I was already against the wall.

"To the party at the Student Center. You?" I looked up at him.

"Really? So are we. Oh, this is my roommate, Hazel. Hazel this is Taylen."

"You can call me Tay," he told her as he stuck his hand out for her to shake. "Nice to meet you Hazel. This is my roommate Bishop. Bishop, this is Pretty - I mean, Karizma and Hazel."

"Hey," the three of us said at the same time. We reached the lobby and the elevator doors opened.

The guys let us exit first. Taylen came up and walked next to me while Bishop walked next to Hazel, putting Hazel and I in the middle.

"It's kinda late ladies. You mind if we walk with you? You know, to make sure you get there safely," Taylen asked.

Hazel and I looked at each other and she shrugged her shoulders.

"Sure, why not?" I answered for us.

We walked out of the building and towards the Student Center.

"So, where are you ladies from?" Bishop asked, looking only at Hazel.

"I'm from Peoria," Hazel answered.

"I'm from Waukegan," I answered, knowing that they probably had no idea where that was.

"Waukegan? Where is that?" Taylen questioned.

"It's a very northern suburb. It's close to the Wisconsin border. Have you heard of Gurnee?" I asked.

"Isn't that where Great America is?" I guess I shouldn't have been too surprised since most people associate Gurnee with Great America or the outlet mall, Gurnee Mills.

"Yeah. But I mostly grew up in Waukegan, which is near there. Where are you guys from? Have you been to Great America?" I asked.

"A few times. We're from Chicago. Southside to be exact!" Bishop said, proudly, for both of them.

"Did you guys grow up together?" Hazel inquired.

"We met in elementary school but didn't start hanging tight until eighth grade. We both play football and lucked up and got scholarship offers to the same school," Taylen answered.

"That's cool. We kinda figured you played football. We're both on the track team," I shared and noticed the look of surprise on Taylen's face. "Why do you look so surprised, Taylen?"

"Huh? Ahh, no reason. But you two being on the track team explains your bangin' ass bodies. No disrespect, just being honest."

Hazel and I looked at each other, smiling, thanking him for the compliment. We were nearing the doors to enter the Student Center and there was a small crowd of people near the entrance and in the lobby area. Bishop held the door for us and we walked in, with he and Taylen coming in behind us. I noticed heads turning and heard a few comments from some guys about how fine we were. None of them were bold enough to step to us because Taylen and Bishop were with us, I assumed.

Pulling Hazel to the side, I whispered, "Let's go to the bathroom." We walked in the direction of the bathroom, without saying anything to the guys.

"Oh my God Rizzy! Them niggas too fine! They seem nice too!" Hazel exclaimed as soon as the door to the bathroom closed.

"Yes, Hazel! They are fine and seem nice. But I'm newly single so I'm not trying to hang with them all night!"

"Well damn Rizzy! They were nice enough to make sure we got here safely and you just wanna ditch them. You cold," she said laughing.

"I mean, they probably trying to find somebody to take back to their rooms tonight. I know I'm not going with them. I don't want to give them the impression that it might happen," I explained, putting my hands on my hips.

"Yeah, you probably right. I might be easy but not that damn easy." She laughed and high-fived me as we walked out of the bathroom.

Taylen and Bishop had an audience of groupies surrounding them as we came around the corner. Hazel and I gave each other a knowing look and made our way to the line to pay for entrance into the party, leaving them to entertain their fans. From the sound of it, the DJ is pretty good. I'm excited to get inside.

The party is live! We walked the perimeter of the room until we found a place that we could chill until we felt like going to the dance floor. With the way this DJ is cuttin' up, it won't be long. He played a nice mixture of old school and new school music.

About ten minutes later, the DJ played one of our jams, "In My Feelings" by Drake, and Hazel and I hit the dance floor. About half-way through the song, Taylen and Bishop found us and danced with us for about three more songs. The DJ slowed the music down and that was my cue to exit the dance floor. Hazel and Bishop were quite cozy with each other and continued dancing to "Best Part" by Daniel Caesar and H.E.R. Taylen grabbed my arm as I tried to walk off the dance floor and pulled me back.

"Hey, I can't get a slow dance?" He asked, smiling wide showing all thirty-two of his beautiful white teeth.

This man is so damn fine, there is no way I can say no to him. He could be dangerous. "I don't slow dance but I guess I can make an exception for you." I flirted.

"Well I feel special." He wrapped his arms around my waist and pulling me close, resting his hands just above my ass.

With him being so tall, he could rest his chin on top of my head. Damn, he smelled so good and I felt like I could melt in his arms as I rested my head on his chest. I was enjoying this a little too much but it was quickly ruined by someone yanking me away from him.

"What the fuck is this Karizma?" Marcus screamed. "What the hell are you doing all cozied up with this nigga?"

"Marcus, what is your problem? Get the fuck away from me!"

"Aye nigga, didn't I tell you to fall back already? She ain't fuckin' with you!" Taylen intervened, getting in Marcus' face.

"And didn't I tell you already to mind yo fuckin' business? This is between me and her. Why the fuck are you all up on my girl anyway?" Marcus yelled, not backing down from Taylen. I moved to stand in between them, facing Marcus and put my hands on his chest.

"Marcus! Just leave me alone please. I'm not your girl anymore. Just accept it and move on. You're ridiculous!" I tried to push him back to create some more space between him and Taylen.

"So this is your new nigga. Your hoe ass moved on already, huh? I knew that good girl role your ass was playing was some bullshit. How the fuck you break up with me and fuckin' around with this nigga already? You ain't shit but a hoe, Karizma. Fuck you and this nigga!" Marcus spat and walked away.

Hazel ran up to me, put her arm around my shoulder and walked me to a less congested area. Taylen and Bishop followed.

"Are you okay?" Hazel asked.

"Yeah, I'm good. I can't believe how he's acting and he called me a hoe! Really nigga, I'm a hoe but we were together for damn near a year and I didn't even let him sniff my pussy. Fuck his punk ass! I'm not about to let him ruin my night!" I grabbed Hazel's arm and was about to go back to the dance floor but Taylen stopped me.

"Aye, lemme holla at you for a minute," he said, with a concerned look.

"I'll just wait over here with Bishop," Hazel said, as she and Bishop walked away.

"What Taylen?" I asked with a little more attitude than necessary. Not that I should have had an attitude with him at all.

"Damn, I'm just trying to make sure you're good." He held his hands up, surrendering.

"I'm sorry. I didn't mean to snap at you. I'm just annoyed about this whole situation. I haven't been on campus for 24 hours yet and it seems like all it's been is drama."

"What's the deal with you two? I'm not trying to pry but it seems like he wasn't expecting the breakup."

"Look, I don't know you well, or at all. I'm not trying to get you involved in my problems. You probably think that I'm nothing but trouble at this point. You don't have to act like you're concerned."

"I'm not acting. I want to make sure you're okay. I don't think you're trouble, although Marcus seems to be. You don't have to tell me if you're not comfortable. Just know that I'm here for you if you ever want to talk." Taylen looked very genuine when he spoke.

"Naw it's cool. I didn't break up with him for any particular reason, honestly. I mean, he is a tad bit controlling and very jealous. I just wasn't that into him and it was time," I shared with him, while looking into those eyes with those gorgeous eyelashes.

"That's understandable. It's clear he doesn't feel the same way. But hopefully it'll sink in soon for him," he replied.

"It may as well. I'm so done with him." I shook my head. "Anyway, I don't want to talk about him anymore."

"Cool. I appreciate you sharing with me. Now, can I have a hug?"

He pulled me close to him and I got chills going down my spine. It felt so good being close to this man, of course he could have a hug. He could have anything he wanted, I thought, as I put my arms around his neck and he slid his around my waist. I can already tell that my willpower is going to be tested around him.

Releasing me from his embrace, we walked towards Hazel and Bishop. She had a smile on her face and Bishop wore a smirk on his. *Why are they looking at us like that?*

We all went back to the dance floor and danced until the party was over. Of course, Taylen and Bishop wanted to walk with us back to the dorm and we agreed. Hazel and I stopped in the bathroom again before exiting the building.

We walked out of the bathroom and just like before the party, Taylen and Bishop were surrounded by a group of thirsty ass girls. Hazel and I looked at each other, rolling our eyes, and walked right on past them, out of the main doors. There were groups of people walking to the parking lots and back towards the dorms, which is where we were going.

"Oh my God Rizzy! Do you see them fine ass dudes by that tree?" Hazel asked.

"Hell yeah," I whispered back to Hazel as I made eye contact with the darker one. I was taken aback a little by how sexy he was.

"Hey Lil Mama, where ya'll headed?" The darker dude directed his question to me while his brown skinned friend looked Hazel up and down, licking his lips.

"Hey, we're headed back to the dorms. You guys?" I answered.

"We're headed that way too. You ladies mind if we walk with you?" the darker one asked.

I looked at Hazel and she looked a little nervous. She turned around and looked towards the doors of the Student Center. I assume she was looking for Taylen and Bishop but clearly, they were still occupied. Since they were nowhere in sight, why the hell not?

"Sure," I answered.

"I'm Keith and this is my boy Trey," the darker one introduced them and we shook their hands and introduced ourselves.

"Did you guys enjoy the party?" I asked, making small talk.

"Yeah, it was pretty lit. The DJ was nice!" Trey responded as we began walking. Keith walked on my left side and Trey walked on the right side of Hazel.

"Sooo, I'm not trying to be nosy, but you look like the girl in that video going around on Snap, arguing with some dude?" Keith stated, curiously.

I let out a deep sigh before answering. "Do I? She must be cute." *Is this situation gonna haunt me all year?*

"Oh, so it's not you? My bad. She cute but you cuter." Keith flirted.

"Naw, it was me. He's now my ex-boyfriend and what you saw in the video was the aftermath of me breaking up with him."

"Word? That means you're single?"

"Yes, but not ready to mingle," I told him, with a little attitude in my voice.

"Okay Lil mama, I just didn't want to step on your man's toes," Keith said, backing off.

Just as I was about to respond, I could hear someone calling my name off in the distance. Then I heard someone say Hazel's name. Keith and Trey heard it too, because we all stopped walking and turned around. It was Taylen and Bishop. Looks like they finally noticed we were gone. I don't know why, but we waited until they caught up with us and apparently, they knew Keith and Trey because they all greeted each other by name and dapped each other up.

"Ya'll ditched us for these niggas?" Taylen joked but I could tell he wasn't joking.

"What do you mean ditch? Ya'll were a bit preoccupied when we came out of the bathroom and we didn't want to interrupt," I answered, a bit harshly.

"So, we made sure ya'll got to the party safely and ya'll found some more niggas to walk ya'll home, huh?" Bishop said, giving attitude right back.

"We didn't "find" them. They asked where we were headed and since we were going to the same place, we decided to walk together. Why the does it matter anyway? Ya'll niggas had plenty of hoes in ya faces that would have gladly allowed you to walk them home," Hazel snapped.

"Hold up!" Trey said, "Is this you, bruh?" He nodded his head towards Hazel. Before Bishop could even answer, Hazel answered for him.

"Umm, no, this ain't him!" She moved her hand down the length of her body as she said it. "This is me!"

"I've had these shoes on long enough and I'm ready to go to bed. This has been the most fucked up day ever!" I turned around and walked towards the dorms. Hazel fell in line next to me, while the guys lagged behind.

"Can you believe these niggas?" Hazel asked.

"Yeah, they got us messed up. You know I'm not here for all this shit right now."

We walked the rest of the way in silence but could hear the guys talking to each other about some football shit. Apparently, they are teammates. They live in another building so when we got to the point where they had to go in a different direction, Hazel and I stopped and talked to them for a moment.

"It was nice meeting you both. I'm sure we'll be seeing each other around campus," I told both Keith and Trey and we turned to walk away.

"Aye hold up! We can make sure it happens if you give me your number? Just on some friends shit, nothing else," Keith tried his luck.

"Yeah, Hazel. Can a nigga get your number?" Trey asked with a wide smile. Hazel and I looked at each other and then dug our phones out of our purses to let them lock their numbers in. They both called their phones so that they could have our numbers as well.

“Sleep well beautiful,” Keith said as he winked, turning to walk away.

Chapter 8

Taylen

"I know damn well they did not just give those niggas their phones. They act like we ain't standing right here!" That pissed me off. I guess Keith needs me to spell out for him that Karizma is off limits. He didn't take the hint when he asked before.

"Hazel made it clear that we weren't together so I'm not surprised at all," Bishop replied.

Karizma and Hazel were finally walking in our direction.

"Oh, you guys didn't have to wait for us. We could have made it from here," Hazel said.

"Yeah, I think we would have made it to our room safely," Karizma chimed in.

"We ain't rude like ya'll so we decided to wait," I stated.

"Rude? Why are you calling us rude? Ya'll were the ones with the bitches cheesing all up in ya faces. You didn't even notice we were gone." Karizma stopped walking, put her hand on her hip and rolled her neck at me. It was actually kinda cute.

"We were just standing there waiting for you and those girls came up to us and started talking. We thought ya'll were still in the bathroom and waited until they told us to leave the building," I defended.

"Yeah, if you say so," Karizma said and started walking away again.

"I do say so. Aye, wassup with you and Keith?" I gently pulled Karizma arm so that she would slow down or stop walking.

"What business is it of yours?" What the fuck? Why is she giving me all this attitude? I should be the one giving her attitude since she thought it was okay to give her number to another nigga and I was standing right there. *Wait, slow down. She's not my girl.*

She yanked her arm away and marched into the building. By the time myself, Bishop and Hazel walked into the building, Karizma had already pushed the button and was waiting for the elevator. The two of us were quiet as Bishop and Hazel laughed with each other about something that we weren't privy to. At least they're getting along. The elevator came and we all got on and pressed our respective floors. When we arrived at the 4th floor, I got off and Bishop lagged behind a little.

"Karizma, I'm gonna chill down here with Bishop for a minute in the commons area. I'll be up in a bit," I heard Hazel say as I continued walking to our room.

"Okay, I'll probably be asleep when you come up," Karizma replied, as the doors closed.

As soon as I walked into my room I locked the door, took off my shirt and flopped onto my bed. Our last day of camp is tomorrow and I should have been had my ass asleep. I got up and grabbed some basketball shorts and went to the bathroom to take a shower so that I could knock out. Karizma and her attitude were still heavy on my mind and it bothered me that I was even thinking about this girl. Why did I even care that she had an attitude? I don't even feel like this when Imani is mad and she's my girl. My shower was nice and quick and before long I was in bed. Just as I was about to doze off, I got a text message.

Pretty Rizzy: Hey…

Me: Hey…

Pretty Rizzy: I just wanted to apologize. Didn't mean to snap at you. This day has just been too much for me. Are we good?

Me: Under one condition.

Pretty Rizzy: Oh God! You can't just forgive me and let's move on?

Me: Do you want to know the condition?

Pretty Rizzy: I guess.

Me: Let me take you out.

It took her longer than expected to reply. Damn, I guess she really had to think about whether or not she wanted to go out with a nigga.

Me: ?????

Pretty Rizzy: Yeah I'm here. Taylen, you know that I just broke up with my bf and he's a little crazy. Are you sure you want to take me out?

Me: Is that a yes?

Pretty Rizzy: Fine. When do you want to go out?

Me: Meet me in the cafeteria tomorrow for lunch and we can discuss the details.

Pretty Rizzy: Okay...so we're good?

Me: Of course. GN Pretty Girl!

Pretty Rizzy: GN Taylen!

I put my phone down with a smile on my face. I don't know what it is about Karizma but I'm feelin' her. She's so fuckin' beautiful and her body is banging. Not just around the way girl banging but track star banging. Not to mention, it sounds like she's a virgin. Man, she could be wifey.

Just as I was dozing off again, I thought I heard a tap on the door. Not thinking it was anything, I turned over and ignored it, then I heard it again. Letting out a deep breath, I got up and looked through the peephole.

"Tay, it's Faryn. I know you're in there alone. I saw your roommate in the commons."

Shit, I thought to myself. What the fuck does she want at this time of night? I don't feel like being bothered. She knocked and called my name again. Against my better judgement, I opened the door. For whatever reason, she was standing there looking like she had just hit the lottery, smiling all in my damn face.

"Hey Faryn, it's late, wassup?" I asked, clearly annoyed, while I stood in the open space, not letting her into the room.

"I thought you might want some company to help you wind down." She ran her hand down my chest and stopped at the top of my shorts.

She looked at me seductively and licked her lips. Just thinking about the head she gave me earlier made my dick jump. But I wasn't trying to go there with her again. Hell, I wasn't trying to go there the first time.

"Naw, I'm good Faryn. Thanks for offering though." I tried to push the door back closed but she stuck her foot in the space.

"Come on, Tay. Let's have a little fun. It won't take long at all and I know you'll sleep better."

Then she grabbed my semi-hard dick and I just said fuck it and let her in. Just like before, she sucked the soul out of my dick and went on her merry way. I hate to say it but I could get used to getting head with no strings attached. Like she said, I slept like a baby. I didn't even hear Bishop when he came in.

Chapter 9

Hazel Isaacs

Although, I'm not trying to get into a serious relationship right now, Bishop seems like he has potential and now I'm curious about him. Last night, we squashed our little beef and sat out in the commons area of his floor and talked for a long while. He's down to earth and I could look at his handsome face for hours.

"What are you over there daydreaming about Hazel?" Karizma said, startling me because I didn't know she was awake.

"Nothing. You startled me."

"Umm hmm. Well something has you over there smiling and staring off into space. You must be thinking about Bishop. How long did you guys talk? I didn't hear you come in."

"Oh my God! We talked for almost two hours about everything under the sun. He's such a sweet guy and seems so genuine. But I don't know, it could all be front, so

I'm treading lightly." I tried to assure myself more than Karizma.

"Hey, it doesn't hurt to get to know someone. No one says you have to marry the boy."

"I know, I know. But he's a starting freshman on the football team and as we saw, he already got groupies. I had to deal with that with Ricky so I'm not so sure I wanna go through that again." We both agreed.

"What do you want to do today?" Karizma asked, changing the subject.

"Let's start with breakfast because I'm starving. I think we should run by the coach's office and find out if there's anything we need to do before practice starts next week. And let's go pick up our books for classes too," I suggested.

"Sounds like a plan. But we have to come back here for lunch, Taylen asked me to meet him," Karizma shared, like it wasn't a big deal.

"Ya'll must be cool again, planning lunch dates and shit." I sat up on my bed.

"I guess. I sent him a text last night apologizing for my attitude. He said he would forgive me if I let him take me on a date." She tried to play it off like she didn't care either way. But I could tell she liked him.

"Wait! Please tell me he's not taking you to the dining hall for a date!" I scrunched up my face because that would be lame as hell.

"Hell naw! We are meeting for lunch to discuss the details." Karizma laughed.

"Oh! I was gonna say." I shook my head. "Karizma, why are you trying to act like you aren't excited? I know you just broke up with Marcus and everything. But I can tell you're feeling Tay and it seems like he's feeling you too." I sat up, swung my legs to the edge of the bed and placed my feet on the floor.

"Just like you, I'm not trying to read too much into this. He and Bishop have the same story. Both starting freshman on the football team with hella groupies. I'm not about to entertain any bullshit so I'm not trying to get excited for no reason." She stood in front of her dresser, leaning back on it, with her arms folded across her chest.

"Yeah, I guess we are in the same boat. Let's just have fun and go with the flow." I stood and walked over to my closet to find something to wear today.

"I just hope Marcus is done acting a damn fool." She shook her head as if she was trying to shake off the memories of yesterday.

"On God, his ass is crazy! I can't believe he's trippin' like that and ya'll didn't even fuck." I laughed.

"Thank God we didn't! His ass would really have lost his mind. You know how niggas get when they get that virgin pussy."

"Yes girl! They do lose their damn minds when they know they are the first and only. I know Ricky sure as hell did. Mind you, he was probably fuckin' other people all along while telling me he didn't mind waiting until I was ready." I confessed to Karizma. Just the thought of my ex-boyfriend Ricky irritated me.

"You know Marcus told me he was fucking other bitches when he blew up at me yesterday," Karizma shared, as she walked towards her closet.

"Are you serious? Do you think he just wanted to piss you off or it's true?"

"I mean, honestly, I don't know. If he was, he has them hoes properly trained because I've never had any issues as far as that's concerned. But shit, at this point, he ain't got no reason to lie." She shrugged.

"True! You never know with these niggas. Once I finally gave Ricky my virginity, he was still sharing his dick with every Kisha, Tisha, and Misha. Nigga still didn't wanna let me go!"

"Right! It wouldn't surprise me if he was getting it from somebody because I wasn't giving up a damn thang!" Karizma expressed while cracking up laughing. "I'm gonna jump in the shower."

While Karizma was showering, I sat back on my bed and grabbed my phone to check Facebook and Instagram. My heart skipped a beat when I saw that I had a text from Bishop.

Bishop: Good morning beautiful! Just wanted to let you know that I enjoyed talking to you last night/this morning. I'm headed to practice. I hope to C U later. Enjoy your day!

Wow! He's so sweet! But let me calm down because I'm not about to let him get me all caught up and he's just playing games. I went to my Snap and it looked like people were still posting on the videos of Karizma and Marcus. It's a shame how much people enjoy drama. Especially other people's drama.

I went to my Instagram as saw that I had a DM. My heart almost stopped when I saw who it was from. Ricky didn't even do social media at all so he must've gotten desperate trying to contact me. I've had to block several numbers that he's used to contact me.

Ricky: I guess you're serious about us being over. You won't take of my calls or respond to any of my texts. I'm sorry about everything. I didn't mean to hurt you. I'll leave you alone since that seems to be what you want. I'll always love you Hazel.

I don't know if I should respond or ignore. As I was contemplating, Karizma walked out of the bathroom.

"Guess who sent me a message," I said to Karizma.

"Who?"

"Ricky." I tossed her my phone so that she could read the message. She sat on her bed wrapped in her towel and tossed me back my phone when she finished.

"Aww Hazel. He seems so sincere. What are you gonna do?" she asked.

"I don't know what to do. I know I can't be with him anymore but I can't lie and say that I don't still love him.

"Aside from his numerous side chicks, which I'm not saying is good, or that you should accept, how did he treat you?"

"I mean, we argued a lot because of his side chicks but he treated me fine. He just let the whole star-athlete thing go to his head and lost himself. If we were having problems in high school, living in the same town, I know a long-distance relationship would never work. He couldn't handle the attention from being a high school basketball star so I'm sure being a college basketball star will magnify his already huge ego. I don't want to deal with that anymore," I confessed to Karizma.

Ricky was the star basketball player on our high school team. He got offered tons of scholarships and ended up choosing University of Illinois. I toyed with the idea of trying a long-distance relationship with him because we aren't that far from each other. But I caught him one too many times in compromising positions with other girls and I was tired.

"Did you ever share how you felt with him?" Rizzy asked.

"Yep. I told him when I broke up with him. He didn't think I was serious but I guess reality is setting in."

"I don't know what to tell you. I wish I could help. You know what's best for you. Just think about it for a little while before replying," Karizma advised.

"Yeah, I guess. I'm gonna jump in the shower." I got up and grabbed my things for the shower, thinking that I was definitely not going to reply to Ricky.

Chapter 10

Bishop Kingston

The last day of camp is over and I'm surprised I got through it. I couldn't stop thinking about Hazel's fine ass. I'm low-key hoping to hang out with her again today.

"Where you headed?" Tay asked, taking me out of my thoughts.

"I don't know. Probably back to the dorms to grab some lunch before I go take a damn nap. I'm tired as fuck."

"That's cause your ass was up talking to Hazel ass all night. What time did you get in?" he said, laughing.

"Shit, about 3:30 and I'm feeling it right now too. You headed to lunch?"

"Yep," he answered with a big as smile. "I'm about to meet Karizma."

"Aw shit nigga! You talkin' about me. Ya'll going on lunch dates and shit?"

"Naw, it ain't even like that. She sent me a text last night, apologizing for snappin' on a nigga and asked if I'd forgive her. I told her that I'd forgive her if she lets me take her out," hc informed me, still smiling.

"So your cheap ass is taking her to lunch in the cafeteria?" I laughed and shook my head.

"Hell naw, I told her to meet me there to have lunch and we would discuss where we are gonna go on our date. I just wanted to make sure I saw her pretty ass today." He had a big ass grin on his face, like he was getting away with something.

"Damn nigga, you got it bad for her ass. I guess I'll roll with you because I'm sure Hazel will be with her," I told him.

"You ain't slick nigga. You know your ass just wants to see Hazel," Tay said, making fun of me. "Sound like you got it just as bad. But did you tell her about Keesha and BJ?"

"Naw man, it didn't come up."

"Fuck you mean it didn't come up. How the hell you leave out that you have a baby mama and son?" Tay was just fucking with me now.

"It just didn't. I didn't ask Hazel to be my girl so it ain't no reason to tell her."

"Yeah okay nigga, if you say so! Let's head on out. Karizma just texted me to meet her in the lobby." Tay grabbed his belongings.

"Yo thirsty ass talking about me. When do you plan to mention Imani?" I asked as I gathered my things.

"Shit, I don't, honestly. Like I told you before, that shit is dead with me and her. Just trying to do the right thing and not break up with her over the phone," he reasoned.

"Yeah, that makes sense. I hope it works out for you bro."

"Hold up! I forgot to tell you I got another visit from Faryn's ass last night," he whispered.

"Are you serious? Did you fuck?"

"Hell naw! I'm not fuckin' that nasty hoe. But that head put me right to sleep!" He smirked.

"Damn nigga! I ain't mad at you. I wouldn't turn that shit down either. But you playin' with fire. I hope this shit don't blow up in your face."

There wasn't much conversation between Tay and I as we walked across campus and back towards the dorms. He was busy texting someone and I was in my thoughts. I'm feeling Hazel but I don't want to lead her on. I shot her a text to see if she was with Karizma.

Me: Hey beautiful! Did you get my text this morning?

Hazel: Hey handsome! Yes I did. It was sweet. Are you done with practice?

Me: Yep. About to go to eat lunch. You wanna eat with me?

Hazel: Sure. Karizma and Tay are meeting up anyway.

Me: Okay, walking over the bridge now.

I don't know what it is about Hazel but I'm excited to see her. This is new for me because I've never pursued a girl. Being a handsome athlete has always made it pretty damn easy. Hazel is different and I like it...a lot.

Chapter 11

Karizma

Hazel and I were getting ready to meet Taylen and Bishop in the lobby so that we could have lunch together in the dining hall. We stopped by our room to drop off our books and freshen up a bit. The Carbondale sun is not to be played with. I was looking for a shirt to change into and heard a knock at the door. I assumed we were taking too long and the guys decided to come up to hurry us along.

"Taylen, you didn't have to come up, I -- Marcus, what the fuck do you want?" My mouth dropped open in surprise.

"Were you expecting me to be that fuck ass nigga? I came to see my girl," he said, basically pushing himself into the room and grabbing my wrist.

"I'm not your girl!" I yanked my arm away from him. "Now can you just go!"

"Man, Rizzy, fuck all this. We need to talk and I'm not goin' no fuckin' where until that happens." He grabbed my waist this time and pulled me close to him. "Tell me what I'm doing wrong and we can fix this shit."

"There's nothing to fix! I don't want to talk. Now let me go Marcus, damn. You said you were fuckin' other bitches anyway, so clearly you will have no problem replacing me!" I yelled as I struggled to get out of his grasp. "Let go Marcus!"

He let me go and walked over to the door, closing and locking it, trapping me. My breathing increased and I wondered why the hell Hazel hadn't come out of the bathroom.

"Just sit down. I won't touch you anymore, I just wanna talk. You owe me that much, Rizzy. I'm not fuckin' anyone else. I just said that to piss you off baby. I'm waiting for you just like I promised."

"I don't owe you shit. I tried to talk to you about this yesterday and you wanted to act stupid and put your fuckin' hands on me and embarrass me in front of all those people. Then you come to the party and do the same damn thing. I ain't got shit to say except get the fuck outta my room and leave me the fuck alone!" I got up and walked towards the door. He followed me and quickly placed himself between me and the door. I unsuccessfully tried to move him.

"Why can't we just talk this out? Is it because of that Taylen nigga? Is he the reason why you broke up with me?"

"No, I didn't even know him before yesterday. I don't need a reason to break up with you. I just know that I don't want to be in a relationship with you. It's over and I'm not going backwards. Now leave before I call security on your ass."

"Man fuck this Rizzy!" He pushed me and I fell back on my bed. "I have been real patient with your ass but you startin' to piss me the fuck off. I don't give a fuck what you say, you mine and you always will be," he continued.

I scooted back on my bed, trying to get as far away from him as possible. "If I find out you fuckin' that nigga, or any other nigga, I'm fucking you and that nigga up. You bet not give my pussy away or I will kill your ass! Try me if you want to!" he spat.

At this point, he was straddled over me and I was lying flat, screaming and throwing punches. Suddenly, I heard a door slam against the wall. He heard it too and turned around. That allowed me the chance to knee him in the nuts and he fell on top of me, moaning in pain. Tay barged in with Hazel and Bishop. He ran towards us and pulled Marcus off of me and immediately threw several blows to Marcus' body. It took Marcus a second to defend himself because he was caught off guard and still holding his nuts. They were in the middle of the floor, swinging back and forth on each other before Bishop got between them and pushed Marcus towards the door and out of the room.

"Don't let me catch your punk ass anywhere near her again or I'm fuckin' you up on sight," Taylen yelled trying to get around Bishop.

"Fuck you nigga! That's my bitch and don't you forget that shit!" Marcus yelled back as he wiped his bleeding mouth.

"Try me bitch ass nigga. Stay the fuck away from her!" Taylen said again.

"Like I said, that's my bitch!" He turned and walked down the hall towards the elevator.

This cannot be my fuckin' life! I never, in a million years, would have thought that Marcus was this crazy and would lose his damn mind if I broke up with him. This is too much! I sat in the corner of my bed, breathing hard, trying to wrap my head what had just happened. I'm so thankful for Hazel and Taylen because I don't know what the hell Marcus would have done to me had they not come in.

"Are you okay?" Hazel asked, sitting next to me on my bed.

"I'm good. I just don't understand what his problem is. Why the fuck is he acting like we were engaged and I left him at the alter? We didn't even fuck! It shouldn't take all of this for him to move on."

"Did he hurt you?" Taylen came over and kneeled on the floor in front of me, grabbing my hand, while Hazel got up.

"I mean, not really. How did you get them up here?" I looked at Hazel, directing that last question towards her.

"Luckily, Jessica, was in her room. I left out through her room and found them in the lobby and came right up," she explained.

"Man, that nigga is crazy as fuck," Bishop commented.

"I'm glad that we were able to get here but it doesn't sound like he's about to let this go," Hazel said.

We were quiet for a moment before I broke the silence. "Let's just go eat lunch. I can't deal with this shit right now."

*****

After lunch, the four of us went to hang out in the commons area of Taylen and Bishop's floor. Bishop and Hazel seemed to be getting along pretty well and had their own little conversation going on.

Taylen and I sat on one of the couches and Bishop and Hazel were across from us.

"You good Karizma? You've been pretty quiet," Taylen asked.

"I'm okay. Thank you for saving me…again." I laughed.

"What are you gonna do if I can't get to you?" He wasn't smiling and his tone was serious. I looked away from him and he grabbed my chin and turned my face back towards him. I swear every time he touched me, I felt a spark. I could get lost in his eyes, with those sexy eyelashes that every woman would die to have.

"Answer me. What are you gonna do if I can't get to you?" he asked again.

"I--I--I don't know. I don't think he would really hurt me. I---," Taylen interrupted me before I could finish what I was saying.

"You don't think he will hurt you? Are you serious right now?" I looked away again and again, he grabbed my chin and turn my face towards his.

"What do you want me to say? I don't know what I'm gonna do, okay. I don't know. If I get a restraining order, it's just a piece of paper. It's not gonna do anything when he's in my face." My mom got a restraining order on my sister's dad when she finally decided to leave him. That shit didn't stop him from getting to her and putting his hands on her again.

"You're probably right. Where I grew up, you don't get the police involved unless it's absolutely necessary. I can have some of my homies take care of him." I didn't immediately respond because I was trying to figure out if "take care of him" meant what I thought it meant.

"What do you mean, take care of him?" I asked, sure that he didn't mean what I thought he meant.

"I think you know what I mean. But never mind. Forget I mentioned it. Just be careful. Make sure that you're always aware of your surroundings. Get some mace. Okay?" He waited for me to answer.

"Why are you so sweet?" I asked after I nodded yes to his requests.

"I'm not like this with everyone. Just with people that I like… a lot." He leaned in closer to me.

"You don't even know me well enough to like me a lot." I'm sure my smile was from ear-to-ear.

"I know enough to know that I want to find out everything there is to know about you." He leaned in even closer and pecked me on the lips. He pulled away quickly, gauging my reaction, then leaned in and kissed me again. This time, it was more than a peck. He let his lips linger on mine and slowly slipped in his tongue inside my mouth. I didn't deny him and allowed his tongue to invade my mouth until we heard someone clearing their throat.

"Excuse me, umm, Tay, what's going on?" This voice startled us out of our kiss and we both looked up.

"Umm, hi Faryn. How can I help you?"

"How can you help me? You can help me by telling me who this bitch is and why she is shoving her tongue down her throat?" Faryn stood there, arms folded across her chest with her weight on one leg, tapping her foot.

“Oh shit!” Bishop said, in the background.

“Bitch! Who the fuck are you calling a bitch? I will beat your ass!” I stood up, ready to knock the taste out of this bitch’s mouth. Taylen stood up and gently pushed me behind him.

“Yo, Faryn! What the hell is your problem? You don’t even know her to be calling her out her name. Get the fuck on man!” Taylen yelled and stood between us.

“You weren’t saying that shit last night!” Faryn said, rolling her neck.

I grabbed Taylen by his shoulder and turned him around to face me. “What the fuck is she talking about Taylen?”

This nigga couldn’t even look me in the eyes. This Faryn bitch just stood there with a smug look on her face. “You know what. Fuck this shit!” I grabbed my purse, ran down the hall and took the stairs up to the eighth floor.

Chapter 12

Taylen

"Karizma, wait!" I yelled as I ran after her. Damn, I can see why she's on the track team. I don't know how she got up four flights of stairs and to her room that fast but she did. She slammed the door just as I reached it. I knocked with no success.

"Karizma, open up. Let me explain. Please!" Silence.

"Come on Karizma." Still silence.

"Okay fine! I'm gonna sit out here until you open the door." I had no plans on doing that. I sent Bishop a text asking him to ask Hazel to come and open the door. There was no way I was about to let Faryn's hoe ass fuck this up for me. I looked down the hall and saw Hazel coming towards me. She looked pissed.

"Look Tay," she whispered, "Rizzy already texted me and told me not to let you in. You're lucky Bishop explained to me the situation with Faryn's thot ass so I'm gonna give your nasty ass the benefit of the doubt and let you in so that you can explain it to her." She unlocked the door and went back down the hall towards the elevators.

The room was dark, except for the light shining from her phone. I could see Karizma laying on her bed facing the wall, with her headphones on. I quietly closed and locked the door and walked over to her bed. She still hadn't realized that I was in her room so I kneeled down next to the bed and touched her shoulder. She damn near jumped out of her skin as she took her headphones off and sat up.

"Shit Taylen, you scared the shit outta me! Why are you here? I told Hazel not to let you in."

"I just want to explain. I think you got the wrong idea." The room was still dark so I reached over and turned on the lamp next to her bed.

"You don't have to explain anything to me. We aren't in a relationship, therefore an explanation is not necessary." She began to put her headphones back on because apparently, she was done talking and didn't plan on listening to me. I grabbed them and threw them to the other end of her bed.

"Please, Karizma, just listen. I know I don't owe you an explanation but I want to explain anyway." I paused to see her reaction and when she said nothing, I continued.

"I just met Faryn yesterday, before the Student Center party. Bishop left the room for awhile and I was going to take a nap before we got ready for the party. She lives across the hall and came over to introduce herself. Before I knew it, the bitch was sucking my dick." I told her all at once. She shook her head and had a look of disgust on her face but she said nothing so I continued.

"I know that sounds bad but I'm just a typical nigga at the end of the day and it's hard to turn down some head with no strings attached. That's all that happened. I didn't fuck her and I don't want to. I don't even know her last name." I decided against telling her about the second time she sucked my dick because that would just make matters worse. She folded her arms across her chest before she said anything.

"You're telling me that this bitch just goes around giving random niggas head and you just let random bitches suck your dick? That's nasty as hell."

Damn! It does sound bad but shit, who passes up head.

"I didn't think of it the way you're thinking. She---" I began before she interrupted.

"Obviously, you didn't but like you said, you're a typical nigga." She rolled her eyes and shook her head.

"I swear that's not something I would normally do. But regardless, she's not my girl so I don't give a fuck about her. Like I said, I met her yesterday. I'm not sure what's going on in her head but I will let her know that she ain't my bitch and to get the fuck on," I said, trying to convince myself as much as Karizma that I wouldn't let Faryn suck my dick again. She's really good at what she does.

"Hey, we aren't together. If you wanna get your dick sucked by random, crazy ass bitches, that's your problem, not mine. However, what I will not tolerate is those same random bitches in my face talking shit, especially about a nigga who ain't mine. We good though. Now can you leave?"

"Damn, it's like that?" I leaned away from her a little bit, shocked by how she tried to dismiss me. But my ass ain't about to leave.

"Yup!" Damn, she is still pissed. That must mean she's feeling a nigga.

"But we never got a chance to plan our date." I need her to move on from this shit. I basically had to beat her ex's ass twice already so there is no way I'm letting her back out of this date. She owed me that much at least.

"Date? I don't even know if I still want to go on a date with you?" she replied with her face all scrunched up.

"Aww, come on Pretty Girl, don't be like that. You promised."

She let out a deep breath before saying, "I don't recall promising but fine Taylen! Plan the date and text me the info so I'll know how to dress. Can you leave please?"

I looked at her with a big cheesy smile on my face. This girl was so fuckin' fine that it ain't even funny. She was gon' have me turn in my player card.

"Aight, cool. I'll text you. But umm, can we finish our kiss before I go."

I stuck out my bottom lip and gave her my best sad face. She just looked at me and I could tell she wanted to kiss me so I laid it on a little thicker.

"Pleeaasse."

"I don't know. Have you been kissing Faryn's nasty ass?" She couldn't be serious. Clearly, she doesn't know how I get down.

"Don't play with me Karizma. Hell naw I ain't kiss that damn girl." I shook my head in disgust.

"Well you let her suck your dick so shit, who knows?" She's trying me right now.

"That's not the same thing! You know what---I don't wanna talk about that bitch anymore. You gon' give me a kiss or what?" I went back to batting my eyelashes and pouting.

She didn't answer me so I pulled her toward the edge of her bed and she put her legs on either side of me. I leaned in and gave her a quick peck. She didn't back away so I leaned in for another peck and slipped my tongue in her mouth. She allowed my tongue to enter her mouth as I pulled her body closer to mine. I leaned forward and pushed her back on the bed and the top half of my body was now laying on top of hers.

I know she felt the hardness of my dick increasing with each second and I was doing my best not to grind against her pussy. The kiss was becoming more passionate and she let out a soft moan. I swear I almost nutted in my shorts. My left and her right hand were intertwined on the bed next to her head. I took my right hand and slowly slid it under her shirt and God must have been smiling upon me because she wasn't wearing a bra. *Thank you!* I took my thumb and rubbed her left nipple and she moaned again, this time a little louder. She wrapped her legs around my waist and I began kissing her neck as I lifted her shirt up to expose her breast. We looked each other in the eyes and I know she wanted me as much as I wanted her. I took her right breast in my mouth and licked around her nipple.

"Taylen….wait, please. We can't," I knew it was too good to be true. I stopped and sighed, laying my head on her chest. "I'm sorry." She continued.

"It's cool. You don't have to be sorry. I just got carried away."

"You should go." She sat up and our faces were now only inches apart. I pecked her lips again and stood up.

"Are you mad?" I asked her.

"No, I'm not mad. I just -- we can't -- you should just go. I'm not mad though."

"Okay. I'll text you the details about our date."

"Okay." She followed me to the door and I turned to face her. We stood there for a second but she wouldn't look at me. I lifted her face so she could look me in the eye.

"I'm sorry about today. Well not all of it but….you know, that stuff with Fa---"

"It's fine. We're good. Let's not bring her up anymore. I'll see you later, maybe."

I turned and opened the door and walked out. I waited until I heard her lock the door before I walked down the hall to the elevators. I don't know what is going on but I want that girl and I'm gon' to get her. I already consider her mine.

Chapter 13

Hazel

"I guess I'll head up to my room to see what's up with Rizzy. Hopefully Tay was able to talk to her." Bishop and I were still hanging out in the commons. I stood up from the couch we were sitting on together and Bishop did the same.

"Yeah, I told Tay that Faryn was crazy. He didn't take me seriously but maybe now he'll listen." There was a short silence. "We've been down here for a while. I like hangin' with you." Bishop said with the biggest smile on his face.

His phone lit up again with another incoming call or text. It had been doing that for the last twenty minutes or more. Just like before, he pressed ignore.

"Me too. It seems as if someone is missing your company though." I tried not to mention it but I couldn't resist. The smile disappeared from his face and I could tell he became uncomfortable.

"Oh yeah, uhh, those are just my peeps back home. I haven't talked to them in a couple of days so they're just hittin' me to see what's up." I knew he was lying. He couldn't even look me in the eyes.

"Well, let me let you go so you can call them back. I wouldn't want them worrying about you for no reason." I guess Keesha could be a relative. But as many times as I saw her name pop up on his screen, if it was a relative, I think he would have answered.

"What are you ladies gettin' into tonight?"

"Not sure. I'll have to talk to Rizzy to see if she's feels up to doing anything. She's had a rough couple of days."

"Yeah, she definitely has. Well, hit me up later. Maybe we can all hook up and hangout again," Bishop suggested.

"Maybe." He walked me to the elevator and pushed the up button. It was a little awkward as we waited and he pulled me close to him by my wrist.

"I know I've only known you for about twenty-four hours but, can I kiss you?" he asked as I looked up at him.

I almost replied telling him that he could do anything he wanted to me. Instead, I stood on my tip toes and kissed him. As he moved his hands up my back, he stuck his tongue in my mouth and I got chills up and down my entire body as we kissed. I swear my lady juices are dripping down my legs from this kiss. Had the elevator doors not opened, I could have kissed him forever. Our lips parted and we both were a tad breathless.

"I gotta go. I'll text you." I stepped onto the elevator and we held eye contact until the door closed. I was thankful yet surprised that no one was on the elevator.

I pushed the button for the 8th floor as leaned my head against the wall on the ride up.

"What the hell is he doing to me?" I said to myself, as I got off the elevator and walked to my room.

When I opened the door, Karizma was laying on her bed looking at her phone.

"What's up?" I asked her.

"Not a damn thing. Just laying here thinking about my crazy life."

"Yeah, you got some shit going on. You didn't tell me that Marcus was this fuckin' nuts."

"Hell, I didn't know. I've never seen him act this way. Shit, I'm glad I broke up with his ass in time. Who knows when that lunatic would have shown his true colors. Wait until I tell my mom." Karizma sat up on her bed.

"Did you give Taylen a chance to explain?" I was hoping that she did.

"Yes and let me tell you what he said about this bitch!" she began.

"Oh, Bishop already told me. She just going around giving head to niggas that she just met. That's nasty as fuck!"

"Hell yeah it is! She don't know Taylen from Adam and she's already sucked his dick. He said he doesn't even know her last name!" We were both shaking our heads in disgust. "You and Bishop are getting real cozy, I see." Karizma smirked, changing the topic.

"Oh my God Rizzy! He seems so perfect...well almost perfect." I flopped back on my bed.

"Why almost?"

"I think he has a girlfriend that he's not telling me about," I shared my concern.

"Why do you think that?"

"The last twenty or thirty minutes that we were hanging out, his phone was blowing up. A few times, I was able to glance at the screen and I saw the name Keesha."

"Ummm….that could be his sister or cousin or some other family member. But why don't you ask him?" Karizma suggested.

"I don't think I should have to ask him. I know it ain't his sister because he already told me that her name is Brianna. I guess it doesn't have to be his girlfriend but she was calling back-to-back and she even tried to Facetime. He didn't pick up so then she started texting." I explained to Karizma.

"Like I said before, just tread lightly. Take it nice and slow with his ass," she advised.

"Are you and Tay cool now?" I wanted to see what was up with them before asking if she wanted to hang out with them tonight.

"We good. I'm gonna still let him take me out on a date."

"Bishop asked what we were gettin' into tonight."

"Regardless of whoever was calling him, he's feelin' you. Ya'll been together for hours and he's still trying to see you later," she teased.

"I know, right! But I can't get too excited over this nigga."

"I'm feelin' Taylen too. But he just had a bitch sucking his dick yesterday so I don't know what the fuck to think about his ass right now." Rizzy did have a good point but ain't no single nigga gonna deny a girl that wants to suck his dick.

"You know what? Let's just have some fun with them. How does bowling sound?" I suggested.

"That sounds good. There's a bowling alley in the Student Center."

"I'll text Bishop and see if they want to join us. If not, we can still go hang out without them." I grabbed my phone to send a text to Bishop. About a minute later he replied that they were down for bowling.

Chapter 14

Bishop

When I got the text from Hazel asking if we wanted to go bowling, I was excited as hell. We have a great connection and want explore it and see where it goes. I have to play it cool in front of Taylen though. I don't need his ass riding me about how much I like this girl already.

"Hazel and Karizma wanna know if we wanna go bowling tonight?" I shared with Taylen as I was lying on my bed.

"Hell yeah! Shit, I'm just glad Karizma still fuckin' with a nigga." Taylen sat up on his bed. Here I am worried about seeming thirsty about Hazel and this nigga over here ecstatic.

"Calm down! Yo thirsty ass!" I laughed at him.

"Man, I can't even front. I'm feelin' her little ass and I didn't think she was gon' fuck with me after Faryn's crazy ass pulled that dumb shit." He smiled showing all thirty-two teeth.

"Yeah. I'm tryin' to see wassup with Hazel too. She cool as hell but I can tell she got some shit about her. She has her guard up."

"What? You think she got a crazy ass ex-boyfriend too?" He laughed.

"Shit, she might! It ain't like it ain't possible." I laughed with him but I wasn't ruling it out. "I don't know if that's it but there's something real guarded about her."

"Man, she don't know you! She should be guarded. Just give her some time. It ain't like you don't have your own little situation goin' on with Keesha," Taylen reminded me.

"Yeah you right. Keesha ass been blowin' me up all day. Hazel peeped that shit too but I played that off like it was just family calling me."

"Yo, you need to just tell the girl about BJ and let her know ain't shit between you and Keesha. If you feelin' her, the sooner you tell her, the better. You know Keesha's ass can get crazy," Taylen advised, just as my phone started ringing. I sat up on my bed and looked at the screen.

"Damn, we done talked her ass up." I shook my head as I answered the phone and put it on speaker. "Wassup Keesh?

"What the fuck you mean wassup? Nigga I been callin' yo ass all day!" Keesha screamed.

"Hold the fuck up! Who the hell you talkin' to?" I yelled back into the phone, pulling it away from me to look at it.

"You know who I'm talkin't to. I know you saw me callin'. Why the hell didn't you answer the damn phone Bishop?" Keesha yelled back.

"Because I was busy Keesha, damn!" I dropped my phone down on my bed and laid back down.

"Yo ass wasn't busy. Probably somewhere up in some bitch face. Them hoes down there more important than makin' sure your son is okay now Bishop? Is that what you on now?"

"Shut that bullshit up Keesha. Ain't shit more important than my son and it ain't none of your business how many bitches I entertain. Now what do you want?"

"Fuck it now! Bye nigga!" Keesha hung up in my face.

Taylen was sitting on his bed, listening to Keesha and I go back and forth. When she hung up I looked at my phone and then at Taylen. He just shook his head.

"I love my son, I swear I do. But I can't deal with her ass. You know, when we first started messing around, I didn't think she was a hoodrat. She's smart, got goals, wanna do something with her life. I mean, Keesha be about her business and she's a great mom. But when it comes to dealing with me, her ass has no chill." I sat up on my bed, putting my feet on the floor, my elbows on my knees and my head in my hands.

"I don't envy you bruh. But ya'll gon' have to figure out a way to co-parent. I think the problem is that you keep giving her hope."

I lifted my head and looked at him. "Naw, she knows what it is. I've made it clear to her several times," I explained.

"It don't matter how many times you make it clear. You keep fuckin' her, she's gon' think she got a shot."

I thought about what he said for a minute. "Yeah, you probably right. She just be throwing it at me and sometimes I catch it. Shit, it's hard to turn it down. But you right, I can't be doing that shit no more."

"It ain't like ya'll got that much history. Shit, ya'll dated for what, a few months, before ya'll broke up? She can't be that damn attached," Taylen reasoned.

"I put this good dick in her life and she can't let go!" I laughed and tried to give Taylen a pound but he gave me that side-eye.

"Whatever nigga! Now your ass can't get rid of her," he replied. "Let's go meet the girls in the lobby."

We both got up and got ourselves together to meet the girls downstairs. I let out a deep sigh as we locked up the room. I need to figure out this shit with Keesha before it gets too out of hand. But first, let me see what's up with Ms. Hazel.

Chapter 15

Taylen

School has officially started and classes are in session. Even after a full week of classes, I'm still surprised at the number of students on campus. There is an abundance of beautiful women in all shades of chocolate, but I only had one on my mind. Karizma! I wish I could tell you what it is about her that has me wanting to be with her, and only her. But she's all I see.

My professor let us out of class early and Karizma's class is in another lecture hall in the same building. I want to catch her before we both go to practice because I won't be able to see her tonight. I took my phone out and shot her a text.

Me: Hey, we got out early.

Pretty Girl: My professor is still talking.

Me: OK. I'll wait for you by the middle exit.

Pretty Girl: K

As I walked around the corner to the lecture hall where Karizma's class is located, I started pulling my headphones out of my bag and I heard someone calling my name. I stopped and turned around to this thick ass light-skinned girl, with shorts on so short that I'm sure her ass was hanging out.

"You're Taylen, right?" light-skinned asked.

"Yeah, wassup?"

"Hi, I'm Diamond." She put her hand out for me to shake and I did.

"Nice to meet you Diamond."

"Sooo, I was wondering if you wanna maybe go out some time?" She leaned in towards me, giving me a great view of her breasts. Now a week ago, I would have taken complete advantage of her forwardness. However, she ain't who I want. The bad thing is, I don't even know how to let her down easy. I don't know if I've ever turned down pussy being thrown my way.

I rubbed my hand over my head and down my face. "Umm, I, uhh, it's pretty busy for me now, with football starting. I don't have a lot of free time."

"I'm sure you don't spend all of your time doing football stuff." She smiled and twirled a piece of her shoulder length hair around her finger.

The doors to the lecture hall opened and students began filing out. Thank goodness! Karizma walked out and smiled when she saw me.

"Hey!" I said to Karizma and leaned in to give her a hug, inhaling her scent. She smelled like vanilla. Her body felt so good in my arms as she hugged me back.

"You ready?" she asked. Then her eyes landed on Diamond. "Oh, I'm sorry. Did I interrupt?"

"Yeah, you did!" Diamond said, laced with attitude.

"Naw, I was just waiting for you, Pretty Girl. You good. It was nice meeting you Diamond." I put my arm around Karizma's shoulder and started to leave.

"Really Taylen? So you're gonna just walk away like we weren't in the middle of a conversation," Diamond exclaimed.

"We were done. It was nice meeting you." Karizma and I continued on our way.

"Fuck you and that bitch," she said under her breath. Thankfully, Karizma didn't hear her and I didn't have time to even address that hoe.

"So how has your day been?" I gave Karizma all of my attention.

"Ugh! These Gen. Ed courses are gonna bore me to death. You?" She turned to look up at me as we walked.

"Same."

"You ready for tomorrow?" she asked.

"Yeah man. I'm geeked. Seems like we've been practicing forever."

"Imagine if you were me. Our first track meet is in December. But I'm excited to see you play tomorrow."

"Aww, you ready to come support your man?" I teased her.

She pushed me away from her and said, "If I had a man, yes, I'd be ready to support him. But I'm excited to support my friend too." I noticed she stressed the word friend.

"Okay. I see how you doing me." I pulled her back to my side.

"I'm just keepin' it real."

"After practice I have to go to our team dinner and then we have curfew. I won't see you until tomorrow after the game then."

"Well, I have plans tomorrow night and I was gonna try to get some studying done before going out. I'll just see you on Sunday for our date. But text me after dinner though, before you go to sleep," she stated.

"Plans? What kinda plans?" I hope she ain't hooking back up with her ex or another nigga.

"You sure are nosey!" She scrunched up her nose at me.

"What? I just want to know what kinda plans you have. You don't want me to know?"

"Hazel and I are hanging out with some of our teammates and their friends. Nothing big. Nosey!"

"Just making sure you ain't giving another nigga time that should be mine." *I don't know why she don't know that she's mine.*

"Yeah, whatever. I gotta go change for practice. Text me later."

I pulled her to me and kissed her forehead. Then I gave her a hug that I didn't want to pull away from but we both had to get to practice. She took a step back from me and looked up. I couldn't resist grabbing her by the back of her neck and planting a lingering kiss on her lips. When I pulled away, she was frozen in place with her eyes still closed, holding the wrist of my hand that held her neck.

"I'll text you later." Her eyes popped open and she took a breath. *I'm wearing her down.*

"Yeah. Okay," she replied.

We both went to our respective practices. I'm thankful that today we were practicing in pads only and no hitting since I can't get my mind off of Karizma.

Chapter 16

Karizma

After practice, Hazel and I met at the dining hall for dinner. I am starving and don't care what they are serving today. I'm eating it!

"What's the plan for tonight?" Hazel asked.

"I don't know. All I can think about is food right now."

"I know, I'm hungry too. I hope they have something good," Hazel commented.

We moved through the line and the only thing that looked good was pizza. I grabbed three pieces and kept it moving. Hazel was taking a chance on the entrée of the day. I can't even tell you what it is but it didn't look edible.

After getting our food we made our way to the table we normally sit. It was noticeably empty in dining hall today because the football players weren't there. I sat down quickly and started eating.

"Why are those girls staring at you so hard?" Hazel questioned. I looked up as I took a huge bite of my pizza and saw the girl that Taylen was talking to earlier.

"Hmm. The one with the big boobs, I think her name is Diamond. Taylen was waiting for me outside of my class today. When I came out, they were talking. He kind of dismissed her and walked away with me. She probably got an attitude because of it," I explained.

"She has a problem with you because Taylen dismissed her ass? That makes a lot of sense," Hazel said sarcastically, looked over in Diamond's direction and gave them all the evil eye. I'm too hungry to be fooling around today.

"I guess. She better keep that shit over there. I ain't got time." I continued to enjoy my pizza, ignoring the stares.

"I know these hoes ain't bringing their asses over here," Hazel said.

I looked up to see Diamond and her little crew walking in our direction. I don't know what business she had with me but she better keep that shit moving. I will fuck her up today. Practice was hard as hell, I am tired, and I am not in the mood.

Diamond and her crew stopped at our table. She put her tray down and stood in front while the other three stood behind her, with two on her left and the other on her right side. They stared at me for a good thirty seconds before Diamond spoke. I just kept eating my pizza like they weren't there.

"Are you supposed to be Taylen's girl?" Diamond asked. I looked to the left and right, then behind me.

"Are you talking to me?"

"Duh! I saw you with him this afternoon. I know you remember!" She was on the other side of the table and leaned forward.

"Naw, actually, I don't." I took another bite of my pizza.

"Whatever! Your ass will remember me when he's my nigga and I'm the one on his arm. Enjoy him while you can. He gon' be mine soon!" She picked up her tray, twirled around and walked away, with her peons following behind her. They were sure to roll their eyes at me as they turned around. They all had on very short, tight shorts. All of their asses were hanging out and I know their kitties had to be suffocating.

"What!" I said to Hazel, because she was looking at me crazy as I finished the last few bites of my pizza.

"What the hell was that? You ain't even check that bitch!"

"Why should I? Taylen ain't my man and I'm not gonna argue with no hoe about a man that ain't mine. What kinda sense does that make?"

"I hear you. But it's the principle. She got some nerve approaching you about him, especially since she is under the impression that you and Taylen are together. I mean, who does that?" Hazel said.

Hazel is right. If Taylen was my man, which he is not, why the hell is she approaching me about my man? I like Taylen and us being in a relationship is a possibility. But I don't know if I want to deal with shit like this. Random girls approaching me making threats. That's that shit I don't like.

"Clearly thirsty ass bitches. But it's whatever. I'm not about to stress."

We finished eating and went to our room to shower and find something to get into. As we entered the lobby of our building, Diamond and the petty crew were sitting on the couches. There were about five guys fawning all over them. Hazel and I didn't pay them much attention and made our way to the elevators.

"Aye Rizzy, slow down." I stopped and turned around to see Keith, with his fine ass, walking away from Diamond. Oh, this bitch is really about to hate me. Keith was dressed in black slacks and a light blue button-down shirt. The football players were required to dress up for the team dinner.

"Keith! How you gon' just walk away in the middle of our conversation?" Diamond yelled across the lobby.

"You good! Give me a minute." Keith turned around and told Diamond.

"Naw, I'm out nigga." She and her crew got up and walked out of the building with all kinds of attitude and talking shit.

Hazel and I looked at each other and started laughing. "I guess I'm just fucking up her whole day." I high-fived Hazel.

"Yeah, you really on her list now. I'm gonna go on up and hit the shower," Hazel told me as she continued walking to the elevators.

"Okay! I'll be up in a sec," I replied to Hazel. "Hey Keith, wassup?" I said as I returned the hug that he was giving me.

"Nothin' much beautiful. How you been? First week of classes good for you?" He licked his lips and I all I could think about was how soft they looked.

"Uh yeah. Classes were fine. Nothing to write home about but I'll survive. How about yours?"

"Boring as hell. I'm just glad it's Friday and we have our first game tomorrow." He smiled with excitement. "You comin'?"

"Yeah. Hazel and I---," I began before I was interrupted.

"Hey Pretty Girl!" Taylen came up behind me, kissing my cheek, and putting his arm over my shoulder, pulling me close to him.

Taylen was much taller than me so I had to turn my head and look up, only to find him grilling Keith. *What's that all about?*

"Hey Taylen! Keith was just asking me if I was coming to the game tomorrow. How was dinner?"

"Did you tell him that you wouldn't miss the chance to come support your man?"

"Seriously Taylen. I thought we talked about this earlier," I reminded him. His ass was still giving Keith the death stare and didn't answer me.

"Keith, it was good to see you. I'm gonna go shower because I went straight to dinner after practice. Good luck tomorrow." I tried to get out of Taylen's grasp to give Keith a hug but he wouldn't let go.

"It was good seeing you too Karizma." Keith replied to me but was matching Taylen's stare. *What the hell is wrong with these niggas?* "Do you still have my number?" he asked.

"Uh yeah." This is beginning to get uncomfortable.

"Use it anytime beautiful," Keith said, as he backed up, still staring at Taylen.

I didn't even say anything. Taylen finally loosened his grip and I ducked under his arm and walked over to the elevator, with him right behind me.

"Wassup with you and Keith?" I asked Taylen.

"What do you mean?"

"You playin' dumb now? I mean, why were ya'll having a stare-off?"

"Cause I told that nigga that you were off-limits!" he stated, looking in Keith's direction.

"What? How the hell? You know what?" I couldn't even find the words to express myself.

The elevator came and I got on and pushed four and eight. Only the two of us were on and once the doors closed, we leaned on opposite walls. His sexy ass was looking at me with a smirk on his face. He was looking fine as hell in some tan slacks and dark teal button-down shirt. Everything fittin' like it was tailor-made.

"You got a problem?" Taylen asked.

"Why would you tell Keith, or anyone, that I'm off limits? What the fuck Taylen?"

The elevator stopped on the fourth floor and he pushed himself off the wall.

"You will be soon enough." He kissed my cheek as the elevator doors opened, then walked out.

"How does he know that I want to be his girl? He got some nerve telling somebody I'm off limits. That nigga really got some balls!" I said all of this to myself as I rode up four more floors. I wanted to be annoyed but walked off the elevator smiling from ear-to-ear.

Chapter 17

Hazel

I'm fresh out of the shower, wrapped in a towel, standing in front of my closet trying to find an outfit for tonight. I heard a key in the door and turned around to see Karizma walk in.

"What's up?" I asked because she had a strange look on her face.

"Girl, niggas are a trip," she replied, shaking her head.

"What happened?"

"You know when you left, I was talking to Keith's fine ass. He asked me if I was going to the game tomorrow." She continued to tell me about what went down in the lobby. I could do nothing but laugh. Taylen was staking his claim to her and wanted everyone to know it.

"Taylen ain't playin' no games. He ain't givin' nobody a chance to snatch you up. Girl, what did you do to him?" I laughed.

"Not a damn thing. I asked him why he told Keith that I was off-limits. His cocky ass said, 'you will be soon enough' and kissed my cheek then walked off the elevator." I could barely control my laughter. Karizma knows she liked that shit. I know it would have turned me on.

"Are you even attracted to Keith?" I asked.

"Hell yeah! Have you seen him?" She had a point. That nigga is fine. But he didn't have nothing on Taylen. Taylen was magazine ad and billboard kind of fine.

"Yeah, he's easy on the eyes, fa sho. But are you attracted to him in the same way that you are attracted to Taylen."

"No, not really. Taylen and I have some kind of crazy vibe connection. I've only known him a week but it feels like we've known each other for years. He's so sweet, protective, smart, ambitious, strong, and do I even need to say how fine he is. Not to mention he saved me from Marcus twice and is willing to do it again."

"Clearly, whether Taylen is blocking or not, Keith don't stand a chance and neither does anyone else. Stop playing!"

"I know right! But it's the principle! You don't get to tell people I'm off limits when I ain't your girl!" She laughed. "Let me hit the shower so we can hit the streets. I'm ready to shake my ass somewhere!"

Karizma got in the shower and I got me an outfit together. As I set the ironing board up, my phone went off, letting me know I had a text message.

Bishop: Hazel

Me: Bishop

Bishop: What r u doin?

Me: About to iron some clothes for 2nite

Bishop: Oh. Ya'll goin' out?

Me: Yep

Bishop: I got curfew in a bit. Wanna c u right quick.

Me: OK

Bishop: Meet me in your commons area

Me: OK

I put on some shorts, a tank top, and my Nike slides and knocked on the bathroom door.

"Hey Rizzy. I'll be right back!"

"Okay!"

When I made it to the commons area, Bishop, with is sexy ass, was already there, sitting on one of the couches.

"Hey Beautiful! I haven't seen you all week. I just wanted to lay eyes on you for a few minutes." He stood up when I made it to the couch and gave me a tight hug.

"Hey yourself! This week has been crazy. Just trying to figure out my life." I laughed.

"Well I hope you can figure out a way to include me in it." We were still standing, so he sat down and pulled me down onto his lap.

"I may be able to arrange that, if you keep acting right." I flirted.

"That won't be a problem at all." He smiled. "So, what are you ladies gettin' into tonight?"

"We haven't figured that out yet. There are a few parties so we have some options," I told him.

"Hmm…what are you wearing?" he asked, while rubbing his hand up and down my leg.

"I don't know yet. Why do you ask?"

He laughed. "You sexy as hell, Hazel. I know niggas gon' be comin' at you left and right. I guess it don't really matter what you wear."

"Aww, are you jealous Bishop?" I teased.

"Naw man, calm all that down. I just know how niggas can be. I'm not gonna be around and I just want you to be careful."

"I will. Karizma and I are big girls. We can handle ourselves."

We sat in silence for a few minutes. He was still rubbing my leg with one hand and started playing with the hair and the nape of my neck with the other. I promise I felt his dick getting hard beneath me.

"Are you ready for the game?" I broke the short silence.

"Man, I'm so ready. You comin' right?"

"Yeah, of course. I'm excited for you. As a matter of fact, you should probably head back down so you don't miss bed check. I don't want to be the reason your ass is sittin' on the bench tomorrow." I tried to get up from his lap but he pulled me back down.

"Never that, sweetheart. I still have some time. Just sit with me for a few more minutes. I'm enjoying just being with you." Shit! I didn't have any panties on under these shorts and they just got wet.

"Me too. I don't want you to get in trouble though."

"I'm good! Don't worry about me."

"I'm not worried. Just lookin' out for you. How was your first team dinner?" I asked.

"It was cool. Way better than the food in the caf'," he replied.

"I bet. Damn near anything is better than that shit," I said and we both laughed.

"Hell yeah! I'm gonna be looking forward to more than just the games on the weekends."

"Yeah, the football and basketball teams get all kind of special treatment around here. I'm sure they ain't gon' lay it out for us like that."

"Ya'll don't bring in no money," he teased.

"So what! We work just as hard, if not harder. Forget you Bishop!" I mushed his head and attempted to get off his lap.

"Aye, cut all that out. Where you going? I'm just playin' with your sensitive ass."

"Whatever. I'm going to get dressed. It's time for you to go anyway." I tried to stand again, this time he let me.

We both stood and he grabbed my hand and pulled me in the direction of the stairwell. We walked down the hall in silence, holding hands, until we got to the door.

"Will I see you tomorrow after the game?"

"Ummm, maybe for a little bit. But Karizma and I were invited to a party. Some guys on the track team that live off campus are throwing it."

"Dang! You just kickin' me to the curb huh?" he teased but looked like his feelings were a little hurt.

"No, it's not like that. They invited us earlier in the week. I didn't know you would want to hang out," I explained.

"Why would I not? But it's cool." He legit looked like he was upset. How was I supposed to know he wanted to do something?

"Why don't you and Taylen come with us? It's not a private party or anything."

"Naw, I told you it's cool. I'll just see you before you go. Let me get back to my room." He pulled me into a hug and kissed my neck. I felt chills all the way down to my toes. Whew!

"Okay. Good luck tomorrow."

"Thanks!" he said as he opened the door to the stairwell and left.

When I got back to my room, Karizma was almost done getting dressed. She had on a yellow maxi dress and it looked so good against her chocolate skin.

"You look cute! What shoes are you wearing?"

"I haven't decided yet. Where'd you go?" she asked.

"Down the hall to the commons area. Bishop wanted to see me before bed check. And you are right, niggas really are a trip."

"Oh shit! What he do?" Karizma questioned.

"He got a slight attitude because I told him we were going to a party tomorrow night. He wants to hangout."

"Taylen and Bishop must be related. I swear they act the same way. Why do they expect us to keep our schedules clear for them?" She shook her head.

"I know, right! I told him that they can come with us to the party but he didn't seem interested so it's whatever." Bishop is going to have to learn how to communicate. He can't just assume that I'm gonna be available whenever he has time. As fine as he is, I've only known him a week.

"Yeah, it's whatever," Karizma agreed.

"Give me twenty minutes and I'll be ready. Let's check out the strip and see what's poppin' tonight."

"Sounds like a plan!"

Chapter 18

Bishop

I don't know why it bothers me that Hazel is going out tonight and tomorrow night. I guess I shouldn't expect her to stay in tonight just because I can't do anything. But damn, tomorrow, I planned on being with her. I might as well get over it though because ain't shit I can do. We aren't a couple and I shouldn't have any expectations of her. Even knowing that, I'm still feeling some type of way. I think I like her more than I care to admit.

"Look Mani, I'm not sure how you think it is down here. But you can't just come here for a weekend during football season. When we have home games, on Friday we have a mandatory team dinner and then bed check and we can't have anyone in our rooms for that. On Saturday, we have games and Sunday we have practice and film. I don't have time to be entertaining you!" I heard Taylen trying to explain to Imani when I walked into our room.

"If I don't mind waiting around until you have some time, why do you care? It sounds to me like you would rather me not come. Besides, Keesha was gonna come too and we could hangout while you and Bishop are gone." I heard Imani whine because the phone was on speaker.

Wait! Hold the fuck up! I must be hearing things. I know damn well Imani and Keesha aren't making plans to come stay with us for no damn weekend. First of all, me and Keesha ain't even together like that. I looked at Taylen and mouthed "no fuckin' way", while waving my arms back and forth!

"This ain't no damn hotel Imani. We barely got room for just me and him. I'll see you when I come home for Thanks---"

"You're okay with not seeing me until Thanksgiving?" Imani interrupted.

"Damn Imani! I don't have a choice. What do you expect me to do?"

"Nothing Tay! Just forget I said anything. I gotta go!" she said quickly and then hung up.

Taylen let out a long sigh.

"I take it Keesha hasn't mentioned anything to you about coming down here, huh?" Taylen asked.

"Hell naw and it would have been a negative for that shit! I ain't even talked to her ass since she hung up in my face last week."

"Them coming here would be a disaster," Taylen expressed with a worried look on his face.

"Who the fuck you tellin'?" I agreed.

Keesha coming here would mess everything up that I'm trying to do with Hazel. I need more time to tell her about BJ. I'm not ready to tell her yet. All I know is I want Hazel and I don't need Keesha fucking it up.

"What's up with Hazel. Ya'll good?"

"Yeah we straight," I answered dryly.

"Damn, it don't sound like it."

"Naw, we good. I'm a little heated about her going to some party tomorrow that some guy on the track team is having. It bothers me that I'm mad about it." I shook my head.

"I think that's the party Karizma told me she was going to?" Taylen sat up on his bed.

"Yeah, her, Karizma and a few other teammates of theirs."

"Hmm…Karizma told me about a party but she conveniently left out whose party it was." Now Taylen sounded like he was in his feelings about it.

Now this is new. Taylen and I have been friends for a long time. Never have either of us ever clocked a girl's moves. I let out a chuckle and Taylen looked over at me.

"What's funny?" he asked.

"The fact that we both sittin' here like our damn dog died over two girls that we've only known for a week. Ain't this some shit?" I laughed again and he joined me.

"Damn! We are, aren't we?"

"Yep! And on that note, I'm taking my ass to bed. Maybe when I wake up I'll be back to the Bishop that don't give a fuck." I heard the words coming out of my mouth but I didn't believe not one of them.

Chapter 19

Taylen

It's Saturday morning and today I will play in my first college football game. I can't lie, I'm nervous as hell but I'm also excited. I'm ready to knock some heads and get this first win under our belt. Growing up, I always thought that I would play basketball in college. I wasn't able to play little league football because I was too tall and weighed too much for my age group. Because of that, my first experience playing football wasn't until my freshman year of high school. That year, I played on the sophomore level and the years following, I played varsity. Basketball took a backseat during my senior because my love for football was so strong. Playing football in college and possibly the pros has been a dream of mine since the first down of football that I played.

The game is at one o'clock but we had a team breakfast at nine. As Bishop and I were getting ready to walk out the door to go to breakfast, there was a knock on the door.

"Shit, I hope this ain't Faryn's ass!" I whispered as I pulled the door open without looking through the peephole. Bishop laughed.

To my surprise, it was Karizma and Hazel.

"Hey! What are ya'll doing here?" I stepped back and gave them room to come in.

"We wanted to come and wish you luck in person." Karizma grabbed my hand.

"Aww shit! Ya'll trying to be all sweet and shit!" Bishop said, grabbing Hazel by her waist and pulling her close to him.

"Whatever Bishop! Are you guys about to leave?" Hazel asked Bishop.

"Yeah. We're headed over to the Student Center for the team breakfast," Bishop answered.

"Daamnn, ya'll get breakfast too?" Hazel asked, surprised.

"Yup and stop hatin'," Bishop told her.

"Ya'll wanna walk with us?" I asked Karizma.

Her and Hazel looked at each other and then looked down at themselves.

"We look a hot mess," Karizma said.

They were both wearing tank tops and running shorts, which I've noticed is their chill mode uniform. Karizma had her hair in a bun and Hazel had a baseball cap on with her afro sticking out around the sides and back. Karizma's not wearing a bra, which I noticed that she rarely does.

"Ya'll look fine to me. Let's go!" I pulled her out of the room. Hazel followed while Bishop locked the door.

The dorms were quiet since it was still early. We took the stairs down the four floors and I grabbed Rizzy's hand as we left the building. As we made it to the entrance of the bridge that took us to the campus, Keith and Trey did as well.

"Wassup," Keith and Trey said, simultaneously.

They all spoke and I gave them a head nod. I'm still not fuckin' with Keith's sneaky ass.

"Rizzy, are ya'll going to the party at Phil's house tonight?" Keith asked.

"Yeah, he invited us. How do you know him?" she inquired.

"He's from my hometown and is good friends with my older brother," he answered, never taking his eyes off of Karizma.

"Oh yeah? So, are you going to the party?"

"Hell yeah! I heard his parties be lit," Keith said, excitedly. He glanced at me and smirked. This nigga ain't slick.

"That's what my teammates said. We're looking forward to it."

"Cool! I guess I'll see you at the party." Keith grinned.

Bishop and Hazel were in their own world, having their own conversation. I was getting more pissed by the second. It's obvious that Keith wants me to beat his ass. I'm gonna have to find out where this party is tonight because I'm not leaving that door wide open for his ass to make a move on Rizzy.

"What did you ladies end up doing last night?" I asked Rizzy, wanting to end the conversation between her and Keith.

"We hung out on the strip. It was crazy down there. The White people were kickin' it hard as hell, weren't they Hazel?"

"Man, they were on ten and you know how drunk White people act. It was pure comedy," Hazel added.

"Hell yeah! My stomach is still sore from laughing." Karizma rubbed her stomach as she thought about last night and laughed again.

"Ya'll up and out pretty early for a Saturday. What time did ya'll get in?" Bishop asked Hazel.

"I don't know. Maybe about 1:30," Hazel replied.

"What do you guys do after breakfast? The game isn't until one, right?" Rizzy asked me.

"We have meetings with our position coaches, ice, heat or whatever in the training room," I told her.

"Oh okay. Did you get a good night's sleep?"

"Sure did. I dreamed about you all night too." I grinned and heard Keith suck his teeth.

"Shut up lying Taylen. You did not!" she gasped.

"I swear I did."

"Tell me what it was about then." She pursed her lips together, waiting for my reply.

"I'll tell you later. Meet me by the stadium locker room after the game so we can walk back together." We made it to the Student Center and was about to part ways.

"I guess I can do that." She looked at me with desire in her eyes. I know she's feeling the kid as much as I'm feeling her.

I leaned down and kissed her on her forehead, then her cheek. "Awight, I'll see you later Pretty Girl. Thanks for walking with me."

"Okay. Good luck again," she said as her and Hazel walked back towards the bridge.

I looked around and saw Keith's punk ass staring in my direction. Our eyes met, then he looked towards the direction that Rizzy and Hazel were walking. He whispered something to Trey, which I'm sure was about Rizzy, and they dapped each other up and laughed. He can play if he wants to. Soon he'll realize that I don't play about mine. Karizma is mine!

Chapter 20

Hazel

Karizma and I went back to our room after walking the guys to the Student Center for their team breakfast. They don't serve breakfast on weekends and brunch doesn't start until 11am.

"Keith is something else huh?" I said to Karizma. We were both lying on our beds on our phones.

"Oh my God Hazel!" She sat up on her bed. "He clearly saw me with Taylen and was talking to me like Taylen wasn't even there."

"But did you notice how he was looking at you. He couldn't take his eyes off of you!" I turned on my side so that I could face her.

"I hope I'm not being too friendly with him and sending him mixed signals. His ass had the nerve to wink at me too. I'm so glad Taylen didn't see it."

"Taylen cock-blocking ass probably would have punched him in that eye." I laughed.

"Yup!" She laughed. "What were you and Bishop over there whispering about?" She changed the subject.

"Shut up! We weren't whispering. I told you that he had an attitude last night. I asked him about it and he tried to deny it at first. But then he finally admitted that he was disappointed about us not hanging out tonight."

"Aww. He really likes you Hazel. Maybe you should hang with him. I can go to the party with the other girls," Karizma offered.

"Hell naw! This is Phil's first party of the year and everyone said it's gonna be lit. I'm not missing it. I told him again that he could come but he said he was cool and told me to have a good time. Shit, Ricky use to try to guilt me into to staying home all the time. I'm not doing that shit again." Ricky had something to say every time I hung out. But I guess it was easier for him to do his dirt if I was at home.

"Awight, I hear you! But I think it's sweet that he's in his feelings about not being able to spend time with you. It's only been week and you got his nose wide open," she teased.

"Maybe so. But right now, I'm about to take a nap. I don't even think I wanna get up for brunch." I got up to close the blinds and then got back in my bed and under my blanket.

"Me either! I'm gonna set my alarm for 11 and we can grab something at the Student Center before the game."

*****

When Karizma's alarm went off, I begrudgingly got up and hopped in the shower. As soon as I was done, Karizma did the same. With this being the first game, I wanted to be cute but it's so damn hot, that was gonna be a challenge.

"What are you wearing?" I asked Karizma as soon as she stepped out of the bathroom.

"I have no idea. It's too hot and I'm already irritated thinking about being out in that sun," she replied.

"Tell me about it! But let's hurry up so we can eat. I'm starving," I told her.

We quickly found something to wear. I decided on a blue and white Adidas tank top and some matching running shorts, with my shell toed Adidas. Karizma wore a green tank top dress that is fitted but not tight. She paired it with some white Converse. As usual, we took some pics for the 'gram and left to go grab a bite before the game.

We decided to eat subway. Once we bought our food, we found a table that allowed us to see the people walking through the Student Center. A few minutes after we sat down, I saw Marcus walking through with a girl on his arm.

"Karizma, is that Marcus?" She looked in his direction and nodded her head but didn't say anything.

"Looks like he found himself a new boo," I commented.

"Looks like it. She looks familiar to me," Karizma said.

"Oh shit. I think he saw you. Don't make eye contact!" I whispered.

We busied ourselves eating our food and trying to go unnoticed but to no avail. Marcus and his new boo were standing in front of us.

"Hey Rizzy!" Marcus said, all chipper and shit.

Rizzy looked up, rolled her eyes, looked back at her phone and took a nice big slurp of her drink. The girl that was with Marcus was pretty but she had a stank look on her face, like she didn't want to be there. I'm sure this is awkward for her.

"It's like that now. You can't even speak?" More silence from Rizzy.

Marcus went to grab Karizma by her arm and his new boo stopped him. She stepped in front of him and I could tell by her demeanor that she was about to go off.

"Really Marcus! Did you forget that I was standing here? What are you gonna do, make her talk to you? Hasn't she rejected you enough?" She yelled after stepping in front of him, between him and Karizma.

"Shut the fuck up Nisha. I'm just trying to say hello." Marcus moved Nisha out of the way.

"I thought we were better than that Rizzy. I miss you," Marcus pleaded.

"Oh hell naw! Fuck this. Your delusional ass can't see that she not fuckin' with you and you think I'm gonna stand here and watch you beg her to talk to you. After giving you all the pussy you could ever want for the past six months, this is the respect I get!" Nisha was standing in front of Marcus again with her hand folded, upset and about to cry. Wait! Did she say the past six months?

Karizma finally looked up again and shook her head.

"I knew you looked familiar. You know him from home?" Karizma stood and Nisha turned around and faced Rizzy.

"Yep! And we've been together for over six months," Nisha proudly answered.

Karizma walked around Nisha and got in Marcus' face.

"I don't want you to confuse what I'm about to say and think that I give a fuck about you. But explain to me how you've been fucking her for six months and we were dating for ten," Karizma said to Marcus.

"Rizzy baby look…it's not what you think. She was just something to do until you decided to give me some pussy."

"What! Wow Marcus. So that's all I am to you. Well fuck you! When I have this baby, you remember that shit!" Nisha yelled and stormed off.

"Wait! What? Nisha what did you say? Nisha! Come back here! You pregnant?" Marcus yelled, running after Nisha.

"Well! That was…interesting," I said to Karizma.

She sat back down and when we made eye contact, we both burst out laughing. I swear, her life could be a damn book.

"So I guess he was fuckin' other bitches like he said. I'm so glad I didn't give his ass my virginity. I dodged a huge bullet!" Karizma declared.

"Hell yeah you did! Let's go so we can get some good seats!"

Chapter 21

Taylen

"That's what the fuck I'm talking about!" I yelled as my teammates and I ran to the locker room. We had just pulled off a surprising win, when I caught an interception and ran it in for a touchdown with twenty seconds left on the clock. Because of me, we won by six points.

"That shit was wild!" Bishop shouted, as we held our helmets up and banged them together.

I couldn't be happier with my performance in the first game of the season. I put up some good numbers and we got the W. The locker room was on ten because we were all excited about the upset. After the coaches said some positive words, reminded us that we had conditioning and film to watch in the morning, they released us. I couldn't wait to shower and find Karizma.

Just as I asked, she was waiting for me. I smiled when I saw her but it quickly turned into a frown when

Keith walked up and hugged her from behind. This nigga here! When she turned around, she was smiling but her expression changed to one of confusion.

"Ayc yo Bishop! You scc that shit?" I askcd Bishop, who was walking next to me. I picked up the pace so that I could get to her quicker.

"Yeah, he foul as hell," Bishop commented.

"Taylen, great game!" Karizma said, nervously. She walked away from Keith and stepped into my waiting arms. "Nice interception!"

"Thanks, Pretty Girl!" I kissed her forehead.

"I'll see you at the party later Karizma," Keith said with a wink to Karizma, and walked away, mean mugging me.

I looked over at Bishop and he just shook his head and put his arm around Hazel.

"What are you ladies about to get into?" Bishop asked Hazel, as they began walking.

"Well, since we're going to that party tonight, we thought we'd hang with you guys for a little while," Hazel responded.

"How nice of you to give us some of your time." Bishop joked, although I think he was a little serious.

Karizma and I were walking hand-in-hand but she seemed a little distracted.

"Wassup? We hanging out or do you have other plans." I asked Karizma. She looked at me and smiled.

"No plans until later. I'm all yours for now." Her saying that made my dick jump.

"I like the sound of that."

"What are you guys about to get into?" Karizma asked Hazel and Bishop.

"Let's go get something to eat at one of the places on the strip," Hazel suggested.

I was hoping to spend some time alone with Karizma but I guess I'll have to wait until our date tomorrow.

"Sounds good," I answered.

We chatted while we walked the rest of the way back to our dorm. Karizma and Hazel sat in the lobby while we took the stairs up to our room to drop off our bags.

"I'm gon' fuck Keith up!" I told Bishop as soon as we were out of the girl's earshot.

"I feel you man. But you really can't do that. Karizma is not your girl. Imani is," Bishop reminded me.

"Fuck that. He can have Imani's ass." We both laughed.

"Seriously though. I know he's getting under your skin. But what can you do?" Bishop asked.

"I guess you're right. I can't do shit until I break up with Imani. But I know one thing for sure."

"What's that?"

"We goin' to that party tonight!" I declared.

"Bet!" Bishop agreed.

We dropped our bags off in our room and went back down to the lobby. There was a small crowd of people hanging out. As we walked to where the girls were waiting, several people, guys and girls, stopped us to congratulate us on the win and shoot the shit. By the time we made it over to the girls, thirty minutes had passed. I was starving at this point.

"Finally! I thought we were gonna have to go without you guys," Hazel told Bishop.

"Our bad. People just kept coming up and talking to us. Let's roll!" Bishop replied.

We left the building and walked in the direction of the strip. It's still hot as hell, even though it's after five o'clock. We decided to eat at Quatro's Pizza. I've heard from others that it's pretty good.

Hazel and Bishop seemed to be enjoying each other's company, talking to each other. Karizma was quiet. I notice she's been quiet after the game.

"So, what's up with you and Keith?" Fuck it, why pretend like that shit ain't bothering me?

"What do you mean? Ain't nothin' up with us. He's my friend, just like you are."

"Oh really? Ya'll hangout and shit?" I pressed.

"No, we've never hung out. I only talk to him when I see him."

"You like him?" I continued.

"Do I like him? I mean, he seems cool." She dodged the question.

"That's not what I mean Rizzy?"

"I don't know him to like him. I just told you we don't hang out. I've only seen him a couple of times," she voiced.

"Do you want to know him?" I know I'm out of order questioning her like this but I need to see what the fuck was up with them. She can't control him talking to her, but she doesn't have to look like she enjoys it. Maybe she wants to get to know him.

"Seriously Taylen! If I did I would be going to get something to eat with him, not you. And why are you questioning me? We've known each other for a week," she scolded.

"What did I tell you last night?" I paused, waiting for her to answer but she said nothing. "I told you that I told him that you were off limits."

"And I told you that you can't be tellin' him, or anyone else, that I'm off limits." Why does she keep saying that? *Maybe because she's not my girl.*

I didn't say anything else until we got to the restaurant. I'm not gonna force her to stop talking to Keith or any other dudes. But I'm gonna take up so much space in her mind that she won't have the time to entertain nobody else.

Chapter 22

Bishop

Quatro's Pizza was busy but we didn't have to wait. We sat in a booth, with Hazel and I sitting on the same side and her sitting on the inside. Karizma and Taylen did the same on the other side.

We ended up each ordering personal pizzas because everyone wanted something different. We were enjoying each other's company, sharing things about our lives, how we grew up, and our families. Thankfully, our dating life didn't come up.

Just as the waitress brought our pizzas out, my phone vibrated on the table. Why my dumbass had it sitting on the table, face up, I have no idea? Keesha's name displayed across my screen? Shit! I hit decline and put my phone in the pocket of my shorts. Taylen and I made eye contact and so did Hazel and Karizma.

I should have called Keesha after the game to avoid her calling me. But Hazel has taken over the forefront of my mind so I didn't think about it. My phone buzzed in my pocket again and all three of them looked at me.

"Maybe you should answer that," Hazel stated, with an annoyed look on her face, giving me the side-eye.

"Naw, I'm good."

Low and behold, my phone went off again. I decided to slide out of the booth and step outside to see what the hell had Keesha calling me back-to-back.

"I'll be right back," I told them. I slid out of the booth and went outside to answer my phone.

"What Keesha!" I yelled into the phone when I got outside.

"Why the fuck are you yellin' at me?" Keesha yelled back.

"Because your ass is blowin' up my damn phone. What do you want? Is BJ okay?" I asked, concerned that something may be wrong with my son.

"BJ is fine! I wanted to see how your first game was," she said calmly, as if she didn't just call me several times in a row like someone had died.

"Keesha, I know damn well you weren't calling me just for that. You couldn't wait for me to call your ass back?"

"Nope! But clearly you're too busy to talk to your son's mother."

"What the fuck man! Don't be blowin' up my phone on no dumb shit no more. I don't have time to be playin' with your ass. Where is BJ?" She was really trying my damn patience.

"He's taking a nap. You'll have to FaceTime me later if you want to see him."

I took a deep breath before I replied to her. I just couldn't understand why she was so damn annoying. Keesha was cool as hell while we dated, after we broke up and while she was pregnant. But after she had BJ, it's like her goal is to be the baby mama from hell.

"Awight, I'll call you in a couple of hours. Make sure he's up man. Bye!" I was just about to hit end and I heard her saying "Wait", so I put the phone back up to my ear.

"What Keesha, damn!"

"Well, I wanted to talk to you about bringing BJ down for a visit. He misses his daddy," she whined.

"First of all, BJ is only four months old. I miss my son but I will be home to see him in a couple of months. My schedule is too crazy for you to bring him right now," I explained to Keesha.

"Fine! I will leave him here and just Imani and I will come."

"Hold the fuck up! That ain't gon' work either. Taylen told me that Imani said something to him about ya'll coming to visit and he shut that shit down. It's football season Keesha. I don't have time to entertain people. Ya'll can't come right now, end of discussion. I gotta go!" I quickly hung up, turned my phone all the way off and went back into the restaurant.

"You straight?" Taylen asked, giving me a knowing look.

"Yeah, it's all good. How's the pizza?" I quickly changed the subject. I didn't want Hazel asking me anything about that phone call. I know she saw Keesha's name and this isn't the first time she has blown up my phone like this. Shit!

Chapter 23

Karizma

Our impromptu double date was nice, although Bishop's phone call did make it a bit awkward for a few minutes. Hazel couldn't see him while he talked on the phone because she was sitting facing the other direction. But I saw it all and it looked intense. I don't think she should worry about it because whoever it was, it didn't look like someone he wanted to talk to at all.

We walked back to the dorms and I was all set to go our separate ways. I wanted to take a nap before the party. However, Taylen and Bishop had other plans. Bishop ended up talking Hazel into going to he and Taylen's room to hangout so Taylen came to our room. I hope he's sleepy because I'm still taking a nap.

Taylen sat on my bed as soon as we entered the room and I went to the bathroom. When I came out, he had found the remote and was watching ESPN.

"I wanna take a nap," I informed him as I washed my hands.

"Okay." He was sitting in the middle of my bed, the short way, with his legs hanging off. There was no way I could lay down.

"I can't lay down with you sitting on my bed like that."

He smirked but didn't move.

"Taylen, I wanna lay down. Can you move?" I whined.

He stood up and took off his shirt and I had to catch my breath. Oh my God! His skin was smooth and the color of dark chocolate. His chest and abs looked like they had been chiseled by Picasso himself. I knew that I was staring but I couldn't tear my eyes away if someone paid me to. He took off his shoes and instead of sitting, he laid down and reach his hand out to me. I was frozen in place, stuck, looking at him with googly eyes. My mouth was watering so I swallowed so that I wouldn't start drooling.

"Come lay down with me," he commanded, still reaching out for me.

He was lying with his back against the wall and I took my shoes off and laid down in front of him, with my back to his chest. *Lord, please don't let me give him my virginity today.* He wrapped his arm around my waist and pulled me closer to him, if that's possible. This twin-size bed ain't made for two people, especially if one of them is the size of Taylen.

My heart was beating fast and I mentally counted to ten, trying to calm myself down. I wonder if he can sense my nervousness. Just being this close to him had my kitty feeling things she never felt with Marcus. How the hell am I supposed to take a nap? I felt Taylen rubbing his nose in my hair and began praying that it still smelled good. I guess it's too late to be worried about that now.

It felt so good being in his arms that I finally began to relax. Just as I began to doze off, my phone, which was on the floor next to the bed, buzzed. I reach down to grab it, which caused Taylen's arm to fall from around my waist and rest on my ass. I turned to look at him and can't believe this nigga is already sleep. It was a text message from Keith.

Keith: Hey do you need a ride to the party?

Me: No, we are riding with one of my teammates.

Keith: Okay cool. I was gonna see if you wanted to go get something to eat before we go.

Me: No, I'm good. I just ate actually. Thx tho

Keith: c u later then.

Me: Yup

"That nigga really wants me to beat his ass," Taylen said very calmly but startled the hell out of me and I dropped my phone.

"Oh my God! You scared me. I thought you were sleep."

"Yeah, I bet you did." He pulled me back close to him.

Taylen is killing me with his attitude towards me being friends with Keith. I ain't gon' lie though, it's kinda cute. I smiled thinking about this fine ass man lying behind me as I dozed off in his arms.

*****

Sometime later, we woke up to Hazel entering our room. Damn! How long have we been asleep? The curtains were open and it was dark outside. I removed Taylen's arm from around my waist, sat up, yawned and stretched. Taylen didn't move.

"My bad! I didn't mean to wake ya'll. Jazmine text me and wants us to be ready in an hour," Hazel informed me.

"Shit! Taylen," I called out and shook him a little.

"What baby?" he answered. *Baby?*

"We gotta get dressed. Our ride will be here in an hour. Wake up," I told him.

"Okay," he replied but still didn't move.

"Taylen!" I shook him again. "Wake up."

"I'm up baby. Just give me a second to focus." He finally opened his eyes. *He called me baby again.*

"I'm about to hop in the shower," Hazel said before going into the bathroom.

I stood up and went to my closet to find something to wear. It's a house party so there's no need to get all dolled up. As I looked through my jeans, I decided on a skinny low-rise pair of ripped jeans and pulled them out. My shirts were stacked on a shelf at the top of the closet and sometimes hard to reach. I stood on my tippy toes when I spotted the crop top that I wanted to wear and started to reach for it when Taylen came up behind me and grabbed me by the waist, startling me yet again.

"You like scaring me, don't you?" I asked as I leaned my head to the side to look at him, noticing that he had put his shirt back on.

"Wasn't trying to. But I'm about to go. Text me later, okay." He kissed my cheeked and then my neck, sending chills through my body.

"Okay. Can you grab that red shirt right there for me?" I asked, pointing to the shirt.

He reached up and grabbed it very easily. Before handing it to me, he held it up and looked at me and then back at the shirt.

"For real Karizma! You're about to put this little bitty ass shirt on," he asked.

"Uhh, yeah. There's nothing wrong with this shirt. It's cute!" I grabbed it from him and tossed it on my bed with the jeans that I was gonna wear.

"Your ass better make sure you wear a bra with it," he commented.

"What?" I asked, confused.

"I notice that you have a habit of not wearing bras. You need to start," he said sternly.

"Uhh, yeah, okay," I replied, not taking him the least bit serious.

Taylen shook his head and walked to the door. "Don't forget to text me." Then he was gone.

Chapter 24

Hazel

I grabbed my towel and stepped out of the shower to dry off, wondering if Taylen had left.

"Rizzy is Taylen gone?" I called out.

"Yeah, it's safe to come out. Sorry about that!"

"No, it's cool. That must've been a good ass nap though." I laughed.

"It really was. I'm sure he was exhausted but I slept like I'm the one that had the game. What did you and Bishop do?" she asked.

"We talked, played Uno, put on a movie and fell asleep," I shared.

"Look at ya'll bonding and shit. All we did was take a nap." I laughed. "Did you ask about Keesha?"

"Naw, I let it ride. It was kind of awkward when we first got to his room. I was so close to asking about her. Then I remembered that we weren't in a relationship," I explained.

"I didn't get a chance to tell you because we haven't been alone. I could see Bishop talking on the phone and it didn't look like a pleasant conversation. I don't know who this Keesha is to him but he ain't happy with her right now."

"Maybe she's an ex that doesn't want to let go. You know how that can be." We both giggled at the reminder of Marcus.

"Don't I though! But I wouldn't give it too much thought. Now let me go shower before Jazmine gets here." Karizma grabbed her toiletries and ran off to get in the shower.

I hadn't thought about the fact that Keesha could be an ex until I said it. I still think it's odd that he wouldn't just say that. But earlier I decided to just let it ride so I'm going to continue to do so.

I decided to wear a pair of ripped skinny jeans and a shirt that opened in the back. I held the shirt up and decided that it didn't need to be ironed. As I began to lotion my body, there was a knock on the door.

"Shit! I hope this ain't Jazmine!" I said to myself as I walked over to look through the peephole. It was Bishop. Hmm, I wonder what he wants. I grabbed my towel, wrapped it back around me and opened the door.

"Hey! You miss me already?" I teased.

"I actually do," he answered, pulling me to him by my waist. "Why are you answering the door half naked?"

"I looked through the peephole so I knew it was you. What's up? I'm getting dressed and Rizzy will be out of the shower soon."

"Oh, you left your phone in my room. I thought you might need it." He reached in his back pocket and handed me my phone.

"Thanks! I didn't even realize I didn't have it." I took it from him tossed it on my bed. When I turned back around, he was still in the doorway, leaning on the frame. This man is fine!

"I'll let you get dressed. Call or text me when you get in tonight."

"It'll be late. Are you sure?" He had me by the waist again.

"Yeah. Taylen and I are about to get into something. Not sure what but I should still be up." He kissed my forehead.

"Okay. Later!"

He made his way to the stairwell and disappeared. I think I really like him.

*****

Karizma and I were waiting in the front of our dorm building for Jazmine to pick us up. It had cooled off a bit since the sun went down but it was still very warm. There was a good amount of people hanging out in the lobby and in front of the building. Groups of people were walking towards the bridge, headed to the main campus.

The outfit I decided to wear looked good and if I needed any reassurance, the looks I got from the fellas did that. One of the best things about running track is the body that comes from all the hard work I put in. Can't nobody tell me shit about my body!

"Where the hell is Jazz?" Karizma asked, looking at her phone.

"She said ten minutes. She should be here in a f---." Before I could finish, her truck rolled down the street. I stepped a closer to the curb and Karizma followed as Jazmine pulled up.

"Hey freshies!" Jazmine greeted us. I got in the front seat, while Karizma took the back. "Ya'll ready to kick it? Phil has a DJ friend from his hometown that comes and sets that shit off."

"We've heard several people talking about how great his parties are so I'm ready to throw this ass in a circle," Karizma replied and did a little dance in her seat.

"Aww shit! Don't hurt nobody." Jazmine laughed. "His family has money so he's lived off campus since his sophomore year. The house he lives in is nice as hell, especially for this area," Jazmine explained.

Jazmine is very pretty but in a traditional kinda way. Today is the first time I've seen her in anything besides workout clothes and she cleans up well. I'm sure she has her share of guys trying to lock her down.

We road to the party with the music blasting and windows down, getting in party mode. When we turned down the street that I assumed Phil lived, there were already a lot of cars parked up and down the street. We had to park a good distance from his house and I was thankful that I decided to wear my wedge Converse instead of heels or sandals since we had to walk.

The party was already live! We could hear the music outside, where there were a few people out front. As soon as we walked in, Phil grabbed Jazmine and pulled her into a hug.

"Wassup Jazz!" Phil said with his arm around her neck. "I see you brought the freshies with you." He looked me up and down while licking his lips.

"Hey Phil!" Karizma and I said simultaneously.

"Let me show ya'll where the food and drinks are. There is alcohol available so ya'll freshies can drink at your own risk. I'll be around, if you need something, come find me. Ya'll cool?" Phil rambled as he walked to kitchen area.

"We good. Let's go ladies," Jazz said and we followed behind her.

Hazel and I grabbed a bottle of water from one of the coolers, while Jazz got herself a wine cooler. We continued to walk through the house, catching a few eyes, until we ended up in the back yard. That's where all the action was.

Phil has a huge, fenced in backyard. He had lights strung all the way around the fence and a huge makeshift dance floor in the center of the yard. That was pretty much it as far as decorations. There were picnic tables and folding chairs set up around the perimeter, some occupied but most of the people were on the dance floor.

"This is really nice!" Karizma commented as she danced in place a little bit.

"Yeah, it's a nice set up," I agreed.

"He only does three parties a year. He'll have another when we come back from Winter break. He sets up a huge heated tent back here and it's pretty nice. Then he does another in May before graduation," Jazz shared.

"Wow! That's pretty cool. Let's go dance, this is my shit right here." Karizma said, dragging me to the dance floor as Jazmine followed. Cardi B's "Bodak Yellow" was on and the crowd went crazy reciting the lyrics and dancing.

"These expensive, these is red bottoms, these is bloody shoes ," the three of us rapped along with the lyrics while we danced.

The DJ followed that song up with three more songs that had us glued to the floor. By the time we left the floor, I had worked up a sweat and drank the entire bottle of water.

"I'm gonna go walk around a little. Ya'll straight?" Jazmine asked.

"Yeah, we good!" Karizma replied.

Jazmine walked in the other direction, towards this fine ass dude that I knew to be one of the star players on the football team. I tapped Karizma on the side and looked in the direction that Jazmine went. She followed my gaze.

"Is that her boo?"

"I don't know. I thought her and Phil were talking," I told Karizma.

"Hmm, gon' head Jazz. He fine as hell," Karizma said.

"Right! Let's go inside. I need another water."

Before we made it to the house, Karizma was stopped by none other than Keith. The dude is persistent if nothing else.

"Wassup Rizzy? You havin' a good time?" Keith ask her.

"It's cool. The DJ is on point!" she replied.

"Yeah! He's from my hometown too. We all grew up together," Keith said, reminding us that he and Phil were long-time friends.

I left the two of them talking and went inside to grab Karizma and I another bottle of water. As I bent over to grab them out of the cooler, I heard someone behind me.

"Damn! I didn't know you had all that freshie."

I got the waters and turned around to see Phil looking me up and down.

"Well, now you know." I grinned.

"So wassup with you freshie. How's college life treating you so far?" Phil asked.

"I love it! I mean, track practice be killin' me but it's what I've always wanted to do so I'm up for the challenge."

"I see you out there at practice. You holdin' your own," he complimented.

"What are you doing watching me? You should be focused on your own workout."

"Aye, sometimes, I can't help it. My eyes are drawn to beautiful things." He flirted.

Phil is a cutie. This is the first time that I've had a conversation with him but I've noticed him at track practice as well. He's the color of caramel, dreads down to the middle of his back, and a goatee that I'm sure would look good as hell if he let it grow into a full beard. He's only about six feet but his body is so lean that he appears taller.

"On that note, I'm gonna go back out and find Karizma." I went to step around him and he grabbed me by the waist.

"Why you running Hazel? I'm not gon' bite. You must got a man or something?" Phil persisted, with a smile, showing off his dimples.

I looked up at him, not knowing how to answer. Bishop isn't my man. I'm single. But for some odd reason I don't know how to answer him.

"I uhhh, I'm---," I stuttered.

"Damn Hazel. Either you got a man or you don't. I didn't realize it was a hard question," Phil interrupted. Still holding me close to him by my waist.

"I know, I just uhh---," Before I could answer, I heard what sounded like Bishop's voice calling my name. I turned myself out of Phil's grasp and saw Bishop walking towards me.

"Hazel," Bishop said loudly, but wasn't yelling.

"Hey Bishop! Umm, you didn't tell me you were coming to the party?" I asked, nervously. *Why am I nervous? I'm single.*

"I didn't know I was coming. Wassup man! I'm Bishop." He put his fist up, as did Phil, and they gave each other some dap.

"Phil, nice to meet you," Phil replied. "Help yourself to some food and drinks. Hazel, I'll check you later." Phil smiled and winked as he walked away.

Bishop pulled me to him by my waist and kissed my forehead. "You two were looking pretty cozy. What were you talking about?" He asked.

"Nothing. He said something to me as I was walking away and I didn't hear him. He grabbed me and pulled me back."

"What did he say?"

"I don't know because then I heard you calling my name and now we are here. Umm, let's go find Rizzy." I changed the subject and tried to walk towards the door but Bishop held me in place.

"I'm sure she's good. Taylen is here too. How well do you know him?"

"How well do I know who?" I asked, playing clueless.

"That nigga Phil. Don't play dumb Hazel."

"I'm not playing dumb. Why are we even still talking about him?" I leaned my butt against the counter while Bishop leaned against me, with his legs on either side of mine.

"Because it looked like ya'll were real friendly."

"Seriously Bishop! I know who he is because he runs track. That was the first time we ever spoke. I'm not about to have this conversation with you. I'm going back outside," I declared and pushed him away.

I walked out of the patio doors to find Karizma still talking to Keith. Oh shit! I guess Taylen hasn't caught up with her yet.

"Here's your water." I handed her the bottle. She glanced behind me and saw Bishop.

"Hey Bishop! Is Taylen here too?" Karizma asked.

"Why? You looked occupied," Bishop replied, glaring at Keith.

"Oooo---kaayy! Keith, I'll check you la---," she began to say but Keith interrupted, pulling her onto the dance floor.

"Let me get a dance," he said.

Before she could say no, Keith dragged her to the middle of the dance floor. I turned around to see that Bishop had spotted Taylen and waved him over to us. This ain't gon' end well.

Chapter 25

Taylen

I had been walking around for about ten minutes looking for Karizma with no luck. I saw some arms waving in the air out of the corner of my eye and looked up to see Bishop and Hazel standing near the dance area. But no Karizma. As I walked towards them, I looked around to see if she was in the vicinity but didn't see her.

"Where's Rizzy?" I asked Hazel.

"She's uhh…," Hazel paused.

"She's uhh where?" I looked around.

"Dancing with that nigga Keith. They out there in the middle of that crowd somewhere," Bishop answered for her.

Immediately, I'm pissed. Clearly Keith doesn't know what off-limits means. Unfortunately, ain't shit I can do about him pursuing her except step up my pursuit. If I'm all she can think about, ain't no room for her to have his ass on the brain. But I'm still pissed!

"Guess I'll wait here," I said calmly, although I wasn't calm at all. I was boiling inside.

Bishop and Hazel wandered off somewhere and I didn't even notice. My eyes were glued to the dancefloor as I waited to see Rizzy emerge from the crowed. Not one, not two, but three songs later, I see her walking my way, but not yet noticing me because Keith had her attention.

"Hey Rizzy," I said when she was practically in front of me.

"Taylen, hey!" she replied nervously. "Keith, I'll talk to you later. Thanks for the dance." She dismissed him.

"Damn, so it's like that Rizzy," Keith said, pissed. "I thought we were having a good time."

"Uhh, yeah. But I'm gonna talk to Taylen. I'll see you later," she told Keith.

"Naw, she'll be busy later," I said, pulling her to me by the waist and kissing her forehead. Keith narrowed his eyes and looked from me to Rizzy.

"Yeah, awight," Keith stated, walking away, looking a little defeated.

"What're you doing here?" Karizma asked me.

"It's a party. I can't come to a party."

"Of course. Why didn't you text me and tell me you were coming?"

"I didn't know this was where we were coming. One of my teammates asked Bishop and I if we wanted to roll. Since we weren't really doing shit, here we are." I lied, knowing damn well I made it my business to get here.

"It's a nice party. The DJ is the shit!" Karizma shared.

"Must be since I had to wait three whole songs for you to get off the dance floor," I teased. "You must have been having a good time with ole boy." I tried to look hurt. Shit I didn't have to try. I'm hurt.

"It was just a few dances Taylen. Geez!" She rolled her eyes.

"Yeah. Okay. I don't wanna talk about that nigga no more." I rubbed my hands up and down the sides of her waist.

"You're the one that brought him up. I never want to talk about him."

"Well shit! Every time I turn around, he's in your face or texting you. You might not want to talk about him but you don't mind talking to him." I tried to let that shit go because honestly, I had no right to be upset. But, I am, so it is what it is.

"Whatever! I'm not about to argue with you about that Taylen. I told you, he's a friend just like you're a friend. I'm not gon---". She started to say before I planted a kiss on those pouty lips of hers.

"Is he the kind of friend that can do that?" I said when our lips parted.

She looked up at me and smiled. "No but--"

"Ain't no buts. Me and him ain't the same kinda friend to you. You can stop saying that shit. But I guarantee he wants to be." I cut her off.

"Listen Taylen, chill out, damn. Let me just be honest with you. I think we could have something special. But we've known each other a week and I just got out of a relationship. I know you feel the need to let all the homies know that I'm 'off-limits'. But that's not necessary. I'm only trying to get to know one person on another level. That person just so happens to be you. Everyone else is just cool. Now can you just chill?"

I can't lie! Hearing her say that had me feeling giddy as hell. But I was kinda shocked with how she just bossed up on a nigga. Not to mention, it made my dick jump.

Chapter 26

Karizma

Last night we got in at about three a.m. and I was so tired that I didn't wrap my hair or brush my teeth. I didn't wake up until noon and that was only because my mom called. After chatting with her for a little while, I decided to get up and get some studying done before my date with Taylen in a few hours.

Speaking of Taylen…I'm afraid that I'm falling for him too hard and too fast. It's scary! We have so much chemistry that it's like we've been dating for years and we just met. I've been trying to figure out what it is about him that keeps him constantly on my mind. I can't even pinpoint one thing. It's nothing and it's everything.

"I can see why Phil's parties are so popular. That shit was poppin'!" Hazel said, pulling me out of my thoughts.

"Yeah," I replied, still thinking about Taylen.

"I like that everyone had a good time and there was no fighting," Hazel continued.

"Yeah."

"Rizzy, are you even paying attention to me?" she asked.

"Huh?"

"I've been talking to you and you over there on cloud nine. What are you thinking about? Or should I say who are you thinking about?" she questioned.

"Girl, nothing and nobody. Just trying to read this boring ass chapter," I lied.

"Yeah right! Your ass got Taylen on the brain and you know it. But I can't say shit because all I can think about is Bishop's fine ass," she shared.

"This is scary Hazel. I don't like that I like him so much so soon," I confessed.

"I wish I could offer you some advice but I'm in the same boat. It doesn't help that they are both so possessive. We couldn't entertain another nigga if we wanted to." She laughed.

"I know right!" I agreed.

"What time is your date?"

"Three. That's why I'm trying to get some studying done now. But I can't focus because I'm thinking about his ass." I laughed.

"Did he tell you what ya'll are doing?" She asked.

"Nope. I guess he calls himself surprising me."

"Aww, that's sweet! I'm sure it'll be fun. Try not to give him the draws just yet!" Hazel teased.

"You laughing but I might mess around and come back in here walking funny!" I joked.

"Girl please! You know you ain't givin' up the goods that quick."

"Naw, I'm not. But he's already closer to gettin' them than Marcus ever was."

We both got back to studying. At least I attempted to study but my mind continued to wander. Taylen seems just a little too good to be true. I need to slow whatever this is we got going down. I don't want to get too deep and he turns out to be a fraud after all. I need to find out if he's hiding something.

"Hey. Have you ever looked to see if Bishop has a Snap or Instagram?" I asked Hazel.

"I did but I didn't find anything. I actually asked him about it too. He said he doesn't do social media. Why?"

"I just realized that I've never asked Taylen or looked to see if he has any social media. That's usually the first thing I do when I meet new people."

"Let's look. I'll look on Snapchat and you look on Instagram," Hazel suggested.

I pulled up my Instagram app and searched Taylen Andrews. Several profiles came up so I scrolled through to see if any of the pictures looked familiar. Low and behold, a profile under the name @mrta38 came up with his picture.

"I think this is him," I told Hazel.

She came over and sat on my bed as I clicked on the profile. It was definitely him but there wasn't much posted.

"Doesn't look like he posts very often." Hazel observed.

"No, it doesn't," I agreed as I continued to scroll through his pics.

"I don't think he has Snap. Nothing is coming up," Hazel remarked.

"Look at this!" I gave my phone to Hazel, showing her a picture of Taylen and what looks to be his prom date.

"Interesting. She's cute. You think she's a girlfriend or just a date?"

I grabbed my phone to take a closer look at the picture. I really couldn't say if it looked like they were dating or just on a date. The way she was posed against him would make one think that they were in a relationship.

"I don't know. Can't really say either way."

I scrolled down to see if he captioned the picture and to look at some of the comments under the picture. Taylen's caption was "Prom". Just like a guy. Moving on to the comments and they were the usual, 'cute pic', 'you guys look great', etc. But one stood out from @manipooh38. It said, "Me and bae killin' it" with heart emojis following.

"I think she's a girlfriend," I said and handed Hazel my phone.

"Ahhh, yeah. How cute! She put his football number in her username too," Hazel said sarcastically.

"He hasn't mentioned having a girlfriend or even an ex. You think I should bring it up?"

"Hell yeah!" she answered quickly.

"Why do you think I should ask him about Manipooh but you won't ask about Keesha?"

"You have proof and you're just getting confirmation that she is an ex and not a current. I have no reason to believe that Keesha is a current girlfriend."

"I don't see the difference Hazel. But whatever. I'll think about it and decide later I guess."

I looked through the rest of the pics that Taylen had posted and there were a few more with Manipooh. She made her presence known in the comments of each picture that I saw. I clicked on her profile and didn't need any more confirmation that she was, at one point anyway, Taylen's girlfriend.

If Taylen has a girlfriend, it's a wrap for us. There is no way I'm about to be a side chick. He's not about to play me and her and get away with it. The thought of ending what we have before it's gotten a chance to get started made me sad. Shit!

Chapter 27

Taylen

It took everything in me to get my ass up and get to conditioning this morning. I knew I should have had my ass in the bed much earlier last night. I had no intentions of staying out until the wee hours of the morning. When I found out that David, one of my teammates, was headed to Phil's party, Bishop and I hopped right in his car. The only thing about riding with someone else is not being able to leave when you want.

The party was nice though. Once I found Rizzy, I chilled with her until David was ready to go. Turns out David and Jazmine, Rizzy and Hazel's teammate, are an item or something. I didn't realize that David had a girl because he seems to have several in rotation. But that's not my business.

After conditioning we had to watch two hours of film. Normally, that's right up my alley but today, I'm just ready to spend some time with my pretty girl, Karizma. We aren't really doing anything special. I reserved us a spot at this place called Panic Room. I think it's something that you do with a group of people but they said they are going to pair us up with or against other people when we get there. I don't know how it works, I just thought it would be something cool and different for us to do. Then we are going to Flame Grill and Bar for a nice romantic dinner. This is the first date I've ever planned so I'm a little nervous.

I have a couple of hours to kill and decided to take a nap. I grabbed my phone so that I could set an alarm to wake me up and saw that I had a text message.

David: Got some bad news. Somebody busted the windows out of my car while we were at practice.

Fuck! How the hell am I going to find a car to borrow on such short notice?

Me: Damn man! WTF!

David: I know man! It was probably one of my side hoes. I know you wanted to borrow it but that's kinda impossible now. My bad bruh.

Me: It's cool. Thanks for letting me know.

I'm screwed. There is no way we can go on this date on foot. These places are too far away. Shit! I fell back on my bed and rubbed my hand down my face. I need to figure something out because I'm not canceling.

I grabbed my phone and texted some of my teammates that had cars to see if I could borrow one and waited. Damn I hope somebody can hook me up!

A few minutes later, there was a knock on the door. I got up and opened it, without checking because I figured it was Bishop because he was always forgetting his key. To my annoyance, it was Faryn.

"What the fuck do you want Faryn?" I yelled.

"Damn Tay! What's your problem?" she asked, giving me the same attitude I gave her.

"Nothin' you can help me with. What do you want?"

"Are you sure I can't help? You seem a little tense," she said, rubbing her hand down my chest, past my stomach and to the waist band of my basketball shorts. This bitch!

"Hell the fuck naw!" I pushed her hand away and backed up, although doing that didn't stop my dick from getting hard.

"Umm, I think he feels otherwise." She nodded towards my dick.

"Listen, unless you have a car that I can use, ain't shit you can do."

"Is that all? You can borrow my car. I don't need it for the rest of the day," she offered with a smirk on her face.

"Are you for real? I got some important shit that I need to take care of and my homey had some shit come up so I can't use his car," I lied.

Faryn looked me up and down, licking her lips. I hope she's not getting any ideas because her ass won't be getting near my dick again.

"Faryn? Can I borrow your car or not?" I asked again.

"Yeah, I guess. But what do I get out of the deal?" She pouted.

"I'll fill your tank up. Let me get the keys though." I need to solidify this deal before she changes her mind.

She dug in her purse and found her keys, handing them to me.

"Here! And make sure my tank is full when you come back nigga!" She started walking away then added, "And don't have that bitch Karizma in my car either!" Then she disappeared into her room.

"Don't be callin' her no bitch!" I yelled loud enough for her to hear me.

I closed the door to my room then checked my phone to see if any of my teammates hit me back. A few of them did but borrowing their car was a no go. Faryn don't know it but she saved my day!

Chapter 28

Bishop

After practice, I decided to get some studying done at the library. I knew that if I tried to study in my room, I'd end up asleep or talking shit with Taylen. By the time I got back to the room, Taylen had already left for his date with Karizma. She had that nigga gone already. That's crazy but I can't say shit because Hazel had me the same way. Let me text her and see what her sexy ass is doing.

Me: Hazel Baby

Hazel: Bishop Boo

Me: Corny

Hazel: LOL

Me: U want some company

Hazel: Nope

Me: Oh it's like that

Hazel: Yep! I'm trying to finish reading this chapter for 2morrow

Me: Well that's all u had to say. Come c me when u done

Hazel: Okay. Give me about 30 mins

Me: Cool. Door is unlocked

I laid down on my bed and smiled, as I thought about Hazel's pretty face. Maybe tonight I can tell her about BJ. It's not like he's going anywhere. If she's gonna be my girl, I can't continue to keep him a secret from her. I need to know, sooner rather than later, if she wants to deal with a dude with a baby and the shit that may come along with it. I already know Keesha is gonna be a problem. BJ isn't Hazel's responsibility so it's not like I'm going to ask her to take care of him. As I went through scenarios of how Hazel could possibly react, I had dozed off. I woke up to Hazel placing kisses all over my face. I'm not sure how much time had passed.

"Wake up sleepyhead," Hazel said. She was leaning over me and I grabbed her and pulled her down to the bed, on top of me.

"I didn't realize I had fallen asleep. What took you so long?" I yawned.

"It was thirty minutes, like I said. You must have fallen asleep right away."

"I guess so. What have you been doing today?" I asked.

"Nothin' really. Trying to study but taking a lot of naps in between. That shit was boring."

"Yeah, I know. That's why I took my ass to the library. Wasn't shit gon' get done in this room."

"You should have told me. I would've come with you." She pouted those sexy lips.

"Naw that wouldn't have worked either. Because then all I'd wanna do is kiss these sexy lips all day," I said as I kissed her. "You would have been a distraction."

"Do you need a distraction now?" She flirted.

"It depends on what kind. What are you offering?" I flirted back and kissed her neck.

"I don't know. I'm kinda liking these kisses though."

"I got plenty of---," I started before we heard a knock on the door.

"Did you lock it?" I asked Hazel.

"No."

"Come in!" I yelled. Hazel was now laying off to the side of me with her leg draped over mine. Both of us were looking at the door.

The door opened and Faryn's ass walked in. Shit! What the hell does she want?

"Aww, isn't this cute? Where's Taylen?" Faryn asked.

"None of your business," Hazel answered.

"Umm, I beg to differ. He's in my car so I think I have a right to know his whereabouts!" Faryn took a few more steps into the room and put her hands on her hips.

Hazel sat up and looked at me. I shrugged my shoulders because I had no idea what Faryn was talking about. As far as I knew, he was using David's car.

"What are you talking about Faryn?" I asked.

"Are you deaf? Taylen asked to borrow my car and he didn't say how long he'd be. I asked where he is?" she asked again.

"Well we can't help you. You just gotta wait until he gets back," Hazel answered.

"I'm not talking to you!" Faryn stood with her arms folded across her chest, looking at me for an answer.

"So the fuck what, I'm talking to you and I said we can't help you!" Hazel snapped back a her.

"Chill Hazel." I shook my head. "I don't know where he is either, Faryn. I'll text him and see when he'll be back," I replied and looked at the door, hoping she take the hit to get her ass outta here.

"Fine!" She marched out and slammed the door.

I got up and locked it and when I turned around, Hazel was looking at me with a scowl on her face.

"What? Why are you looking at me like that?" I walked back over to the bed and laid down next to where she was still sitting up.

"You know exactly why I'm looking at you?" she said, giving me undeserved attitude.

"Actually, I don't. The last time I talked to Taylen about his date with Karizma, he was gonna use David's car. I ain't seen or talked to him since I left for the library, so you can lose that attitude," I expressed.

"I can't believe that Taylen would have the audacity to take Rizzy on a date in another girl's car. Especially Faryn's!" she exclaimed.

I agreed with Hazel on that. This was about to be all fucked up. I grabbed my phone off the floor to shoot Taylen a text.

"What are you about to do? Warn him that he's been found out?"

"I'm just trying to see what's up. Faryn's ass is crazy so I'm not gonna just take her word," I explained.

Me: Faryn just left here asking when you would be back with her car

Tay: Tell her in a couple of hours

Me: So you do have her car? I thought she was talkin shit. What happen with David?

Tay: Tell you later

Me: FYI, Hazel was here when Faryn came. She knows

Tay: Fuck

Me: Yeah

"What did he say?" Hazel asked as soon as I put my phone down. I wanted to lie to try and cover for Taylen but there was no way around this. I'm not about to have Hazel pissed at me for some shit that ain't my business.

"To tell her he'd be back in a couple of hours."

"You're telling me that he is in Faryn's car on a date with Rizzy? You've got to be kidding me!" she said in disbelief.

I could sense the change in her attitude. I'm going to legit fuck Taylen up if my time with Hazel is screwed up because he did some dumb shit. She grabbed her phone and started typing out a text, shaking her head the whole time.

"Are you texting Rizzy?" I asked.

"Hell yeah! She deserves to know." I snatched her phone from her hands before she was able to send the text.

"You're not about to tell her. That's not your job. This ain't our business," I told her.

"It is my business. She's my roommate and Taylen is shady as hell for this shit. Give me my phone Bishop!" She held her hand out.

"Naw, I'm not giving it back unless you promise not to text or call Karizma and mind your business."

"Ugh Bishop! This ain't right! If she finds out that I knew and didn't tell her, she's gonna think I'm bogus. I would want her to tell me!"

"How about this? If Taylen doesn't tell her by the time you see her again, you can tell her. I'm not talking about this shit anymore because this ain't our business and it's fuckin' up my time with you."

She folded her arms across her chest. "Fine! Now give me my damn phone!" She held her one of her hands out while leaving the other folded across her chest.

"Nope! You can have it back when you leave. Now let's talk about something else." I told her, putting her phone on the floor next to mine.

"You are so annoying!" She said but smiled.

"Yeah but you like my annoying ass, don't you?" I said as I laid back down on my bed and pulled her on top of me.

"I'm starting to but I don't know why!" she teased. "What do you want to talk about?"

This would be the perfect opportunity for me to tell her about BJ. But like a dumbass, I punked out. I need to make sure she's fully vested in pursuing a relationship with me and I need to make sure this shit with Keesha is completely over. Keesha ain't my girl but I did give her a good ass dick down before I left for camp. I can tell just by the way she's acting that she read too much into it. As soon as I make sure that Keesha knows that we are strictly co-parenting, I'm locking Hazel's fine ass down.

"What was your last relationship like?"

After a long sigh, she replied, "You mean my only relationship. It was cool, I guess."

"You guess?" I pressed.

"We went to high school together, same grade, had a few classes together. He played basketball and we both ran track. We were just cool at first. The summer after our junior year, right before school started back, I saw him at a party and he shot his shot. Stayed together until this summer."

"That sounds like a normal boy mccts girl, they fall in love type of story."

"Yeah, I thought it was love. By the time we graduated, we had broken up so many times, but I kept going back. He was the star basketball player, on varsity since his freshman year. Had hella groupies and couldn't be faithful. I dealt with it for too long but finally called it quits for good this summer." She told me, in such a way that I knew she was done talking about it.

"Yeah, well, I'm glad he fucked up because his loss is my gain," I said, kissing her lips.

"Your gain huh?" she said, after kissing me back.

"Ya damn right!" I said, tapping her ass. Before she could respond, one of our phones vibrated. She tried to reach down on the side of the bed but I tossed her on the side of me, next to the wall.

"Nope. You still can't have your phone until you leave." I rolled over to see which of our phones was buzzing and it was hers, with at text from Phil. Ain't this some shit.

"Wassup with you and Phil?" I asked.

"Huh? Are you really still on that? I told you we are just cool," she answered, irritably.

"Then why is he texting you and why is he saved in your phone as Phine Phil?" We both sat up and I gave her, her phone.

"What?" She laughed and looked at the message. "He's goofy. He must have done that last night."

"Oh ya'll exchanged numbers last night?" I'm pissed now.

"Uh no! I sat my phone on the counter at some point and walked away. A few minutes later he brought it to me so I'm assuming that's when he put his number in it," she explained.

I guess that sounded believable enough. "You need to put a passcode on your phone Hazel."

"Yeah, I probably should," she answered as she replied to his text.

"Hazel, are you fuckin' serious right now." I yanked her phone out of her hands.

"What Bishop, damn!"

"You just gon' reply to his text right in front of me? That's rude as hell."

"My bad! I forgot your ass be jealous." She laughed and planted kisses all over my face before she landed on my lips. "Stop being a baby!"

"Whatever man! Let's just watch a movie." I got up to see what the choices were from our collection of DVDs.

Hazel ass got me acting out of character, like a jealous boyfriend. Not to mention I ain't even sampled the pussy. *What the fuck is really going on?* I need to settle this shit with Keesha as soon as possible so that I'm not sitting around here getting mad about shit I have no right to be mad about. I need to lock Hazel's ass down quick, fast, and in a hurry.

Chapter 29

Taylen

So far, everything has been perfect. We had a great time at the Panic Room and we are now enjoying our dinner at the Flame Grill and Bar. Karizma ordered shrimp fettucine alfredo with garlic bread and I ordered a steak with a baked potato and sautéed vegetables.

"You ready for week two of classes?" I asked.

"It don't matter if I'm not, I still have to go." She laughed.

"True! Hopefully they will get better because it's gonna be a long semester if they don't."

"Right! I ain't gone make it if they don't," she agreed.

"What's your major anyway?" I asked.

"Exercise Science. I want to own a fitness center for kids one day."

"That's cool. Mine is Business. Specifically, Finance," I shared.

"You must like working with numbers. I can't do it. I'm okay at Math, I just don't like it that much."

"Yeah. It takes a special kind of person." I laughed.

We continued to eat and it was quiet for a few minutes, while we enjoyed our food.

"I have a question Taylen." Karizma broke the comfortable silence. Her tone made me a little nervous. She didn't sound upset, maybe a little concerned, which made me concerned.

"Anything."

"Who is Manipooh?" She asked very calmly. I almost choked on my drink but I covered very well.

"Manipooh?" I repeated.

"Yes. Manipooh38 on Instagram to be exact," she clarified.

I knew exactly who Manipooh was the first time she asked. I was just stalling so that I could figure out if I was gonna lie or tell truth. It was clear that Karizma had looked at my Instagram.

"You can answer any day now Taylen," she urged.

"Umm, Manipooh is Imani, my uhh, ex-girlfriend," I finally responded.

"Your EX-girlfriend, you say?"

"Yes, we broke up this summer," I lied.

"Oh. Why'd you break up?" she grilled me.

"Uhh, no reason really. She's only a junior in high school so I figured it was only fair, since I was going away to school."

"So you broke up with her?" she probed.

"Yeah. I thought it was best." I haven't been on my Instagram in months and I pray that nothing on it negates what I'm saying. *I need to delete that damn Instagram!*

"Make sense," she agreed. I breathed a sigh of relief. It appears that I dodged that bullet.

"Any other questions?"

"Nope, I'm good. I had to make sure you weren't playin' me. I like you a lot Taylen. But I don't want to get to know you on another level if you already have a girlfriend. I trust that you are being honest with me."

"Of course! I'm glad you asked. Now that that's out of the way, have you heard from Marcus, since we're talking about exes," I quickly changed the subject.

"Ugh! I forgot to tell you that Hazel and I ran into him before the game yesterday," she shared.

"And?"

"Nothing. He was with this girl named Nisha that's from back home. Apparently, they've been fuckin' around for the past six months and she's pregnant."

"What?" I whispered yelled.

"Yup!"

"Well damn! That's, uhh, messed up. How do you feel about that?" I asked. I know that she broke up with him but she might feel some type of way about the fact that he was cheating on her for most of their relationship and the girl is pregnant.

"I couldn't care less. Just glad to be rid of him, honestly."

"Understood. But that's still messed up," I repeated.

"Yeah, but it is what it is," she agreed as she took a sip of her water. "I'm gonna go to the bathroom before we leave."

She scooted out of the booth, stood and smooth out her dress. Even though she was dressed casually, she looked good as hell in an orange fitted dress with orange flat sandals. With her body, I can't imagine her ever not looking good.

As she walked away, my phone buzzed with a text from Bishop.

Fuck! I dodged one bullet with the whole Imani situation. Now I gotta explain why the hell I'm using Faryn's car. I can't get a break. I stood and stuck my phone in my back pocket as Karizma came back from the bathroom.

"You ready?" I asked her.

"Yep! What's up next?" she asked as we walked hand-in-hand to the door.

"Nothing much! I brought a blanket and thought you might want to go sit by the lake on campus after we go get some ice cream."

"I'm cool with getting the ice cream but it's getting dark outside and you know these mosquitoes have no mercy. I'm not trying to get attacked." She made a good point. I hadn't thought about that.

"Cool, then ice cream it is." I opened the door for her and waited as she got in before I closed the door and walked over to the driver side. Hopefully, Bishop will keep Hazel from texting Karizma. I'm going to tell her but not until this date is over.

We rode in silence all the way to Dairy Queen. I was distracted with my thoughts of how she was going to react to this being Faryn's car.

"You're pretty quiet. What's on your mind?" I asked her.

"You actually. I've enjoyed this a lot. Thank you for planning it."

Damn! She had a nigga feeling good. With this being the first date that I've ever planned, it was nice to hear her say that.

"I'm glad you had a good time. But it's not quite over yet. Let's go get some ice cream." We pulled at Dairy Queen and I got out and went to the other side to open her door.

There was no line so we placed our orders right away. Karizma ordered a strawberry and pineapple sundae with caramel topping. Weird combination but if that's what she likes, I'm cool with it. I ordered a banana split. There were some benches on the side of the building and we decided to sit there and eat, instead of in the car.

"Pineapples, strawberries and caramel huh? That's and interesting little creation," I teased.

"I love fruit and these two are my favorite. If I'm gonna eat all of these calories, at least a few of them will be good for me." She laughed and held a spoonful out to me. "Taste it."

I ate the spoonful and it was good. But I still preferred chocolate over caramel.

"It's decent. But my banana split is better."

We finished up our ice cream while making small talk and went back to the car. I walked to the passenger door with her and turned her around to face me before she opened the door. She leaned her back up against the car and I put my hands on the hood, on either side of her.

"I guess it's almost time for our date to end. I hope you had a good time."

"I had an amazing time. Best date I've ever been on," she confessed.

"Oh really? Well if that's the case, can I have a kiss?"

Instead of answering me, she stood on her toes, wrapped her arms around my neck, and planted a nice juicy kiss on my lips. When she tried to pull away, I held her neck in place and pushed my tongue into her mouth. Thankfully, she was receptive and mirrored my actions. As our tongues intertwined, I pressed my body against hers while her hold around my neck tightened. I almost forgot where we were until I heard her moan, then I pulled away. Both of us were a little breathless and I had to adjust my dick.

"We should probably get going," Karizma stated.

I agreed by opening her door and letting her into the car, closing the door once she was settled. I walked over to the driver side, quickly adjusting my dick again, with a huge smile on my face, until I remembered that I had to tell Karizma that this was Faryn's car. Shit!

Dairy Queen isn't far from the dorms and the parking where the students that lived in the dorms were allowed to park. Before I knew it, I was parking and walking over to passenger side to let Karizma out of the car.

"You're awfully quiet," she said as we walked hand-in-hand back to the dorms.

"Yeah. I was just thinking about how much I enjoy spending time with you and hoping that you feel the same," I replied.

"I do, Taylen. This was nice."

"That's good to know." *Just tell her now Taylen. If you wait and Faryn says something later, it's gonna be worse.*

"Look, Rizzy, I need tell you something," I finally said, as we neared the door to our building.

"Oh shit. This doesn't sound good. Is it about Imani?" she asked, nervously.

"Imani? What? Oh no. It's not about her." I shook my head. I had forgotten all about her asking about Imani earlier.

"Okay. So, what's up?"

"Well, when I planned this date, I was---," I began before I heard my name being yelled from a distance.

"Taylen! I know you hear me calling you!" I looked around and saw Faryn coming towards me with two other girls. Fuck! This cannot be happening!

Karizma and I turned in her direction and watched her and her friends marching towards us like they were on a mission.

"Not this bitch again," Karizma said.

"Wassup Faryn?" I said when she was in front of us.

"Nigga what the fuck you mean 'wassup'?" her dramatic ass said, doing the air quotes when she said wassup. She stepped even closer, now in my personal space, which meant, she was also in Rizzy's personal space. This shit ain't gon' end well at all.

"You asked me to use my car hours ago. When I agreed---," she continued until Karizma stopped her.

"Wait a minute, hold the fuck up. Please don't tell me that you just took me out on a whole damn date in this bitch's car!" Karizma yelled.

"First of all, who you callin' a bitch?" Faryn yelled back, getting in Karizma's face.

There was no way I was about to let them fight. I stepped in between them and pushed Karizma behind me as they continued to argue back and forth.

"Faryn shut the fuck up!" I screamed in her face. "Yes, you agreed to let me borrow your car and I appreciate it. Here are your keys!" I grabbed her hand a placed them there. "Thank you!"

"Nigga when I told you that you could borrow my car, I specifically told you not to have that bitch in it." Faryn just had to throw that out there as I tried to pull Karizma in the opposite direction.

She yanked her arm away from me and popped Faryn in her face so damn quick. Faryn didn't even see it coming.

"I told your ass the last time I would beat your ass. Don't fuckin' call me out my name again, hoe!" Karizma spat and walked away.

Faryn didn't even attempt to hit her back. She was too busy holding her damn nose. Her so-called friends did nothing. Karizma tried to walk past me but I grabbed her arm. She yanked it away from me again but stopped in front of me, folding her arms across her chest.

"Let me explain. That's what I was trying to tell you," I pleaded.

"I'm listening."

"Come walk with me over to this bench," I said, pulling her arms from her chest, surprised that she let me touch her.

When we sat down, I turned to face her but she was looking straight ahead.

"Look at me Pretty Girl." I tried to pull her by the chin but she moved her head back.

"I don't need to see you to hear you Taylen. Talk!"

"Okay. When I planned this date, David said that I could use his car. Earlier today, he texted me and told me that his windows were busted out. I didn't want to cancel so I texted some of my teammates to see if they would let be borrow their cars. Only a couple responded saying no, the others didn't respond at all."

"So you went to Faryn? You know I don't like that hoe! Why would you---," she ranted before I interrupted.

"Let me finish, Rizzy. I didn't go to Faryn. She just so happened to knock on my door and when I opened and saw it was her, I asked her what the fuck she wanted. I knew she was on some bullshit because she always is. I told her that if she didn't have a car I could use then it wasn't shit she could do for me. Then she offered to let me borrow it," I explained, hoping she would understand.

"We could have just canceled the date. I can't believe you thought it would be cool to take me out on a date in that bitch's car!"

"I know! I just…I was really looking forward to being with you, getting to know you, and showing you a good time. I thought you were just as excited as I was and I didn't want to disappoint you. I didn't think it through and I'm sorry, Rizzy."

"Why didn't you just tell me this before? Then I could have told your ass that I wasn't going anywhere in that hoe's car!"

"That's why I didn't want to tell you. It would have ruined the whole date. Didn't you have a good time?"

She sat her fine ass over there pouting, not wanting to look at me, with her arms still folded across her chest. She didn't answer me for a good minute.

"Just because we were in Faryn's car, you saying you ain't have a good time?" I pressed.

"Yes Taylen! I had a great time. I just don't like being caught up in drama and you know damn well, you taking me on a date in her car creates drama!" she pointed out.

"I know and I'm sorry. I didn't plan on you finding out like that. Since I'm being honest, I didn't plan on you finding out at all. Bishop sent me a text saying Faryn came to our room wanting to know when I'd be back with her car and that Hazel was there. I knew there was no way you wouldn't find out. I decided to tell you at the end of our date," I confessed.

"Wow! Just…wow!" Rizzy looked at me, shaking her head in disappointment . "You do know that you could have called an Uber?"

"What can I say? I didn't even think about an Uber. I was desperate and I didn't want to cancel. I didn't even know she had a car and I never would have known had she not come knocking on my door. I know it was fucked up but I meant well. I just wanted to give you the perfect date and see you smile. It worked, up until now. Do you forgive me?"

I gave her the saddest, puppy dog eyes that I could and put my hands together like I was praying.

"Please! Baby I swear it won't happen again." I continued batting my eyelashes and pouted my lips for a more dramatic effect.

"Okay fine! I forgive you. But you need to stay away from Faryn's ass. Don't borrow shit else from her. Not a cup, a spoon, water, milk, nothing!" she demanded.

"That won't be a problem. I don't deal with her anyway. Now let's go inside."

We stood from the bench and walked towards our building, with my arm around her shoulders. When we got to the lobby, Faryn was holding her nose, sitting in the lounge area with her friends. They all looked in our direction and watched us as we waited for the elevator. Karizma turned to face me, wrapped her arms around my neck and pulled me in for a kiss. I know she only did it to piss Faryn off but I took full advantage and grabbed a handful of her ass. We kissed until we heard the elevator doors open.

From our first encounter, I knew that there was something special about Karizma. I immediately felt the need to protect her and keep her safe. I also felt…possessive, like she was already mine and I didn't even know her name. The time we spent together today confirmed what I already knew.

Chapter 30

Karizma

The first month and a half of school and track practice has flown by. Classes were going smoothly so far. However, the track workouts are ridiculous. Each day I'm pretty sure I'm going to die but I always live to practice another day.

Taylen and I are still getting to know each other. People around campus assume we are a couple and neither of us correct them. There is something about him that I can't seem to resist and it's scary. He's so damn fine and charming. I can't begin to explain our connection. However, he hasn't asked me to be his girlfriend and until he does, I'm technically single.

Today is Friday and I'm so glad because I am exhausted. I'm about to hit the shower and go to bed. I began getting my toiletries together and Hazel walked in our room.

"Hey Rizzy," she said as she collapsed on her bed.

"Hey! Are you just getting out of practice?"

"Yes. Well, no. I just came from dinner and I damn near missed it. You know I practice with distance girls on Fridays and my ass got lost on this damn route we went on. Them bitches be running too damn fast. Me, Leah and Bailey got lost because we were so far behind."

"Geez! Are you serious?" I laughed.

"Hell yeah! I was so pissed. We probably ran two extra miles trying to figure out where the fuck we were. I'm glad I'm not the only slow running bitch because I'd still be out there if I was by myself!" She laughed at herself and the possibility. The distance runners run too damn much for me.

"Better you than me. I would die. I'm barely making it through the sprint workouts now." I continued laughing at her. "I'm about to hop in the shower."

"Okay. I'll be doing the same after you. Bishop wants me to come up to his room before their bed check. You know they have a home game tomorrow."

"Of course and I'll be front and center to watch my boo do his thing. But I can't fuck with him tonight. I'm tired as hell and I just want to sleep."

The shower was just what I needed and gave me a little bit of energy. When I got out, Hazel got in and I decided to go down to Taylen's room to see what he was up to before I took my ass to bed for the night. I threw on some black leggings, tank top and slides. My hair was still wet and my natural curls were on display because I washed it while in the shower, so I put it up in a bun.

"Hazel, I'll be back. I'm about to run up on Taylen." I poked my head through the bathroom door.

"Okay!"

I decided to take the stairs down the four flights instead of taking the elevator. When I got to his room, I knocked on the door and it opened. *That's strange.* I walked in slowly and could hear the shower going.

"Taylen!" I called out and got no answer. I was pretty sure it was him that was in the shower because I saw his bag on his bed and his phone and keys were on his desk. Bishop's side of the room looked like he hadn't been there for a while.

"Taylen!" I called again and tapped on the bathroom door before turning the handle and opening it. What I saw when I opened the door pissed me off to no end.

"Taylen! What the fuck is going on?" I could see through the glass that his back was facing me and when I yelled his name, he turned around with shampoo still in his eyes and reaching for his face towel to wipe his face off.

"Rizzy? Hey, what are you do--Faryn! What the fuck are you doing?" he yelled and tried to cover himself up.

Faryn stood there, naked as the day she was born with the biggest smile on her face. Taylen looked just as surprised as I was.

"What do you mean Tay? You told me to come and shower with you after we made love." Faryn smirked, still standing there as if she wasn't naked.

"What? Bitch you know damn fuckin' well I ain't never fucked you and I ain't gon' fuck you. Get the fuck out!" Taylen turned off the shower and made an unsuccessful attempt to use his face towel to cover up his dick. This nigga is packing so it did didn't work too well.

"Why do you always do this when she's around?" Faryn said, giving me the evil eye before bending to pick her clothes up off the floor.

"You know what? Fuck this shit! I'm out!" I slammed both the bathroom and the dorm room door and took the stairs back up to my room.

"Hazel, you ain't gon' believe this shit!" I yelled as soon as I opened the door to our room.

"Damn, what happened that quick?"

"When I got down there, the door was cracked so I went inside. I could hear the shower so I called Taylen's name. I knocked on the bathroom door before I opened it and when I did, Faryn's ass was standing there fuckin' naked, like she was about to get in the shower with Taylen." I paced back and forth in front of my bed.

"What?! You lyin'!" Hazel was in shock.

"I wish I was. Taylen seemed surprised when he saw her and told her to get the fuck out. But she said he told her to come shower with him after they fucked. We she actually said 'made love'!" I shook my head again.

"You've got to be kidding me! What did he say?"

"He said she knows they've never fucked and she asked him why he always acts this way in front of me. I just said fuck it and left. I don't have time for this bullshit. I should have taken my ass to bed like I was gonna do in the first place. She's gonna make me beat her ass but I'm not about to fight over a nigga who ain't mine for real."

Suddenly, our room door swung open and Tay stood there with just a pair of basketball shorts on, looking like a whole got damn meal. He still had droplets of water on his chest. As my eyes gazed up and down his body, I would swear he wasn't wearing any underwear...and I got wet down below. But I couldn't let him know all that.

"Taylen, you can't just be barging up in here! What the fuck?" I stood with my arms folded, leaning on my right leg.

"Rizzy, I promise you I didn't know she was in there. I'm not fuckin' around with that girl!" Taylen began to plead his case, holding on to my shoulders. I didn't respond because I was so mesmerized with his body. My thoughts were in the gutter and my words were stuck in my throat.

"Baby," he tried again, "I swear to you, I have not had sex with her and I did not tell her to come shower with me. I didn't invite her into my room. I don't even know how she got in there." He looked so cute as he kneeled in front of me when I sat on my bed. I still didn't respond and he put his head in my lap, still pleading. "Please baby, you have to believe me."

Finally, I decided to put him out of his misery. Honestly, I did believe him. The whole scene looked suspect. But what convinced me was how he called my name when he heard my voice and the look of shock on his face when he saw Faryn's ass standing there naked.

"I believe you," was all I said. He looked up at me smiling, batting those eyelashes that women would kill for.

"You do? Good because I was gon' have to beat her ass and I don't even believe in hittin' females."

"You need to do something about her," I told him.

"Yeah Tay! For her to only have sucked your dick, she sure is psycho over you," Hazel chimed in.

"Right! Are you sure that's all that happened between you two?" I teased.

"Man, ya'll go head on with that shit. I don't even want to think of her nasty ass no more." He shook his head in disgust.

"She wasn't nasty when she was slobbin' all on your knob!" I laughed and Hazel and I gave each other a high-five.

"Bishop just texted me so I'm going downstairs for a few. I'll check ya'll later," Hazel said as she left the room.

"Are you sure you believe me, baby?"

"Yes, I believe you."

He leaned in and kissed me, gently at first. Then his tongue penetrated my lips as he pushed me back on the bed and laid on top of me. I opened my legs enough for him to lay between them as our tongues continued to wrestle. I could feel his dick getting hard and I wrapped my legs around his waist as our hips grinded together. His mouth found its way to my ear and my neck and the way he worked his tongue had my pussy leaking.

He lifted my shirt and took turns playing with my nipples, one getting the tongue, the other, his thumb. My brain was telling me to stop him but my body was saying the opposite. What he was doing to me felt so damn good. His fingers made their way into my leggings and he pressed his thumb on my clit. I was about to fucking lose it. I had never let a guy get this far and now I'm wondering why. This feeling was unreal. Our make out sessions have been getting more and more heated. I'm contemplating giving him my virginity—when we become an official couple that is.

"Ahhh, shit! It feels so good."

He spoke in between licking and sucking my nipples. "You like that huh?"

"God yes!" The next thing I felt caused me to tense up. I think he stuck his finger in my pussy while he continued to rub my clit.

"Damn baby, relax. Shit, you so fuckin' tight!" He moved his finger in and out as his thumb went in a circular motion on my clit. I swear to God, if this is what heaven feels like, I'm ready to go now. All of a sudden, my body starting jerking and I wanted to scream but I was afraid people would hear me.

"You cumin' baby?" he asked me like I knew what the hell was happening.

"I I I don't---It feels---ahhh Taylen! What is --- Oh-my-God!" I couldn't even finish a thought. This was the best feeling ever. My body finally stopped seizing and I just lay there, out of breath. Taylen took his hand out of my leggings and smiled.

"Damn baby!" he said as he looked at the clear fluid on his hand. Then he licked it and said, "You taste almost as good as you look!" I didn't know if I should be disgusted or turned on at that moment.

"Oh my God! I'm so embarrassed." I put my hands over my face. Taylen came back from washing his hands and pulled them away.

"Why are you embarrassed?" He laid on top of me.

"Why do you think? I don't even know what just happened."

"What happened was you had an orgasm. I assuming that was your first?" I don't know why this fool was smiling at me with those perfect white teeth.

"You assume correctly." I shook my head and covered my face again with my hands.

"Wow! I feel so honored to have given you your first. Don't be embarrassed. I hope to give you many more in the future." He pulled my hands away and looked directly into my eyes and kissed my lips.

"Maybe. Now get off of me so that I can clean myself up." He rolled off of me and I went to wet a towel with warm water so that I could wipe between my legs. I'm gonna need to go get some birth control because if this nigga made me feel like that with his finger, I can only imagine what that dick do.

"I have a question." I heard him say.

"Shoot," I said as I peeked out of the bathroom.

"Why the hell don't you have on a bra or panties?" His tone seemed a little agitated.

"Huh? Why do you ask that?" Confused, I walked back over to my bed.

"Because you're walking around here with your ass and titties all out!"

"I rarely wear bras because they are uncomfortable. As for the panties, I usually do wear them but I was planning to go to bed after I showered but decided to come see you and you know what happened with that," I informed him.

"You need to start wearing bras. I can't have my girl out here with her shit all out."

"First of all, you can't tell me what to do. Secondly, I didn't realize I was your girl, so until that is officially the case, this conversation never happened." How is he trying to regulate me and I'm not even his to regulate? Boy Bye!

"You not my girl?" I hated when he gave me the sad face. Those eyelashes and dimples would make you do anything he asked.

"Not unless I missed something."

"Even after I just made you cum for the first time?" I was still standing in front of my bed and he grinned and looked up at me.

"Nope," I repeated.

"Why is a title even necessary? We know what we are?" he asked.

"I don't but it's cool. I'll see you tomorrow." I walked towards the door.

"You puttin' me out? It's like that?"

"Just like that." I don't know what he expected me to say.

"Awight then. I'm gonna head upstairs and knock out. I'll text you in the morning and see you at the game tomorrow, okay." He got up and put his hand around my waist.

"I guess."

"What do you mean, 'I guess'? Aren't you coming to the game, Pretty Girl?"

"I guess I'll be there. Not too much else going on around that time." I tried to hold my fake pout without laughing. He and I both knew I was gonna have my ass at that game, front and center.

"Don't play with me Rizzy. I'll be looking for you in your usual spot."

He kissed me on my forehead and cupped my butt cheeks with his large hands. I stood on my tippy toes and gave him a long peck.

"Make sure your ass wears a bra to my game Rizzy!" He opened the door and walked out, going towards the stairs.

"Yeah, whatever." I dismissed him as I closed the door.

I gave that nigga the perfect opportunity to make us official and he didn't take it. He'd better hope another nigga don't snatch me up. Ha! Who am I fooling? I don't want nobody but him. I went and brushed my teeth and before finding something that I could watch on TV until I fell asleep.

Chapter 31

Hazel

The football team has had three homes games so far this year and played their asses off, getting the wins. Karizma and I will be sitting right at the 50-yard line just like before.

"Rizzy are you almost ready?"

"Just about. Trying to decide what shirt to wear. It's hot as hell and you know I hate bras!"

"Well your boobs are the perfect size. I don't need a bra but I wear one for the extra padding!" I laughed but I was so serious. Bigger breasts wouldn't benefit me as far a track is concerned but I hope they get a little bigger before it doesn't matter anymore.

"Taylen was talkin' shit to me about not wearing bras last night. I told his ass that I wasn't his girl so he can calm all that down."

"I'm sure you told him that too, but you know that's your boo." Karizma is one of the most blunt and forward people that I know. She has no problem expressing herself at all.

"I sure the hell did and he talking about 'why do we need a title, we know what we are'. I'm not worried about Taylen's ass. I'm about to wear this shirt with no bra just to let his ass know he don't run shit."

She held up a maroon shirt, which is university colors, that had three slits in the back. When she put it on, it hugged her upper body perfectly. It looked hot with distressed denim shorts and denim Converse.

"Alright now! You about to get some shit started! You look cute!" I told her as I gave her a high-five.

"So do you! Let's take a pic for the Gram!"

I wore a white, fitted tank top that said "Salukis" along the sides, in maroon, some dark denim shorts and my white Converse. My hair was in my signature free flowing afro, as usual, and my curls are poppin'. We took a few pics to post to our social media pages and left for the game.

Surprisingly, the elevator wasn't packed and we were the only ones on it. Usually before games, everybody was headed to the stadium and the same time. Just our luck, the elevator stopped on the fourth floor and that stalker bitch, Faryn, and two of her minions, got on.

"Well, well, well, fancy running into my man's side chick. We should sit next to each other at the game and cheer for our man together," Faryn said to Karizma as she stepped on. Her little puppies laughed like she had just told the funniest joke ever.

"Bitch, if you don't shut your crazy, stalkin' ass up talkin' to me!" Karizma said as she rolled her eyes.

"Are you mad because I had him first?" I don't know why this bitch thought Taylen was her man. He has made it clear that he don't fuck with her.

"Get the fuck off before I pop you in that dick suckin' mouth again!" Karizma had her fists balled up but I'm glad she didn't use them. Thankfully, we made it to the lobby without incident but Faryn is asking for a real ass whooping.

There was a large crowd of people already in the lobby getting ready to walk over to the stadium. I was happy that Faryn and her friends mixed in with them and wouldn't be near us.

"I need a favor, Hazel," Karizma asked with a strange look on her face.

"What?"

"I need you to come with me to get some birth control," she whispered.

"What! Are you serious?" I was surprised.

"Yep!"

"But why? Are you thinking about giving it up to Tay? Were we not just talking about how you two weren't official?"

"I know but…let me tell you what happened last night before he left," still whispering, she pulled me closer.

"Oh shit."

"After you left, we were just talking and of course, we started kissing and it got pretty heated. He was grinding his big ass dick all up against my honey pot and Hazel, if felt so fuckin' good!"

"Oh my goodness! It felt that good and ya'll ain't even do the do."

"Let me finish! So, the next thing I know, his hands are in my pants and he was rubbing my clit and fingering me." She squeezed my arm as she described.

"What! And you let him do it. Your ass was with Marcus for damn near a year and he didn't get that far."

"I know! It just felt so good that I couldn't stop him if I wanted. But the best part is," she paused and looked around for a second, "I came!" she whispered.

"Karizma, was that your first orgasm?" I wanted to laugh but I didn't want to make her feel bad. Shit, I was pleasuring myself long before Ricky came along and popped my cherry.

"Sshhh Hazel!" She looked around to see if anyone heard. "Yes, and that shit felt good. I didn't know what the hell was happening but I want to feel it again. But let me tell you want this nigga did afterwards though."

"Do I wanna know?"

"He licked his fingers and said I taste good. I didn't know if was supposed to be disgusted or not but that shit kinda turned me on."

"Damn! Well alrighty then. Yeah you go ahead and make that appointment ASAP. I have a feeling once you two become official, I may need to find another room, with yo hot ass!"

"Shut up Hazel!" Karizma said as she punched me gently on my shoulder. Hell, I was serious. Her ass was going crazy over his fingers, she's gonna lose her damn mind when she gets the dick. I know from experience what good dick can do to you.

*****

"What a great game!" I said to Karizma as we left the stadium and walked towards the locker room area to wait for the guys outside.

"Yeah, it was. I could have gone without the close score. I swear I had three heart attacks. Glad we got the win though!"

"It's too damn hot. I'm ready to shower and take a nap. This sun has me drained." I fanned myself with the football program.

"You act like you were the one playing in the game," Bishop said as he came up behind me, dropping his bag and putting his arms around me, kissing my neck.

"Shit! You startled me!" I turned to face Bishop to give him a quick peck on the lips.

"Why? Who else would be kissing you on the neck?" he questioned.

"Nobody but you still scared me. Ya'll played a good game." I addressed both Bishop and Tay.

Tay didn't even respond because he and Karizma were all hugged up. Yeah, she needs to get on the pill quick, fast, and in a hurry. She's about to let that nigga bust it wide open.

"Aye, ya'll ready to head back to the dorms or should we leave you two alone?" Bishop yelled over to Taylen and Karizma.

"Shut up nigga! Let's go!" Taylen yelled back, grabbing Karizma's hand and walking towards the bridge that leads the dorms.

The walk back to the dorm was long because the guys kept getting stopped by people that wanted to congratulate them for their win or just talk to them. I was getting annoyed but I guess if I'm going to date a football star, this is what I should expect.

"Rizzy, where's your bra?" I heard Taylen ask.

"Oh shit," I said.

"What are you talking about Taylen?" Rizzy replied innocently.

"Oh you wanna play dumb now?" Taylen continued but didn't push the subject.

We finally made it to our building and was about to get on the elevator. From a distance, I heard someone call Bishop's name.

"Bishop, I know you hear me!" the female voice yelled.

We all turned around to see where the voice came from. This beautiful, brown-skinned girl, with weave down to her ass and an hourglass shape, came marching towards us. The girl that was with her marched right up to Tay. I knew it was about to be some shit.

"Bishop, is this bitch the reason you hardly take any of my calls?" the girl yelled.

"Tay, who is this hoe?" the other girl yelled to Tay.

Karizma and I looked at each other. If she was thinking the same thing as me, she was probably ready to start swinging.

"Keesha, what the fuck are ya'll doing here? Where is my son?" Bishop screamed back.

Did this nigga just ask about his son? Oh hell naw! I guess I know who Keesha is now.

"Son? Bishop, you have a son and a whole damn baby mama?" I was heated at this point.

"Answer the bitch, Bishop!" Keesha said.

"Look hoe, I don't even know you but I ain't gon' be too many more bitches!" I snatched my hand away from Bishop's and walked towards the elevator and I could hear him right behind me.

"Hazel wait! Don't leave. I need you to hear this because from this point forward, I don't want any more secrets or misunderstandings."

I thought about it for a second and decided to stay in the lobby to see what he had to say to his baby mama. We walked back towards Keesha, as she stood there with an attitude and her hands on her hips.

Chapter 32

Bishop

"Why are you here Keesha? Where is BJ?" I don't know what the fuck is going on but this shit ain't good. Yes, I've been avoiding some of her calls, but Keesha knows the deal with our situation.

"I didn't bring him because I knew you were down here on some bullshit!"

"Why did you even come?" I asked.

"Bishop, I thought we were working on us. I guess I was the only one doing that since you down here acting like you don't have a son and a girl at home."

"Naw Keesha, don't do that. I have a son and a baby mama at home. You not my girl!" I can't believe that Keesha is acting like we are together. She knows that we are just co-parents that fuck occasionally.

"Damn! It's like that! You come down here and forget you got a whole fuckin' family at home. That's fucked up Bishop!"

"Keesha, stop fuckin' playin' with me. You know damn well that we ain't together like that. The only reason why we even communicate is because of my son!" He got in her face and pointed his finger down at her.

"I guess fuckin' is part of how we communicate?" I should have known her ass was gonna throw that in there. "What's wrong Bishop, cat got your tongue?" she said with a smug look on her face.

"Listen! We dated for three fuckin'months. It wasn't working and you know that shit. A month after we broke up, you say you're pregnant and it's mine. I'm not some bitch ass nigga so I wasn't gon' kick you to the curb when you could be carrying my seed. I believed you when you said it was mine and agreed to help you out while you were pregnant. Don't stand up here and act like I made you any promises about us being a couple because you know that shit never happened!"

"But Bishop---"

"Naw, shut the fuck up and listen! Yeah, we fucked around a few times after you had my son and I had the DNA test. But you knew what it was. You can take your ass on back to the Chi with this bullshit and go take care of my son!"

I was done talking to her ass. She thought she was gonna come down here and check a nigga but that ain't even happening. I wasn't trying to embarrass her ass in front of all these people but she fucked that up by coming down here and coming at me sideways.

"Fuck you Bishop. I'm gon' put your ass on child support with yo broke ass. You ain't shit for this. I'll find another nigga to take care of me and my son!" Keesha continued to scream as I turned to walk away.

I let Hazel's hand go and got right back in Keesha's face. So close that our noses were almost touching.

"Do what the fuck you think you have to do. But don't you sit up here and act like I don't take care of my son. I will fuck you up about my son Keesha and that's on my mama. Don't fuckin' play with me!" Keesha had me on ten. If I knew I could have gotten away with it, I would have choked her ass out.

I turned around and grabbed Hazel's hand and damn near had to pull her to the stairwell.

I'm stressed the fuck out. I know what just went down is gonna interfere with me seeing my son. I need to figure how to make this shit work without having to fuck Keesha up. I just hope now that Hazel knows everything, that she would still give me a chance.

"Hazel, I'm sorry," I said as we walked into my room.

"Sorry about what Bishop. Forgetting to tell me that you had a son and a girlfriend?" She is pissed. I sat on my bed and she stood by the door, looking like she didn't plan to stay long.

"She's not my girlfriend. What I said down there is true and she was trying to make it seem like more than it was." I need Hazel to believe that Keesha and I weren't a couple because it's the truth.

"How could you not tell me that you had a son though, Bishop? If you and Keesha aren't together like that, why would you hide the fact that you had a son?"

I couldn't answer that without seeming like a fucked up nigga. I knew that if I told Hazel about BJ that she would want to know the status of my relationship with his mom. I was one of those niggas that fucked their baby mama from time-to-time and I knew I couldn't lie about it.

"Because even though we weren't together, we did have sex on occasion. I knew that if I told you about BJ that I'd have to tell you that too. I wanted to make sure that I broke things off completely with Keesha before I told you about BJ," I explained.

"So, you were in a relationship with her then?" She folded her arms across her chest.

"No, I was not. She knew what it was Hazel. I told her and I made no promises about us being together. She was cool with that, I guess, until it looked like I might have somebody else."

She didn't respond and remained by the door.

"Come here," I commanded. She didn't move.

"Haze, come here please." I asked again. She came and stood in front of me as I sat on my bed. I pulled her close to me and rested my head on her stomach.

"I'm sorry baby. Don't let this situation fuck up what we're building. I like you…a lot," I pleaded.

"Then why couldn't you just be honest?"

"I thought me having a son would scare you away." Being with someone that has a kid can be a lot and I know that Keesha has crazy tendencies.

"Well it doesn't. But how you deal with his mother just might," Hazel said.

"I swear it ain't shit between us. Honestly, there never was. In the three months that we dated, I strapped up every time. One time the condom broke and here we are."

I was laying it all out and hoping that Hazel would understand. I pulled her down to my lap and buried my head in her neck, waiting for her to reply.

"How can I trust that you won't fuck her when you go home? You know baby mama's are easy pussy and she will most definitely be throwing it at you."

"You just have to trust me. I don't even want her like that anymore. I swear I don't." This girl ain't even gave me the pussy yet and here I was, begging her to give me a chance. What's really going on?

I looked her right in the eyes while she played in my hair.

"You promise?"

"I promise," I replied, feeling relieved.

"Look, I had to deal with Ricky cheatin' on me for damn near our whole relationship. I can't do that shit no more. If you can't be with only me, don't make promises you know you can't keep. It's cool how we are now, with no title."

I didn't answer her right away because I honestly need to think for a second.

"Listen Haze. If you be my girl, you will be my first real girlfriend. No other girl has had that privilege, not even Keesha. I've never promised a girl monogamy."

"Bishop, if you can't promise me that, then we can just be friends. But I will date other peop---,"

"Oh hell naw! Ain't gon' be none of that. I promise it's just me and you." I couldn't even let her finish that sentence because there was no way that shit was happening.

"Okay, I guess we can see where this goes."

"Does that mean you'll be my girl?" She didn't answer right away.

"Are you asking me to be your girl?

"Hazel, will you be my girlfriend?" I asked her.

"I just want to make sure we were on the same page. Ricky didn't seem to understand the concept of monogamy," she clarified.

"Aye, don't compare me to that bitch nigga! I ain't him!"

"I know, boyfriend."

"Gimme a kiss." I told her with my lips already poked out and ready. She was always trying to give me little ass pecks but I wasn't having that right now.

I grabbed the back of her neck and kissed her more passionately than I ever have. She turned her body to face me so that she could straddle me on the bed. I slid my tongue in her mouth and pulled her hips closer, rubbing my hands up and down her back. She let out a soft moan when my tongue traveled down the side of her face and made its way to her neck. I lifted her shirt so that I could give some attention to her breasts. Pulling one out of her bra, I licked around the nipple. I know she felt my dick on rock underneath her.

"Bishop," she moaned.

Everything about Hazel seemed right. Her personality, her goals, her ambition, and I won't even get started on her body. I could see a future with her. So many things were going through my mind as my tongue explored everything from her mouth to her breasts.

"Bishop," she moaned again.

"Yeah, baby?" I lifted up and flipped her over, so that I was on top. My dick is at full attention at this point. I ain't had no pussy in almost two months.

Hazel opened her legs so that I could lie between them. Our hips were in sync as we grinded against each other. My tongue continued to attack her body, moving down to her abs, which were perfectly toned. I began to unbutton her shorts and suddenly I heard her say my name again.

"Bishop, baby, we should stop."

As disappointed as I was, I stopped.

"Okay." I continued kissing back up her stomach until I reached her mouth. My dick was still hard as fuck but there wasn't shit I could do about it. Pecking her one last time, I got up.

"We not ready for all that just yet."

"Who ain't?" I looked at her and smiled. "Naw, I'm just fuckin' with you. You right." I laughed, trying to convince myself, more than anything.

"Bishop!" Hazel stood up and mushed me in the head.

"I was just playin'. I can wait as long as you need me to. No pressure," I assured her.

"I won't make you wait too long!"

"Word?" I said, surprised. "How long?"

"I'm not telling. You'll just have to wait," she said, giving me a peck on the lips.

As much as I wanted to feel her pussy wrapped around my dick right now, I also wanted to prove to her that this is more than that. This is new for me because I've never had a girl make me wait.

"I guess so!"

Chapter 33

Taylen

"Tay, you ain't got shit to say?" Imani yelled as she stood right in my face, pointing her finger into my chest.

"Why the fuck are you here, Imani?" I pushed her hands away with my free hand while I held Karizma's in the other.

"What do you mean, why am I here? I'm your girlfriend. Do I need a reason?" She rolled her neck and folder her arms across her chest.

Karizma tried to snatch her hand away from me but I wasn't having that shit. Imani can go kick rocks right now for all I care. This breakup shit is just formality. Karizma needs to stay her ass right here so that she can see for herself.

"Don't do that Rizzy, I want you to stay here." The look on her face softened a bit so I'm hoping that if I let her hand go that she doesn't take off.

"This bitch is the reason you be sending all those dry ass text messages and can never talk on the phone?" Imani questioned.

"You know what Imani. I was trying to wait until I came home to do this, I felt like I owed you that much. But since you're here now, showin' your ass, after I told you not to bring your hardheaded ass down here, I might as well do it now."

"Do what Tay?" She rolled her neck again and leaned towards me, arms still folded.

"It's over between us. It's a wrap!"

"Really Tay! For this bitch!" Imani screamed.

"Look bitch---" Karizma started to say. But I cut her off.

"Imani, don't call her out of her name again. This ain't about her."

"We've been together for over a year and you're about to throw it away for somebody you just met. That's real fucked up Tay." Her breathing picked up and I could see her chest going up and down. I could see the hurt on her face but in this moment, I had to follow my heart, and it was with Karizma.

"Imani, this ain't how I was trying to do this shit. I'm not breaking up with you for Karizma. That was gonna happen regardless, when I came home for break. It should have happened before I came to school but I thought that would be a little fucked up," I explained.

"Oh, like this ain't? You know what? Fuck you nigga and this bitch. I'm over this shit!" Imani yelled and tried to walk away but Karizma punched her right in her face and her nose immediately started bleeding. The same way she'd finished off Faryn.

"Call me out my name again and I'm gon' tap that ass for real!" Karizma spat as I pulled her towards the elevators, leaving Imani there with a bloody nose and yelling obscenities. Karizma is good for a quick punch to the face.

Imani put me in a fucked-up position and I didn't want to do her like that. But it is what it is. I'm trying to make shit official with Karizma so there is no way I was about to let Imani fuck it up, especially when I planned to break up with her anyway. It just happened sooner than I thought.

When we got on the elevator, I could tell Karizma was fuming. Her leg shook, arms folded across her chest, as her head swayed side-to-side in disgust. We got off on her floor and went to her room. I collapsed on her bed and she sat on the end, with her back against the wall. I know she had questions and I was going to answer them. I just needed a minute to collect my thoughts.

"You've had a girlfriend this entire time?" She finally broke the silence.

"I'm sorry. I know I should have been honest when you asked me about her but I planned to break up with her when I went home for Thanksgiving," I explained.

"Taylen, Thanksgiving is a month and a half away. Are you serious?"

I didn't answer her because that's exactly what I planned to.

"Just so you know, there is no way that I would have waited that long for us to become official. You basically made me a side-chick without my knowledge!"

I sat up and looked at her. She looked pissed but she was so damn cute. I couldn't even take her mad face seriously.

"You wouldn't wait for me Rizzy?"

"Hell naw!" she stated, scrolling through her phone.

"I thought you liked me." I pulled her chin up so that she could look at me.

"I do. But not enough for me to be giving you boyfriend privileges when you ain't my boyfriend. Nigga you crazy." She rolled her eyes and looked back at her phone.

I laid back down and put my hands behind my head. If that's the case, I'm glad things happened the way they did. Now I don't have to wait until November. I just took this as a sign that we were meant to be together.

"Come here," I told Karizma as I motioned for her to come lay on top of me.

"I'm right here. I can hear you." I wish I could put this dick on her and help her lose this damn attitude. She continued looking at her phone.

"No, I want you right here." I pointed to my chest. "Come lay on me."

She looked up from her phone, rolled her eyes, and then went back to messing with her phone.

"You're gonna ignore me Rizzy?"

"I'm not ignoring you Taylen."

"Who are you texting that's so important?" I was getting a little irritated.

"Nobody important."

She put her phone on the floor and came to lay top of me, with my legs on either side of hers.

"Gimme a kiss," I said poking my lips out.

As soon as her lips touched mine, I grabbed the back of her neck and I pushed my tongue into her mouth. This girl had me gone. I didn't feel like this with Imani at any point during the time we were together. I can't imagine how gone I'm gon' be once she gives me the pussy. After a few minutes of kissing, I pulled away and looked into her eyes.

"Rizzy, I want you to be my girl. I want to make this shit official."

"Taylen, you just got out of a whole relationship two minutes ago. Didn't you tell me yesterday that we didn't need a title. You don't know what you want!"

"I know I want you to be my girl." I meant that shit too. "Besides, like I told Bishop, it's been over between Imani and I for a while."

"Clearly it hasn't been. Not as far as she's concerned. Are you sure this is what you want?" She asked with a look of concern.

"I'm positive."

"How can you be positive? Imani was your girlfriend for what, a year? But you were down here with me acting single as fuck."

"Yeah, but we haven't had sex so technically I didn't cheat on her."

"Nigga, you know damn well if I would have given you the pussy, you would have taken it. And let's not forget you lettin' Faryn suck your dick!" Shit, I had forgotten about that.

"Okay you got me! I've never been faithful to Imani but that was when I was on some little boy shit. I'm on my grown man shit now," I tried to explain.

"Letting random girls suck your dick is grown man shit, Taylen?" This was not going well. She tried to push herself off me but I held her down.

"That only happened a couple of times. I ain't---" Karizma sat up so quick and got off the bed that I couldn't even finish explaining. She stood over me with an angry look on her face.

"A couple of times! Nigga you let her suck your dick again. You told me she only did it once. When the fuck did this happen, Taylen?"

Damn! I forgot that I didn't tell her about the second time. How the fuck can I explain this without letting her know that I lied to her the first time. Shit! I sat up and grabbed her wrists to pull her close to me.

"Rizzy, baby listen. She did it twice. The first time was before the Student Center party and then later that night, when we got back from the party and Bishop and Hazel were down in the commons area talking. She knocked on the door and I tried to close the door on her but her foot stopped it and she grabbed my dick and---"

"You know what, you don't have to explain. We weren't a couple then, just like we aren't one now, so it's whatever." She tried to pull away from me but instead, I pulled her down on my lap.

"So…," I was still waiting for her to let me know if she wanted to make this shit official.

"So, what?"

"You gon' be my woman?"

"I don't know Taylen."

"What's there to know? You feelin' me, I'm feelin' you."

Before she gave me an answer, her phone buzzed and she reached to grab it but I got it before she did. I had no intentions on reading her message but as I was passing it to her, I saw Keith's name.

"Why the fuck is Keith texting you?" I was heated.

"What do you mean? We're cool." She opened the text message and smiled before she replied back.

"How cool?" I said, snatching her phone away from her.

"Taylen, stop playing and give me my phone. We're just cool. He's a nice guy."

"You think it's okay for you to be texting back and forth with one of my teammates?" Is she trying to piss me off on purpose? She had to know that I wouldn't be cool with that.

"We're just friends, Taylen. He just texts every now and then to say what's up. Besides, didn't you just have a whole damn girlfriend?"

"Man, whatever! I just asked you to be my girl. You're too busy trying to text the next nigga to give me an answer." I gently pushed her off me, stood up and walked towards the door, tossing her phone on her bed.

"Taylen, where are you going?"

"I'm leaving so you can have some privacy while you text your 'friend' back."

She smiled like she thought I was playing but I'm pissed off.

"It's not even that serious."

"I want you to tell me that you will be my girl and then tell that nigga that you my girl and stop texting him," I demanded.

"You know what! I asked if Imani was your girlfriend over a month ago, and you lied to me about it. Now you have the nerve to be trippin' because another dude is texting me." I know that shit don't make sense but I'm serious as hell. I didn't even answer her.

"Now your ass ain't got shit to say! This whole time that we've been 'kickin' it', you've basically been lyin' to me. You lied to me about Faryn, you lied to me about using Faryn's car, you lied to me about Imani being your girlfriend and I gave you the opportunity to come clean about that and you didn't take it. You have no right to be mad about who I communicate with because I'm sure you talked to Imani all the time!" she pointed out. I still didn't say a word because I had no argument for her. She's right.

"You still ain't got shit to say?" she continued.

"Look, baby, I'm sorry about all that. The way I feel about you is new for me. I don't know what to do with all these feelings. All I know is I want you. I want to be exclusive. Can we give it a shot?"

She was quiet for way too long before she finally said, "I don't think so Taylen. Not right now. I don't think you're ready for all that. You just broke up with Imani. You don't know how to say no to random girls that want to suck your dick. Maybe you need some time alone to be sure that I'm what you want."

"Man, Rizzy! Don't do this. I fucked up, I admit that. But I know that you're who I want to be with," I pleaded.

"I don't think you know what you want. Let's just cool off on each other for a minute so that you can be sure."

"Naw fuck that Rizzy! I'm sure right now."

"Well I'm not sure! You need to give me a minute to figure this shit out!" she yelled. "I'll talk to you later." She dismissed me.

I stood by the door for a minute, hoping she'd change her mind. When she wouldn't look at me or say anything, I left. If this is what she wanted, there wasn't shit I could do about it. At least not today. I decided to let her cool off but this shit is far from over.

Chapter 34

Karizma

Last night, I didn't get much sleep. All I could think about is Taylen. I don't know if I did the right thing but I went with my gut. I can't make this too easy for him and if he thinks that he can continuously lie to me or tell me what he thinks I should know, he can think again. If we find our way back to each other, then fine, but if not, that's fine too.

"You woke Rizzy?" Hazel said from her bed.

"Yeah, I ain't so sure I went to sleep. I had Taylen on the brain all night."

"Because your ass wants to be with him so I don't know why you did him like that," Hazel reasoned.

I sat up in my bed. "Hazel, I explained to you last night why I did what I did. You said you understood."

"I do. But the more that I think about it, I can kinda understand why he did what he did."

"You understand why he lied to me repeatedly. I gotta hear this. Please explain." I can't believe Hazel is siding with Taylen.

"Okay, fine. The shit with Faryn don't even matter. You barely knew him when all that shit went down so it's really irrelevant. Now him taking you on a date in her car was kinda foul, but not towards you, more towards her. It was just a means of transportation for him to do something nice for you," she explained her point of view.

"Yeah, okay. But even if I disregard all that, I asked him straight up about Imani and he lied," I reminded her.

"Yeah, he did. But I was talking to Bishop after Taylen came his lovesick ass to the room last night and told us what happened. He said that Taylen has been done with his relationship with Imani for a minute. He just felt like breaking up with her over the phone would be bogus."

"He told me that bullshit too. It's not that I don't believe him. It's that he lied. He basically tried to make me a side chick. Then tried to say since we didn't fuck he didn't cheat on her. Whatever nigga!" I continued to explain my position.

"Well, he didn't. At least not with you." I gave her the side-eye. "Look Rizzy, I'm not trying to tell you what to do. I just think you are being too hard on him. Just think about what I said. You don't have to give in to him right away but don't make the poor man suffer too long. His ass was sick last night!" She laughed.

"Serves his ass right! He sent me over twenty text messages apologizing last night."

Just then, my phone vibrated. Hazel and I looked at each other and laughed. "I know this is him texting this damn early." It's only eight-thirty in the morning.

I grabbed my phone from the charger and looked at the notification on the screen.

TayBaby: Good morning beautiful! I hope you slept well cuz I didn't. I'm so sorry baby. Can we just talk later today?

I read the text to Hazel and she shook her head. "Girl, if you don't take that man out of his misery and talk to him."

"I'm good on him for now," I stated, putting my phone down and flopping back on my bed. I let out a long, deep sigh.

"I'm not saying he's not wrong Rizzy. But now that everything is out in the open, at least give him a chance to prove he's worthy of your forgiveness," Hazel reasoned.

"I'll think about it," was all I said.

I knew I wouldn't hear from Taylen anymore until after their practice. That would give me a few hours to take a nap and find somewhere to hide out. Hazel didn't say anything else about the situation and I was thankful for that. I'm annoyed that she seems to be more on his side than mine, but I guess it's not about taking sides. Everyone is entitled to their own opinion, so I can't be mad at her for having a different one than mine.

*****

A few hours later, I woke up from my nap and Hazel was gone. I looked at my phone to see that it was after eleven. Taylen would be out of practice soon and I need to get out of dodge. I don't want to see him just yet.

After taking a quick shower, I threw on some leggings, fitted t-shirt, some running shoes, and a fitted baseball cap. I grabbed my phone and backpack and stuffed my laptop inside. I'm not really sure of my destination but I left the building and walked towards the bridge. I had about twenty minutes before football practice would be over so I need to hurry up and get across this bridge if I don't want to run into Taylen.

I put my headphones on and quickly walked over the bridge to get to campus, deciding I would find a quiet spot on the upstairs level of the Student Center, to get my studying and homework done, instead of meeting Hazel at the library like we had planned. I sent Hazel a text letting her know so that she wouldn't be looking for me. I know I'm being petty but I ain't feeling her ass right now.

When I made it inside of the Student Center, my stomach began to growl, so I stopped and ordered a sandwich from the deli. As I waited for my sandwich to be made, I took one of my headphones off so that I could hear when my order was up and I sat at one of the tables next to the windows. From a distance, I could hear male voices talking loud and coming in my direction. Shit! I bet that's the football team.

The deli wasn't that big so there was really nowhere that I could hide. I was just praying that Taylen wasn't with this group of guys. I got up and walked over to the register, hoping that if Taylen was in the group, that he wouldn't recognize me from behind and just keep on walking.

"Karizma, your order is up!" The girl behind the counter yelled, as if there were ten people waiting, just as the group of guys were walking by. I grabbed my food, hoping to make a quick getaway.

"Karizma!" I heard my name being yelled but it wasn't Taylen's voice. I turned around and saw that it was Keith. I don't feel like dealing with his ass right now either.

"Oh hey Keith. What's up?"

"Nothing but you beautiful," he said, pulling me into a hug. I didn't hug him back because I had my backpack on one arm and my food the other hand.

"How was practice?" I asked, just to be polite.

"It was cool. Coach was actually a little easy on us today because of the win yesterday," he replied, licking his lips and looking at my boobs. This nigga! Maybe I do need to start wearing bras.

"That's good. Umm, okay, I'm about to get some studying done so I'll talk to you later." I turned around to start walking away, but Keith pulled me back by the arm.

"Wait Rizzy! I wanted to ask, what's up with you and Tay? Is that your nigga?" he asked.

"Naw. But I need to go Keith. Hit me up later." This time, he let me leave but kept talking.

"My bad. I know you need to study. I'll hit you up," he said.

When I turned around to wave, he was still licking his lips and rubbing his hands together. That was kinda creepy. I quickened my pace and found a place to study for the next few hours.

Chapter 35

Bishop

Yesterday was crazy! I've been trying to contact Keesha since before I left for practice this morning but her ass ain't replying to my calls or texts. Even though shit went left with us yesterday, I still need to get some shit straight regarding my son. She's never been one to be petty enough to use my son as leverage but the way shit went down yesterday, I have no idea what she's gonna do now. Since Keesha wouldn't answer my calls, I FaceTimed my sister Brianna to see what she knows.

"Hey B!" Brianna answered, looking all grown and shit. *Have I been gone that long?*

"Hey Bri! Wassup?" I asked.

"I don't know, you tell me. Keesha came over here yesterday morning and left BJ and she ain't been back yet," she informed me.

"That's because her ass drove down here with Imani's messy ass acting crazy."

"Are you serious? She's in Carbondale?" Bri questioned.

"I don't know if she's still here. That's why I'm calling you. Shit didn't go well with her poppin' up on a nigga like that so I don't know where she went when she left," I shared.

"Damn Bishop! What did you do?"

"Bri, I don't even wanna really get into that shit. Just know she tried to boss up on me like I was her man and it didn't end the way she probably expected. How's my son doing?" I changed the subject.

"You know my nephew is straight. He always good when he's with us," she answered. That made me feel so good. I owe my family everything for picking up my slack while I pursue my dream and get my education.

"Let me see him," I asked. I watched as she got up and walked to where he was. Since I wasn't there, they made my room his nursery for the most part.

"Hey nephew! You wanna see your daddy," Bri cooed to him. He is only five months old so it wasn't like he could talk back to me. But I wanted him to hear my voice on a regular basis so he wouldn't forget me.

Bri held the phone up by his face so that I could see him. It's been about two weeks since I last saw him because Keesha been tripping. He looked so different in that short amount of time. His face is chubbier and his hair has grown. He had his whole fist in his mouth as he squirmed around. Man, I missed him so much.

"Hey lil man! How's daddy's big boy?" When he heard my voice, he took his fist out of his mouth and looked in the direction of the phone.

"You know daddy's voice huh, man. Daddy misses you, but I'll be home soon! I love you, son," I continued.

BJ flailed his arms and kicked his legs, and made some cooing sounds, as if he understood what I was saying.

"Kiss my baby for me Bri. And make sure you FaceTime me whenever he's there because I know Keesha is about to be on some bullshit. Tell everybody I said wassup!"

"Okay! Love you B!" Bri ended the call.

I laid back on my bed and closed my eyes. As long as my son was good, I wasn't gon' worry about Keesha's ass. He is my main concern. Now that Hazel knows about him, that's a huge weight off my shoulders. I'm glad she took the news well and didn't kick a nigga to the curb like Karizma did Taylen. I laughed just thinking about his ass. Hopefully they can work that shit out. I'm not gon' stress myself about his shit but I do feel bad for him. My phone vibrated and it was a text from Hazel.

MyHaze: Bishop

Me: Haze

MyHaze: Where u at?

Me: My room.

MyHaze: Okay. I'm still at library. I'll be done in about an hour.

Me: Come see me when u done

MyHaze: Okay

Just as I sent the last text, Taylen walked in the room, looking mad at the world.

"The fuck you cheesin' at?" he barked.

"Nigga don't come in here with no attitude because Karizma ain't fuckin' with you!" I snapped back.

"My bad man! I'm just irritable. I went to her room and either she ain't there or she ain't answering. She won't reply to my texts! I don't know what else to do," he complained.

"Ain't shit else you can do bruh. Just give her a minute. She'll come around." I tried to console him but I wasn't so sure how their situation was gonna turn out. I haven't seen Karizma or talked to Hazel about it since Hazel talked to her.

"But what if she doesn't? This is really fuckin' with me. More than I care to admit," he confessed as he sat on his bed and rubbed his hand down his face.

"I can tell. Your ass was a zombie at practice today. Good thing we were just conditioning and watching film. You would have got your head knocked off otherwise."

"I know. I couldn't focus because I was trying to figure this shit out!" He sounded so frustrated and didn't know what to say to help my boy out.

"Like I said, just give her a minute," I advised as I grabbed my backpack off my desk. "I'm gonna head over to the library to meet Hazel. I'll check you later." I gave him some dap and left. I know Hazel said she'd be done in an hour but Taylen's ass is depressing and I don't feel like being stuck in the room with his ass cry baby ass.

When I made it over to the library, I realized I had no idea where Hazel was. Morris Library is huge and she could be anywhere. I pulled my phone out to shoot her text but caught something from the corner of my eye. When I looked up, I was surprised to see Hazel in one of the private study rooms, with Phil. *Now ain't this some shit.*

My first instinct was to barge in there and snap the fuck off. But I thought better of that and walked up a little closer, standing behind one of the shelves. I could see them but they wouldn't be able to see me if they looked towards the window.

Phil was sitting across from Hazel and they were talking. It didn't look like they were studying because every other minute they were laughing about something. Every time they laughed I got more pissed. I know they didn't have a class together because Phil is junior. So why the fuck is he in there? I sent Hazel a text.

Me: Haze

MyHaze: Bishop

Me: U almost done

I'm watching her as she reads my texts and puts her phone down to continue her conversation with Phil. They laughed about something else and she picked her phone up again to reply.

MyHaze: Yeah leaving in a few

Me: If u not done I can just meet you there. I got a few things to read

MyHaze: No it's fine. I'll meet u in ur room

Yeah! I bet it is fine. I watched them for a few more minutes. I know Phil was trying to shoot his shot but that shit ain't happening. Fuck it, I thought, as I walked up to the door of the room that they were in. They were so into their conversation that neither of them heard the door open or saw me coming until I was standing right next to Hazel.

"Uhh, hey Bishop. What are you doing here?" Hazel asked nervously.

"I have some work to do and I didn't want you to rush so I decided to meet you here. But it looks like I'm interrupting something," I stated calmly, looking Phil directly in his eyes.

"Not at all," Phil stood and grabbed his bag. "I was walking by and I saw Hazel in here. Just stopped in to say hello."

"Yeah. Phil was just saying hi and we started talking about track and school. We're in the same major so he's had my classes," Hazel explained.

"That's cool. Good seeing you again bruh," I said, knowing damn well that ain't all he stopped in to do.

"You too. Ya'll be easy," Phil said as he left the room.

I bent down and kiss Hazel on her temple before I pulled out the chair next to her and sat down.

"Why didn't you just say you were here?" Hazel questioned.

"I don't think you're the one that should be asking questions Hazel. I came up here because I had a few chapters to read and to my surprise, I catch my girl giggling in another nigga's face when she told me she was studying."

"Really Bishop! You know it wasn't like that. I was studying," she defended.

"That didn't look like studying to me."

"Aww, is my baby jealous?" She turned her body towards me and put her arms around my neck.

"Do I need to be?" I turned to look at her and she had the nerve to be smiling.

"Bishop, Phil and I are cool. He knows that I'm with you."

"I know what a nigga that wants to fuck looks like and he definitely wants to hit it," I told her.

"What? It ain't even like that with me and Phil," she tried to explain.

"It might not be like that with you but it is with him. Take my word for it baby. Now leave me alone so I can read and you can finish your work."

She leaned in and gave me what started off as a peck, but I slid my tongue into her mouth and it got heated. I had to tell my dick to calm down.

"We need to stop before they kick us out and I still have to finish some stuff." She pushed away from me.

"You weren't worried about finishing that shit while you were laughing all in Phil's face." I joked but I was serious as hell.

"Bishop! Don't do that. I was minding my own business when he came in here. It's not like I met him here."

"Yeah, okay. You just be careful around him," I warned.

Hazel is too naïve to peep Phil's game but I can see that shit a mile away. At his party, I caught him checking her out one too many times from across the room. He may not be trying to be in a relationship with her but he is definitely trying to fuck. We ain't even been official for twenty-four hours and Hazel got my ass about tripping. I will definitely be keeping my eye on Phil.

Hazel and I both focused on our work for the next forty-five minutes. I may need to get my ass out of my room to do my reading and studying done all the time. I'm always a lot more productive at the library.

"I'll be back, I'm gonna go to the bathroom," Hazel said as she stood and push back her chair.

As she walked towards the door, my eyes were fixed on her. I took in her body and how good her ass looked in the leggings she had on. I watched her through the window until she turned the corner and I couldn't see her anymore. I had to adjust my dick because it was hard. Damn! I need some pussy.

When she came back from the bathroom and tried to sit down, I pulled her onto my lap.

"Bishop, stop before they make us leave!" she said as she giggled.

"I don't care. I'm done anyway." I told her as I held her in my lap and eased my hand up her shirt, squeezing her breast. "Gimme a kiss," I demanded with my lips poked out.

She planted her lips on mine, putting her arms around my neck, deepening the kiss. Her lips were so soft and plump, I ended the kiss by pulling her bottom lip with my teeth.

"You do realize there is a window right there?" Hazel asked.

"So?"

"People walking past can see us," she stated, as if I didn't know that.

"So?" I grabbed the back of her neck, pulling her into another kiss. This time, taking full advantage of the position she was sitting on my lap, with her legs facing away from the window. I pulled down the waist of her leggings and panties, pressing my thumb against her clit, in a circular motion.

"Hmm…" Hazel moaned and opened her legs just a little bit.

She pulled me closer by the neck, pressing her body against mine. I took it little further and slid my hand down further into her panties, pushing one finger, then another, into her pussy.

"Ah shit Bishop!" she mumbled against my lips.

Hazel's pussy was slippery and my dick was throbbing to be freed. I knew that wouldn't be happening so I focused on the task at hand…releasing Hazel's waterfall. She grinded against my hand, making the sexiest sounds as she did.

"That feel good baby?" I asked against her lips.

She didn't respond but her grinding against my fingers got harder and faster. I knew she was on the verge of releasing.

"Fuck Bishop!" she moaned, as she released her juices on my hand. Her breaths came out fast and deep when she buried her face into my neck.

"Damn baby! You drowned my hand." I laughed as I pulled my hand out of her pants. I don't know how she's gonna get home because I'm sure he leggings are soaked.

"Oh my God! Shut up! I can't believe you did that in here." She spoke into my neck, trying to hide her embarrassment.

"Man, that's my shit. I'll do that anywhere I feel the urge. Now let me see if you taste as good as I think you do." She looked up at me as I stuck my two fingers in my mouth, sucking off all of her juices, then licked the palm of my hand, making sure I got every drop.

"You like it?" she asked with her nose frowned up.

"Delicious. Just like I imagined." I gave her a wink.

"Here!" she said, handing me some wipes that she got from her purse. Then she grabbed some for herself and tried to discreetly clean herself up with as well.

"Take this," I told her as I handed her a long sleeve t-shirt that I had in the bottom of my backpack. "You may want to just tie that around your waist until you get back to your room baby."

"You better hope nobody saw us!" she warned.

"Why? We ain't do shit. They couldn't see nothing anyway." I laughed. She tied the t-shirt around her waist and put her backpack on her shoulder.

"That's just what I need, people thinking I'm a hoe or something." She pouted as we walked out of the door.

"You know that shit felt good. Stop complaining!" I put my arm around her shoulders as we walked out of the library. "Wait until you see what this dick do though!" I added. She pushed me.

"Whatever!" she said, shoving me away but I grabbed her hand and pulled her back into my arm.

"Yo ass gon' fall in love!" I smirked.

She looked at me and smiled but didn't respond. I don't know when she gon' be ready to give me some pussy but I sure hope she don't make me wait too long. A nigga is backed up like a muthafucka. But I'm not gon' pressure her. I don't want her to think that's all I want. We can take it as slow as she needs to but I can't lie, I'm praying it's not too slow.

Chapter 36

Taylen

It's Monday morning. The start of a new week. I haven't seen or talked to Rizzy since Saturday and I'm going crazy! She's ignoring my texts, hasn't returned any of my calls, and she hasn't been in her room any time that I've gone by there. But I got something for her ass this morning. Her first class today is at eight o'clock. It's seven fifteen and I'm about to go wait for her in front of her door. Luckily, Hazel is on my side. I had Bishop text her to find out if Rizzy was still in her room, and Hazel said that she had just gotten out of the shower.

"Aye man, I'm about to go run up on Karizma," I told Bishop as I opened the door to our room.

"Yo stalking ass!" He shook his head and laughed at me.

"Whateva nigga, I'm out!" I closed the door and walked to the stairs to take to the eighth floor.

When I got to the door, I could hear music playing. She would probably be leaving in about fifteen minutes so I made myself comfortable outside the door. While I waited, I scrolled through my text messages. Imani had been blowing me up since Saturday but she was the least of my worries and I didn't read any of her messages. Since I had time now, I read a few.

Mani: I can't believe u wld do this 2 me

Mani: How can u just throw it all away

Mani: I love u Tay!

Mani: Ur gonna just ignore me

Mani: Ur an asshole

Mani: I hate you Tay!

Imani's messages went on and on. I couldn't even read them all because there were so many. I scrolled down to the last message and when I saw it, I almost passed out! I immediately felt light headed but didn't have time to process the information because the door opened and Karizma walked out, wearing her headphones. She didn't see me until she turned around to lock the door.

"Damn it Taylen, you scared me!" she screamed, pulling her headphones off.

"My bad Pretty Girl! Why haven't you been responding to my texts and answering my calls?" I started as we began to walk to the elevator.

"Because I don't want to talk to you!" she spewed, marching down the hallway.

"But you said that I needed to take a minute to be sure I want to be with you. It's been a minute and I'm sure. Can we just stop the bullshit?"

"Taylen, it hasn't even been two days," she said, rolling her eyes.

We stood facing each other, with some distance between us, waiting for the elevator. I stared at her and she acted like I wasn't there.

"Rizzy, don't do this. Gimme a chance to make it right. I know I fucked up but I've been miserable not seeing or talking to you," I confessed.

She bit her bottom lip and looked in my direction. I took a few steps to close up the space between us and she put her hands up, stopping me from coming any closer.

"Don't Taylen. I just need some time. I'm not saying that it's a wrap between us. I'm just saying that before I make a decision, I want you to be sure. I'm not dealing with the back and forth with your ex or any other girl. I don't need you lying to me about anything else. Figure out what you want."

The elevator opened and I took this opportunity to get as close to her as I could. I let her get on first and she walked to the corner. When she turned around, I was standing so close to her that we were touching. She looked up at me and opened her mouth to say something but I pressed my mouth against hers, shoving my tongue inside. Fortunately, she didn't deny me, and her body melted against mine. The kiss was so intense, that we didn't realize that the elevator wasn't moving. She came to her senses and forcefully pushed me away. Her breathing was labored so I knew that kiss did something to her.

"I know what I want Rizzy!"

"Taylen, why would you do that?" she screamed and took a few steps to press the lobby button.

"You didn't like it?"

"I…that's not the point Taylen," she said, touching her lips as if she was savoring the way mine felt against them.

"It is the point, Rizzy. Why are you denying yourself something you know you want? I apologized and I swear I'll make it up to you. Just stop ignoring me. Can we at least be friends while we take our break? A break doesn't necessarily mean we can't talk to or see each other." I grabbed her wrist and pulled her to me, wrapping my arms around her waist. Surprisingly, she didn't fight me.

"Okay fine. It's not like you're gonna leave me alone anyway. But…" she began, "all of this touchy, feely, and kissing can't happen. That's not what friends do." She took my hands and removed them from her waist and stepped back, just as the elevator doors open into the lobby.

"Yeah, okay!" I said with the biggest smile on my face. If I'm in her presence, I can't keep my hands to myself. But I'll let her believe what she wants to for now. I put my arm around her and we walked out of the elevator, through the lobby, and out of the building.

"I'm serious Taylen. Maybe we moved a little too fast." She reasoned, moving my arm from her shoulders. That kinda pissed me off but I let her be for now. I'm just glad she's talking me. These past two days have been the worst.

"There's no such thing as moving too fast when you know what you want. I want you and you want me. End of story!"

"You sure have a funny way of showing it," she commented, rolling her eyes.

"Are you saying I didn't do a good job of showing you that I wanted you to be mine?"

"That's not what I'm saying."

"If you're not saying that, then that means I did a good job. If that's the case, nothing else matters."

"It matters that you lied to me, on more than one occasion. I don't wanna talk about this right now," she stated, ending that conversation.

We walked over the bridge to campus. Our classes are in different buildings and we had to part ways. I want to give her a kiss but since she said kissing wasn't allowed, I decided against it.

"Can we talk later? What time are you done with classes today?" I asked.

"Twelve-fifty. Then I need to try to eat something light so it will be digested before practice," she told me.

"Awight, cool. I'll just text you later. I gotta go straight from classes to practice." I took her hand and gave it a squeeze.

The look in her eyes said she was conflicted but I'm following the rules. I turned and walked in the direction of my class. Before I got too far, I heard someone call my name. When I turned around, Rizzy did too, but it wasn't her that called me. It was Diamond. Fuck she want?

"Hey Tay, wait up!" Diamond yelled again as she came in my direction with a light jog.

I don't know why I waited because I wanted nothing to do with this girl. I had enough problems trying to get back on track with Karizma, not to mention this situation with Imani, which I've chosen to ignore for now.

"Wassup Diamond?" I spoke, keeping my eyes on Rizzy, who still hadn't started back walking to her class. Instead, she was watching me.

"Hey umm, I know that you said you were busy with football and shit. But I was wondering if you were any good at Math?" Diamond asked. This hoe knows damn well that all she wants from me is the dick. She stood in front of me, wearing little bitty ass shorts and a tight ass shirt, licking her lips and twirling her hair in her fingers. I don't think she has any clothes that actually fit.

"Yeah, I'm pretty good at it. Why?"

"Really? Do you think you can tutor me? I mean, if you have time." She undressed me with her eyes, while she stood with all of her weight on one leg and her hip sticking out.

"Uhh, I ain't so sure that's gonna work. I still have another month or so left of football and I don't have a lot of time." I told her as I looked up at Karizma still staring at us. She wasn't close enough to hear what we were saying but if looks could kill, I'd be a dead ass.

Diamond put her hand on my chest and leaned forward. "Ahh come on Tay. I really need help. I've been asking around campus and everyone keeps telling me that you're the best."

I sighed deeply, knowing that her ass is lying and that this is not going to end well, but still telling Diamond to take out her phone and giving her my number to lock in. Karizma watched the whole thing go down and after she'd seen enough, she turned around angrily and marched towards her class. I guess I'll be explaining this too. Fuck!

"Thanks, Tay! I'll give you a call. I owe you big time!" Diamond said. I hardly noticed her walk away as I took my phone out to text Rizzy.

Me: Baby, it's not what u think. She needs help in her math class and someone told her I could help.

Pretty Girl: Yeah I bet

Me: I swear that's all it was. I don't like that girl

Pretty Girl: Ur free to like who u want just like I am

Me: Stop playing with me

I hope her ass knows she is not free to like nobody but me. She didn't reply to that last text. I'm happy she replied at all because it's more than I've gotten the last two days. Hopefully, she'll be even more receptive later on tonight. If she wants to chill on some friends shit, that's what we will do. Best friends!

*****

The day was slow as hell. My classes were boring and I couldn't focus at practice so I kept fucking up. I fucked up so much that coach put me on the sidelines and went in on me towards the end of practice. I gotta get my shit together. I still haven't replied to Imani, mainly because I don't believe her ass. But regardless, I need to address it.

"Damn man! You was fuckin' up out there today," Bishop said when he caught up with me walking out of the locker room.

"I know. I don't need you tellin' me. Coach already cussed my ass out. This shit with Karizma is fuckin' with me. Not to mention Imani's lying ass."

"Wassup with her?" he asked.

I pulled out my phone and pulled up Imani's text messages. I didn't even want to say that shit out loud. I gave my phone to Bishop and watched him as he scrolled through her messages.

"Just go to the last one," I told him.

"Hell naw!" he exclaimed, handing me back my phone after looking at the message again.

"I don't believe that shit."

"Well you can't ignore it." Bishop stated.

"I know and I'm not. I'm just not dealing with her ass right now."

"What the fuck you mean man? You need to call her ass right now. This ain't shit to play with," Bishop pressed, pushing me on the shoulder.

"I know nigga. I'm gon' call. But I need a minute. And to be honest, Imani ain't my first priority, regardless of that bullshit ass text."

"I feel you. But that's kinda fucked up," he expressed his opinion.

"It is what it is bruh," I told him as we walked into our building.

We took the elevator to our room and left our backpacks, then went back down to catch dinner before they closed. There weren't many people in the dining hall since it was nearing closing time. After getting my food, I entered the dining area, with one person on my mind. It didn't take long for me to find her but I definitely didn't like what I saw.

"Hey Pretty Girl! How was your day?" I interrupted Keith as I sat down, kissing Karizma on the forehead.

"Uh…it was fine. Umm, did you hear Keith talking?" She nodded her head towards him.

"Naw, I didn't actually. I was too focused on you to hear anything." Continuing to ignore Keith I asked, "Is this shit good?" I asked about the meal of the day before eating a forkful.

"It's okay," Rizzy replied, looking down, moving the food around on her plate.

"What's going on with you bruh? I thought coach was gon' send yo ass home today, as much as you were fuckin' up," Keith commented.

"Mind your business. I'm good," I answered, keeping my eyes on Rizzy. She gazed up at me, with a concerned looked on her face.

Bishop finally made his way to our table and sat next to Keith, giving him the side-eye.

"Wassup Rizzy? Where's Hazel?" Bishop asked.

"She had a study group so she showered and said she was gonna grab something from the Student Center," she informed him. "She didn't text you?"

"Probably. I left my phone upstairs and I didn't check it after practice."

"Awight, I'm out. Rizzy, I'll hit you up later." Keith got up, grabbing his tray and winking at Rizzy before walking away.

"Why do you keep entertaining that nigga?" I asked Rizzy.

"What do you want me to do Taylen? I was sitting here, by myself, eating my food, and he sat down."

"I'm gon' beat his ass. Maybe then he'll get the picture."

"It would be kinda silly for you to be fighting over a girl that ain't yours to fight over." She got up and yanked her tray from the table, giving me the evil-eye before turning to walk away.

"Then call me silly!" I called after her.

"You got enough problems. You might wanna let Rizzy be for a minute and figure out this other shit."

I finished my food without any more words. *How the fuck did my life become this complicated?*

Chapter 37

Hazel

I've never been so happy for a Friday to come in my life. My first big project is due today and putting the finishing touches on it this week has been rough. Every night this week I've been working with my group, which consisted of three other people, late into the evenings. Bishop has been very understanding of not seeing me that much this week but I miss my baby. To make matters worse, they have an away game tomorrow and are leaving in a few hours.

After meeting up with my group members to make sure everything was good with our project before we turned it in, I decided to skip my last class for the day and go lay up with my boo for a few minutes. I pulled out my phone to send Bishop a text as I walked back to the dorms.

Me: Bishop
Bishop: Haze
Me: What u doin
Bishop: Packin

Me: Comin to see u

Bishop: Don't u have class

Me: Skippin

Bishop: Baby go to class. I'll c u when I get back

I'm not even gonna reply to him. I'm only missing a lecture class and I can get the notes from somebody on Monday. This week has been hectic and I need this little break before I go die at track practice.

I perused through Instagram as I took a shortcut through the Student Center. Suddenly, I bumped into a hard chest, dropping my phone. I bent down to pick it up, before I looked up to see who it was.

"Oh hey Phil! My bad. I wasn't paying attention," I apologized, taking in his handsome face and inhaling the scent of his cologne.

"No problem beautiful. Where you rushing off to?" He paused to look at his watch. "Shouldn't you be in class?"

"Uhh, it depends. Are you a snitch?" I said nervously.

"You playing hooky huh? What's so important that it has you skipping class?" He folded his arms across his chest and looked me up and down. *Why did I feel like I was being reprimanded?*

"Umm, nothing is really that important. I…uhh…was just going to see Bishop before they left for their game," I explained, still a bit apprehensive about telling him.

"Damn! That nigga got you skipping class and shit," he teased.

"Not exactly. He told me to go to class. But this week has been so crazy with that project that I was telling you about, I haven't had a lot of free time to see him." I don't know why I felt the need to explain myself to him.

"Oh yeah! How'd everything go with the project. Your group members pull their weight?" he asked, seeming genuinely interested, stepping into my personal space.

"They were great. Project turned out really good." I took a deep breath and swallowed. Phil's ass is fine and him being all up in my personal space is doing something to me. I think my nipples are hard.

"That's good. I'll let you go." He stretched his arms out for a hug so I hesitantly gave him one. When I tried to pulled away quickly, he held me tighter and whispered, "Let me know if you ever wanna come over and chill," with his lips so close enough to my ear that I could feel the warmth from his breath. Then I felt his soft lips graze my neck and I think I stopped breathing.

He pulled away and winked before he walked away, leaving me standing there wondering what the hell just happened. Maybe Bishop is right. I gotta stay away from him. I damn near sprinted to the dorms and up the stairs to Bishop's room. I knocked on the door and Taylen answered.

"Wassup Hazel? Bishop's in the bathroom. Where's Rizzy?" Taylen asked, walking back over to sit on his bed after opening the door.

"I guess she's in class. How you been?" I sat on Bishop's bed next to his duffle bag.

"Been better. Ya girl still trippin' but I'm wearing her down," Taylen replied, with a slight grin.

"I wish ya'll would hurry up and figure this shit out. She's been cranky as hell all week and I know it's because she misses your ass."

"Word? Hell, I was beginning to wonder if she gave a damn. She's stubborn as hell."

"You in here sharing intel on ya girl!" Bishop said as he came out of the bathroom. He walked over to the bed and pulled me up into a hug, kissing me in the same spot as Phil, making me become very tense.

"Hell yeah! Anything to get her out of this mood. I don't like the mean and cranky Rizzy. I need my old roomy back asap!" I spit out all at once, trying to play it off, moving out of Bishop's embrace. He gave me the side-eye and pulled me back into his arms.

"Wassup with you Hazel? Acting all nervous and shit," Bishop questioned with a frown on his face.

"Huh? I'm not. I was just---," I started before Taylen interrupted me.

"Aye, I'll give ya'll some privacy." Taylen left the room.

"Continue, you were just what?" Bishop reminded me of what I started to say.

"I was saying that Rizzy is really cranky and---," I began again but this time Bishop didn't let me finish.

"I'm not talking about that. I'm talking about how tense you got when I kissed your neck and you acting all nervous and shit." He was looking me right in my eyes. I looked away but he lifted my chin with his finger, making me look at him. I was trying to think of something to say but no words came to mind.

"Why do you smell like cologne that doesn't belong to me? You been letting some nigga get close to you?" Bishop continued since I was on mute.

"What? Of course not. Why would you say that?" I tried to move from his embrace again but to no avail.

"Because I can smell it Haze. Wassup?"

"Okay. When I was on my way here, I walked through the Student Center. I wasn't paying attention to where I was going and I ran into a body and dropped my phone. When we collided, he hugged me so I guess it's from that," I lied.

"Who is he, Haze?" Bishop asked, finally releasing me from his arms.

I know when I tell him the he is Phil, he's gonna start talking shit. Maybe I can tell him I don't know the guy's name.

"Hazel?"

"Phil," I blurted out.

He looked at me with a frown. "Why does that make you nervous?"

"It doesn't. I know you don't trust him and I don't want you mad for no reason."

Pulling me back into his arms, he kissed my forehead. "I can't get mad because you're clumsy baby. But I still don't want you hangin' with that nigga." He sat back on his bed, with his back against the wall and reached his hand out to me. I straddled him, then put my hands on each cheek.

"You have nothing to worry about," I let him know, kissing him between each word.

"Bet not!" he said, palming my ass and pushing me against his growing dick.

Our tongues intertwined as I pressed my body against his. His lips moved down to my neck as he kissed, licked and sucked. I'm sure there will be marks on my neck but it felt too good to stop him. He stuck his hands down the back of my leggings and I was wearing a thong so they were on my bare ass. Our lips found each other's again and I couldn't stop myself from moaning into his mouth.

"Fuck Haze! When you gon' give a nigga some pussy," Bishop let out between kisses.

"Today if we don't stop," I admitted.

He pushed me back and looked at me. "Don't play with me."

"Who said I'm playin'? I want this dick just as much as you want this pussy." I leaned forward and kissed him again. He grabbed the back of my neck and aggressively shoved his tongue in my mouth.

I managed to find the hem of his shirt and he let me lift it over his head. Just as he was about to do the same to mine, the door opened and Taylen walked in.

"Ohh shit! My bad ya'll," Taylen apologized. "Bishop, we gotta go." Taylen grabbed his duffle bag off the bed. "I'll meet you in the lobby. Hurry up!"

I was so embarrassed. I kept my face buried in Bishop's neck and didn't move until Taylen was gone.

"Fuuuuccckkkk!" Bishop yelled.

I kissed him on the cheek and moved to get up but he held me in place.

"Bishop, you gotta go," I told him.

"I don't want to go. I want some pussy!" he whined. All I could do is laugh.

"I gotchu baby. When you get back tomorrow," I promised him, pecking his lips.

"But I want some now. Let's just do it real quick Haze," he begged.

I couldn't control my laughter. He looked so cute, begging me for pussy.

"I don't think so baby. It's been awhile for me and you gon' have to take your time. Can't be no rushing. Our first time together should be special," I informed him. He finally let me get up and I felt so bad for him. His desire for me was very apparent because his dick was fully erect when I stood.

"You see this shit Haze. I'm gon' have blue balls." He pointed to his dick creating a tent in his sweats.

"I'm sorry baby. But you need to go. Get up!"

He slowly stood and I had my eyes on his dick. I don't know what the hell I've done. He's going to tear up my insides. I thought Ricky was big but I was wrong. I mean, he's not small but Bishop looks like he's on another level.

He stood and made an adjustment in his pants, picked his bag up from the floor and put it on his shoulder. "Come with me to the lobby?" he asked.

I grabbed my bag and we left the room, taking the stairs to the lobby. When we reached the front doors, he turned to me and warned, "I'm gon' tear this pussy up so you better get ready." He kissed my forehead.

"Oh, I will be. I'll see you tomorrow. Text me whenever." I tried to give him a quick peck and walk away. Bishop wasn't haven't that though. He pulled me back and gave me a nice, juicy kiss that would last me until I saw him again tomorrow.

Chapter 38

Karizma

This week, the days seemed to drag by without the constant interaction with Taylen. He still texted me regularly, he walked me to my eight o'clock class on Monday, Wednesday and Friday, he popped up on me at dinner a few times. But it hasn't been the same. I miss him and I want things to go back to how they were.

I realize I'm the one that holds the cards and whenever I decide that we can be together, we're together. I think I've made him suffer long enough. I know I'm tired of torturing myself. When he gets back from the football game tonight, I'm throwing in the towel.

"Okay Hazel!" I called out to her. She had her headphones on so she didn't hear me. "Hazel!" I yelled again.

"What?" She sat up pulling her headphones off.

"I can't do this anymore. I want Taylen back," I confessed.

Haze flopped back on her bed and began laughing hysterically. “Rizzy, I can’t tell you how happy I am to hear you say that. You have been acting like a bitch all week. Taylen has been walking around looking like he lost his best friend. Both of ya’ll been miserable. I’m surprised you held out this long.” She went on and on as she laughed.

“Shut up!” I shouted, throwing one of my throw pillows at her. “I haven’t been that bad!”

“Like hell you haven’t!” She disagreed, and threw the pillow back my way, still laughing.

“Whatever! What time will they be back tonight?” I asked her since I’m sure Bishop kept her informed.

“Why don’t you text Taylen and asked him? I’m sure he will be more than happy to tell you.”

“Why would I do that and you already know?” I asked. “Stop being difficult and just tell me.”

“You’re no fun,” she teased. “Bishop said they should be here by eight.”

“Oh my God! That’s so long from now,” I whined.

“You’ve survived all this week barely talking to or seeing Taylen. I’m sure you’ll live.”

Hazel put her headphones back on and resumed her previous position. I need to find something to do while I wait the next five hours for Taylen to get back. Maybe I’ll take a nap. Sleep was the only thing that would make the time not seem as long. But I’m not sleepy.

“Hazel!” I yelled so that she could hear me over her music.

She sat up and pulled her headphones off. “What Rizzy?”

"Dang, Hazel, you ain't gotta be rude. Let's go to the Student Center and go bowling," I suggested. "I need a distraction."

"We can do that. But I'm not about to be bowling for the next five hours. We can go in a couple of hours." She put headphones back on and laid back down, seemingly irritated.

Hazel has been getting on my nerves this week. But I haven't been the easiest person to get along with either. I'm not gon' snap on her for her attitude since she's been so patient with me. Since we aren't gonna go bowling for a couple more hours, I found a book to read on my Kindle. Mr. Right.com by Rebecca K. Watts. This will definitely keep me occupied for a while. Before I got started, I got a craving for some chocolate.

"Hazel, I'm about to go to the vending machine real quick. You want something?" I asked her after tapping her shoulder.

"Yeah, I do. Can you get me a Reese's?" She requested and went to get some money and I stopped her.

"I got it." I grabbed some cash out of my wallet and went to the lobby vending machine.

As usual, the lobby is buzzing. I don't get why people like to hang out down here. They probably just being nosy and want to see who's coming and going, and with who. I went to the vending area and looked at all of the options. Putting the money in for Hazel's Reese's, I pressed the option number and bent down to get it out of the slot.

"Damn!" I heard from behind me. I stood and turned around.

"Hey Keith? What are you doing here?" I questioned.

"I pulled my hamstring at practice yesterday so they decided not to let me travel."

"Oh, that's too bad. Pulling a hamstring sucks. I pulled mine my junior year and it took months to get right." I shared as I decided to get a Twix and a bag of microwave popcorn. We need to go to the grocery store.

"Yeah, I don't think it's a bad pull but I'm taking it easy for now and getting treatment in the training room."

I got my snacks from the vending machine, being careful not to bend in Keith's direction, and walked out of the vending area, with Keith behind me.

"What are you about to do?" he asked, following me through the lobby and to the elevators.

"Eat my snacks and read a book," I replied as I stepped on the elevator. Keith stepped on right after me.

"That sounds fun," he said, sarcastically.

"I'm just trying to chill. Hazel and I might go bowling later."

I pushed the number eight for my floor and stood opposite Keith, leaning against the wall.

"What floor you need?"

"Eight is cool," he answered after looking at what floor I had pushed.

The last few times I've talked to him, I got a weird vibe and I'm feeling it now. I looked up at Keith and he was staring at me, licking his lips. Creepy ass! I looked down at my feet because his stare made me uncomfortable.

All of the sudden, Keith pushed the emergency stop button on the elevator and was in my face. I was so startled, I dropped the snacks and put my hands up to his chest, keeping him from getting close to me.

"What the fuck is your problem Keith?" I tried to push him away but he didn't move. Keith's massive frame towered over me. Since pushing him away didn't work, I reached for the emergency stop button but he grabbed my hand and pinned it above my head.

"You've been teasing me for weeks Rizzy," he whispered, menacingly.

He used his other hand to hold me in place by my neck. Leaning his face down to mine, our lips touched and he forced his tongue in my mouth. I moved my head from side-to-side, trying to get out of this forced kiss, but he was kissing me so hard, it was pointless. The more I moved, the tighter his grip on my neck became, the harder he kissed. I took my free hand and swung it, hitting him on his arm and shoulder. A million things were going through my head, thinking of what I could do to get myself out of this situation. One of my punches landed on his ear at the same time that I kneed him in the nuts and bit his tongue. He let me go and bent over, holding his dick with one hand and his ear with the other.

"Fuck Rizzy!" he yelled.

I pressed the emergency stop button and the elevator started moving again. My heart raced, my breathing was hard and tears began to fall. I can't believe this nigga just attacked me.

"If you ever fuckin' put your hands on me again, you will regret it. What the fuck is wrong with you?"

"You know you like that shit!" he grunted, still holding his balls.

"Fuck you sorry ass nigga!" The elevator doors opened and I darted towards them but Keith grabbed me by the back of my shirt and pulled me back in.

I turned around and just started swinging on him, landing punches any and everywhere. He was caught off guard. When my fist landed on his jaw, he slapped the shit out of me. I fell back against the door of the elevator, dazed.

"Bitch! Calm yo hoe ass down! You think you can just lead a nigga on like you been!" he yelled.

At that moment, the elevator doors opened again and I fell out, onto the floor. I don't know what floor we were on but I got up as fast as I could and ran. I turned the corner in the hallway and ran to the first stairwell. Luckily, Keith didn't follow me. I was on the twelfth floor so I ran down four floors and all the way to my room. I pushed through the door with such force, Hazel was startled.

"Rizzy, what the fuck happened?" Hazel came to me and held my shoulders.

As I tried to tell her what happened, I couldn't control my breathing, tears ran down my face. I was hysterical.

"Oh my God, Rizzy. Please calm down and tell me what happened." Hazel hugged me and rubbed my back. I tried to calm myself but every time I think back, I shed more tears.

"Keith…he, he att--acked me," I began.

"What? Oh my God Rizzy! What happened?" Hazel pleaded.

I tried to level out my breathing but it wasn't working. "I saw him in the lobby," I paused, taking a deep breath, "he followed me on the elevator. It was just us on there. He said…he said I've been teasing him."

Hazel stood there, looking shocked. "I can't believe this. He's crazy as hell. So being friendly is teasing now?" she said, trying to calm me.

"He forced me to kiss him, he choked me," I cried, "he slapped me because I was fighting him back."

"This is crazy Rizzy. Your face is bruised. Your lip is bleeding. He must have lost his mind. What the fuck?" Hazel ranted. She had worked herself up so much and began pacing back and forth.

I sat on my bed and attempted to put my face in my hands. I couldn't because my lip and left side of my face is sore and swollen. I didn't want to look in the mirror because I was afraid of how my face looked.

"Bishop, how far away are you guys?" I heard Hazel say and I looked up to see her on her phone.

"That far? Shit!" Hazel expressed her frustration.

"Is Taylen by you?" She paused, waiting for an answer. "Because some shit went down that he needs to know about."

"Wassup Hazel?" I heard Taylen's voice after Hazel put her phone on speaker.

"Keith attacked Rizzy!" she said, hurriedly.

"What?" I heard Taylen and Bishop say.

"Keith attacked Rizzy in the elevator," she said again, giving more details.

"The fuck? Where is she? Is she okay? Put her on the phone!" Taylen demanded.

"She's right here and she's not okay. She's calmed down but he choked her and slapped her. Her lip is busted and her face is bruised," Hazel informed him.

"What the fuck man! Rizzy baby, talk to me," Taylen begged.

Hearing him so worried about me made me tear up again. Hazel walked over to me and handed me her phone. I took it off speaker and put her phone up to my ear.

"I'm here," I spoke, weakly.

"Baby tell me what happened," he said, softly.

I didn't want to relive it but I told Taylen what happened, giving more details than I did when I told Hazel. She sat on her bed, listening intently, shaking her head.

"I'm gon' kill that nigga," Taylen said, quietly.

"Naw, we gon' kill that nigga!" Bishop said in the background.

"No! I don't want you to do anything and get in trouble. I'm gonna go to the campus police and let them handle it," I told them.

"Naw, fuck that. We ain't fuckin' with the campus police. I got this baby. Stay in your room until we get back. We should be there in about a couple of hours," Taylen told me.

"But---," I began.

"Rizzy, ain't no but, just listen to me. Please!"

"Okay," I hung up the phone and Hazel came over to my bed to get it.

"Are we going to the campus police?" she asked.

"Taylen told me not to. He said he was gon' take care of it."

"I don't know if that's a good idea Rizzy. Keith needs to be punished," Hazel reasoned.

I didn't say anything as Hazel sat on my bed, next to where I was laying. I'm not sure what to do. Odds are, nothing would happen to him.

"Let me just take pictures of your face and neck, just in case," Hazel suggested.

"I don't even want to see my face. But okay, that make sense." I sat up and scooted to the edge of the bed.

Hazel used her phone to take several pictures of my bruised face and neck, and my busted lip. She took several close ups and some zooming in on the specific injuries. When she finished, I washed my face, very gently because it hurt like hell, while Hazel left the room to go find some ice. When she came back, I put the ice pack that she had found on the side of my face and my lip. I took four ibuprofens and fell asleep soon after.

*****

I not sure how long I slept, but I woke up to someone banging on the door. I popped up on my bed out of my sleep and my body felt sore. The room was dark but I could see Hazel's shadow because of the glare from her phone.

"Rizzy, open the door baby. It's me." I started to get up but moved slowly because of the soreness. Hazel got up, turned on the light and opened the door.

Taylen charged in, damn near knocking Hazel over, with Bishop right behind him. Taylen kneeled in front of me and lifted my face by my chin.

"What the fuck? What kinda punk ass nigga does this to a female?" Taylen said, turning my head to the side so that he could see my injuries.

"Ouch, Taylen! My neck is sore," I yelped.

"My bad baby. I can't believe this shit. I'm about to go find him and beat his ass."

"Taylen, no! I don't want you to get in trouble. If you get caught or if he snitches you can lose your scholarship," I pleaded.

"If you think, for one second, that I'm about to let this nigga get away with puttin' his hands on my girl, you better think again. If you want to go to the campus police, you can. But I'm still fuckin' him up when I lay eyes on him," Taylen fumed.

"Hell yeah!" Bishop chimed in.

"You guys, we need to think about the bigger picture. His ass will be still walking around this campus like ain't shit happened after you beat his ass. She will still have to see him," Hazel told the guys.

Everyone was quiet for a minute, thinking over what Hazel said.

"She's right. I don't want to see him walking around campus like he didn't violate me. He needs more than his ass kicked but that ain't enough," I agreed with Hazel.

There was another bout of silence. Since Taylen didn't want me to go to the campus police, we need to come up with a plan that will to get him off campus.

"Okay. After a beat his ass, I'm gonna give him a choice to withdraw from this school or you're going to the police," Taylen suggested.

"Do you think he'll leave his scholarship and education in the middle of the semester and the football season?" Hazel inquired.

"Rizzy going to the police would be much worse," Bishop said. "I think that might work."

"What do you think Rizzy? If he doesn't leave, we got the pics I took and we can go to the police," Hazel asked.

"We can try that," I said after a long pause.

"Cool! I'm about to go find this nigga and beat the fuck outta him. Let's go Bishop!" Taylen said, getting up and gently pulling me with him. "I'll be back, okay. Don't leave this room. Here's some money so ya'll can order in."

Taylen reached in his pocket and gave me forty dollars. I'm not sure what he thought we were gonna order that cost that much. Not to mention, Bishop gave Hazel money as well.

"Thank you Taylen. You too Bishop," I said, quietly, as tears began to form again. I wrapped my arms around myself as I stood in front of Taylen.

"You know I gotchu Pretty Girl. No more tears," Taylen said, using his thumb to wipe my tears. "I'll be back soon." He kissed my forehead and him and Bishop left.

I sat back on my bed and let out a huge sigh.

"I think that man loves you!" Hazel blurted out.

"Girl, he barely knows me." I tried to laugh.

"Don't matter how long he's known you. I know what I see. Are you ready to stop playing with his emotions?"

"I think so. Hell, I've been ready!" I confessed.

"Good! I'm tired of your irritable ass. Now let's order some food," Hazel said.

Chapter 39

Taylen

Bishop and I left Rizzy and Hazel's room on a mission. We dropped our bags off in our rooms and went directly to the building that Keith lives in.

"Do you know his room number?" Bishop asked.

"Naw, you know I don't fuck with that nigga like that," I replied.

"Well where the fuck we going?" Bishop snapped back.

"I'm about to find this muthafucka!" I said through gritted teeth as I snatched the door open to Keith's building."

As luck would have it, his roommate Trey was in the lobby talking to some other guys.

"Aye, Trey, let me holla at you for a minute," I yelled over to him.

I ain't never had a problem with Trey, aside from the fact that he was cool with a fuck boy.

"Is Keith in ya'll room? I need to talk to him about something," I asked Trey when he made it over to me.

"Naw man. When I made it to our room, he left. He didn't say much and he took a bag with him," Trey shared.

"Fuck! Awight, thanks man!" I said, pissed off.

"Everything cool?" Trey asked.

"Yeah, it's straight. I'll holla atchu later," I replied, not wanting to give him any clues to the fact that I wanted to murder his boy.

Bishop and I left the building and walked over to the Student Center to see if Keith was hanging out over there. Unfortunately, after looking in the commons area, the bowling alley and the pool hall, we still didn't find him. We decided to go back our dorm. I have no idea how the hell I'm gonna catch up with this nigga, but Keith's days around here are numbered. He can't hide for long.

"So, what's the plan?" Bishop inquired.

"I don't know. Trey said the nigga took a bag so he probably ain't planning to go back to his room tonight. I don't even know where to start looking for him," I answered.

"Let's just lay low for tonight. We got conditioning tomorrow. If he shows up at practice, at least we know he's around. You can't beat his ass at practice but we can keep eyes on him," Bishop suggested.

I appreciate how Bishop seema just as pissed as I am about Keith putting his hands on Rizzy. I guess she's become somewhat of a sister to him since we had all been spending so much time together before I fucked up.

We walked into our dorm building and went straight to the elevator. I don't feel like doing shit but laying up under Rizzy. It's been a week since she stopped fucking with me. I hate that this shit happened to her but since she was allowing me to be in her presence, I'm taking full advantage. Her stubborn ass might kick me to the curb again once this is over.

"Taylen!" I heard behind me.

When I turned around, Diamond's annoying ass was coming towards me.

"Wassup?" I turned to face her, not hiding my annoyance.

"When are we gonna hook up?" she spoke with seduction in her voice. I heard Bishop clear his throat and I looked at him telling him this ain't what it looks like.

"Hook up?" I questioned, with my arms folded across my chest. Diamond was standing in my personal space, so I took a step back, keeping my arms folding.

"Uh yeah. You know, you promised to help me with my Math class." She smiled and twirled her hair around her finger. She seemed to do that every time I talked to her.

"I don't remember promising you anything. I told you my schedule is tight." I dismissed her and turned to continue my walk to the elevator. She followed me and is once again in my personal space.

"Well what are you doing right now? I can come to your room," Diamond offered.

Just my luck, the elevator doors opened and Hazel and Rizzy stepped off, just in time for them to hear Diamond's offer to come to my room. They both looked at me and rolled their eyes and proceeded to the front desk. Rizzy is wearing a hoodie and has the hood pulled up and I can barely see her face. But I saw enough to let me know she heard Diamond. My eyes followed them to see where they were going because I know I told Rizzy not to leave the room. They walked around the front desk to meet the pizza delivery guy and grabbed the boxes of pizza and a couple of two-liter pops.

Once they paid the man, they walked back in our direction. Bishop took the pizzas from Hazel and I reached to take the drinks from Rizzy and she snatched away from me and gave me a dirty look.

"Taylen, do you want me to come to your room or not?" Diamond continued talking to me as I got on the elevator with Bishop, Hazel and Rizzy.

"Naw man! You gon' have to find another tutor. I told you my schedule it tight." I told Diamond as the elevator doors closed. I heard Diamond smack her lips in disappointment. I couldn't care less though. I told her ass I was too busy anyway.

"Rizzy, I didn't invite her to my room. She's trying to get me to tutor her in Math. I never agreed but she keeps bothering me," I explained.

Rizzy looked at me but didn't say a word. I reached for the drinks again and she let me take them this time. We got off on the eighth floor and went to their room. As soon as we closed the door, Hazel began grilling me, while Rizzy attempted to get the food together.

"Taylen, what the fuck happened? Did ya'll find him?" Hazel asked.

"Naw. We saw Trey in the lobby of their building. He said Keith left and took a bag with him. Didn't even say nothing to Trey," I told her.

"If he's not on this campus anywhere, he's probably at Phil's. I mean, they're like family." Rizzy spoke up.

"Shit! I need a car!" I said.

“I’m sure Faryn won’t mind letting you borrow hers,” Rizzy said sarcastically, rolling her eyes.

“That shit ain’t funny Rizzy. I ain’t fuckin’ with Faryn’s ass like that,” I shot back, grabbing the plate she made for me with several pieces of pizza on it.

“Text David to see if you can borrow his car,” Bishop suggested.

I put my pizza down and grabbed my phone, going to the texts and shot David a text.

“Do you really think fighting is a good idea? If I go to the campus police, I don’t have to worry about you getting expelled or arrested,” Rizzy tried to reason with me again.

“I thought we were done having this conversation. I know I am,” I spouted, letting her know that me beating his ass is not up for debate. It’s gonna happen.

I picked my plate up and sat in the chair in front of Rizzy’s desk. Hazel and Bishop were sitting on Hazel’s bed and Rizzy sat on her own. We ate in silence for a few minutes until my phone buzzed with a notification.

David: My car is still in the shop. Sorry bruh

“David’s car is still in the shop. I don’t think it’s meant for me to lay hands on this nigga tonight,” I spat, shaking my head frustration.

“It’s probably for the best,” Rizzy commented.

“He gettin’ fucked up sooner or later, so don’t even sweat that shit Tay,” Bishop stated as he stood from Hazel’s bed and pulled her up with him.

“You gon’ be down here for a minute?” Bishop continued, addressing me.

"I don't know. You gon' put me out?" I directed to Rizzy. She didn't say anything at first as the three of us looked at her, awaiting her answer.

"Rizzy, what did we just talk about earlier today?" Hazel reminded her.

She sighed, deeply, before she replied. "No, I'm not gon' put you out."

"Awight, I'm going with Bishop. See ya'll later," Hazel said, much too quickly.

"Much later!" Bishop added. "Like in the morning kinda later!"

"Boy hush! I ain't spending the night with you. My roomy needs me," Hazel said, pushing Bishop jokingly.

"She got everything she need right here. I'll see ya'll in the morning," I affirmed, smirking at Rizzy. I was surprised she didn't say anything.

"Now let's go," Bishop commanded, tapping Hazel on her ass. "Why you always got these lil ass clothes on Haze," he fussed at her as they left the room.

They closed the door and we could hear their fussing fade away as they got further down the hallway. I got up and locked the door and sat on the bed next to Rizzy.

"You good?" I asked her. She was sitting on her bed, against the wall with her knees to her chest and her arms wrapped around them.

"As good as expected, I guess. I thought I was done dealing with crazy shit after the whole ordeal with Marcus died down. Now this nigga!" She shook her head.

"I'm gon' beat that nigga's ass just like I beat Marcus', but far worse." I stated, very calmly.

We sat in a comfortable silence for a while, both of us in our own thoughts. I'm sure she's probably thinking about why these things are happening to her and I'm thinking about the depths I would go to protect her.

"I'm sorry that I keep getting you involved in my craziness. You've been protecting me since the first time we met."

I pushed myself back on the bed, so that my back is against the wall, and pulled Rizzy sideways onto my lap. She put her arms around my neck and her head on my shoulders. I gently rubbed her legs that were stretched out in front of her, on the bed. Of course, she was wearing some little ass running shorts.

"Since the first time I laid eyes on you, I've felt a strong need to protect you. I don't know if it was because of the situation you were in or not. I can't say I wouldn't have done the same thing for any woman that I saw in that situation. But even after it was over, I had to make sure you were safe. Since I wasn't here to protect you from Keith, I'm about to beat his ass and use him as an example to all these other niggas and bitches around here not to fuck with you."

Rizzy didn't comment. "Are you still mad at me about the whole Imani thing?" I asked.

She lifted her head off my shoulder and looked at me. "You mean the whole girlfriend you had but failed to tell me about?"

"I'm not about to rehash it. Are you still mad?" I asked again.

She put her head back on my shoulder. "No, I'm not still mad. I was gonna call you tonight so we could talk. Hazel told me that I've been being a bitch all week and she was tired of my attitude. Told me I needed to stop being stubborn."

"I can't say that I disagree agree with that last part." I laughed. "I know that what I did was wrong and I'm sorry for that baby. I want you to be my girl and I've wanted that since the day we met. I forgot all about Imani's ass. Like, no joke, Bishop had to remind me about her a few different times. In my mind, we've been broken up since I made you mine in my head. I just failed to take the necessary steps to do it in real life," I explained.

"I don't like the secrets and the little white lies you keep telling me. If we gon' be together, you can't be keeping secrets and shit."

"I know, I know. At the time, I thought it was best. I see how wrong I was now." I kissed her forehead, still rubbing my hand up and down her thighs. "You forgive me?"

"Before I do, is there anything else you need to tell me? I don't want any more surprises Tay."

"Tay? Oh, I'm Tay to you now?" I teased. She never calls me Tay, always Taylen.

"Just answer the damn question," Rizzy demanded.

We sat quietly for a minute. I was contemplating whether or not I wanted to tell her about the bullshit going on with Imani. If I don't tell Rizzy and she finds out later, she may not give me another chance. I guess I better get it over with.

"There is one thing. I don't even know what to make of it because I don't believe it's true," I finally blurted out.

She let out a deep, long breath. "Just tell me."

"After I broke up with Imani, she called me repeatedly. When I didn't answer, she sent me text after text. I ignored all of them. I was so fucked up about you kickin' my ass to the curb, I didn't want to hear or see anything she had to say," I sighed deeply before I went on. "I finally decided to see what the fuck she was talking about in the text messages."

I grabbed my phone and when to my text messages, finding Imani's name. I went to the last text that she sent me and handed my phone to Rizzy. I still couldn't even say the shit out loud. Rizzy took my phone and read the message. She tossed my phone on the bed and put her head on my shoulder.

"I don't think it's meant for us to be together," she said, softly.

"What? Why would you say some shit like that?"

"Because shit keeps happening to keep us apart," she declared, trying to get up from my lap but I held her in place.

"Oh, hell naw! We not about to do this Rizzy. I'm not about to let you use this as an excuse to not give me a chance baby," I pleaded.

"It's not an excuse Tay. It's a whole damn baby!" she yelled.

"Stop fuckin' callin' me Tay. And I know it's a baby but I think she's lying about being pregnant or it ain't mine," I told her.

"Why would she lie?" She looked at me, her eyes becoming teary.

"Because she wants me to be her meal ticket. Imani is a straight up hood chick. No goals, no ambition, no plans for her future. She thinks I'm going to the NFL and if we had a kid together, she'd be set for life," I explained to her.

"But that doesn't mean she's not pregnant. Were you fucking her?"

"Yes, but I never fucked her raw and I still pulled out. The last time I had sex with her was in mid-July. It's October. If she were pregnant, do you think she'd be still wearing a half shirt and booty shorts."

Rizzy didn't respond immediately. The shirt Imani had on that day was basically a bra and her shorts were little as fuck. I've thought long and hard about this shit. There is no way Imani could be pregnant with my seed. Her ass was up to something and I wasn't about to let her get my ass caught up.

"She would only be three months or so and maybe not showing yet," she finally said.

"Yes, she would be showing. She's not an athlete like you. Her ass probably would be showing at conception."

We both laughed, which broke the tension a little bit.

"Listen baby. I haven't even responded to her telling me that she's pregnant because I think it's a bunch of bullshit. I know I probably shouldn't be that way but it's how I feel right now. My main priority has been getting back in your good graces and now, beating Keith's punk ass. But don't let this situation change your mind about giving me a chance to be your man."

Rizzy looked up at me and kissed my lips. I think she meant for it to be a quick kiss but I grabbed the back of her neck pressed my lips against hers, pushing my tongue into her mouth. Our tongues twirled around each other's as I ran my fingers through her hair. A soft moan escaped her mouth and she pulled away. Both of us breathless, looking into each other's eyes, but saying nothing at first.

"Please Pretty Girl. Just give me a chance," I begged.

"I don't think I could deny you if I tried. But I'm not trying to be a stepmother and I don't fuck around with deadbeat dads. So you better hope this bitch is lying."

"Thank you baby!" I hugged her and dug my face into her neck, taking in her scent.

Rizzy just made my fucking life right now. Once I beat Keith's ass and prove Imani is lying, everything will be gucci. *Lord, please let Imani be lying.*

Chapter 40

Bishop

After leaving Hazel and Karizma's room, we took the stairs to my room. I'm not trying to be insensitive about what happened to Rizzy but I'm on a mission right now. It's been a minute since I got my dick wet and I've been thinking about the possibility of getting acquainted with Hazel's pussy for a minute.

"You miss me?" I asked her, pulling her close to me as we stood in middle of the room.

"A little bit. You weren't gone that long." She laughed.

"Oh, it's like that? I miss you a lot anytime we aren't together. You hurt a nigga's feelings." I pretended to be sad and gave her my best sad face.

"Aww, I didn't mean to hurt your feelings. What can I do to make you feel better?" She played along, kissing my lips first, then my cheek, nibbling on my ear, then making her way to my neck.

"I don't know, what do you have in mind?" I whispered, walking backwards until my legs hit my bed, pulling her along with me.

"Well," she began, "I think I promised you a lil something. Do you remember what it was?"

We stood right next to my bed, her arms around my neck, mine around her waist, with my hands cupping her ass and pressing her against my erection.

"I think I do remember," I said, lifting her shirt over her head and tossing it to the side.

I took a minute to admire her modest-sized breasts held up by a black lace bra. My eyes went to her stomach and took in her well-defined abs. I've never fucked with a girl that was an athlete. Don't get me wrong, having a banging body was necessary for me to even give a girl the time of day. But I'm use to girls with a fat ass and big titties, a flat stomach but with no muscle definition anywhere on their bodies.

Hazel's body is different and more amazing. Looking at her, you could tell that she spends a lot of time working out. Her muscle definition was visibly present. She is evenly proportioned and has enough curves to catch any man's eye. She's perfect for me. Now I'm ready to see what kind of treasure she holds between her legs.

I grabbed the back of her neck and pulled her face to mine, smothering her lips with mine and pushing my tongue into her mouth. Her arms are wrapped around my waist and she pressed her body against mine.

"Mmmm," she moaned. Grabbing the hem of my shirt, she lifted it and our lips parted briefly, to pull it over my head. Our lips immediately reconnected.

Hazel is a lot more aggressive than I imagined. She pushed me back and I fell onto my bed. I looked up and followed her gaze, to the tent in my basketball shorts. Our eyes met again and I smirked. Never been one to brag on my dick but I'm blessed. When I looked back up at Hazel, she was easing her running shorts down her hips, revealing the black lace panties, that matched her bra.

"C'mere," I commanded, reaching my hand out to her. She straddled me and our mouths devoured each other's once more.

I could only pray that I didn't bust a nut prematurely. It has been too long and I'm long overdue. I need to take control of this or it will be over before it gets started. I wrapped my arms around her body and flipped her over so that I'm on top. Never missing a beat, my mouth moved down to her neck, then licking between her breasts. Pushing one of her breasts up so that her nipple is exposed, my tongue circled around her nipple.

"Shit!" she breathed.

I continued exploring her body with my tongue, making my way down her stomach, to the waistband of her underwear. Instead of pulling them off, I pressed my nose against her center, inhaling her scent. Hazel released another moaned as my tongue glided up and down the inside of her thighs.

"Bishop, please," she whispered.

"Please what?" I looked up at her, with my head between her legs.

"I'm ready."

I grinned and pulled the crotch of her panties to the side. Shit! This pussy is wet as fuck. I slowly slid one of my fingers inside of her wetness and am amazed, once again, by her tightness. As one finger slipped in and out of her drenched opening, Hazel's breathing picked up. I added another finger and dipped my tongue inside of her folds. She began to grind harder against my tongue and fingers.

"Shit baby! Ahh!" she uttered softly.

"You 'bout to cum Haze?" I said quickly, in between licks.

"Ahh, yes!" she hissed as I continued to give her pleasure.

"Let that shit go Haze. Give it to me!" I demanded.

Let it go is just what she did. Her juices dripped from my hand and mouth and I kept licking as if this were my last meal. Hazel tried to scoot away from me but I gripped her thighs and held her in place.

"Baby please, I can't take no more!" she breathed.

I looked up and her chest heaved up and down while she shook her head from side- to-side.

"You can't take it Haze?" I teased.

"I need---a--minute," she panted.

While she caught her breath, I eased her panties over her ass and pulled them off. I reached underneath her back and undid her bra, taking it off her shoulders and tossing it on the floor. I paused for a second to just take her in. She looks drowsy, with her eyes barely open and she's still breathing hard. That must have been one helluva nut. I took a condom out of the top drawer of my dresser and slid my shorts and boxers down. As soon as my dick was free, Hazel must have opened her eyes because I heard her gasp.

"What's wrong Haze?" I smirked.

"Umm, whatchu gon' do with that?" she asked.

"Let me show you."

I slid the condom down the length of my dick and gently laid my body on top of hers. She immediately opened her legs and I fit perfectly in between them. Tilting her head towards mine, she found my lips and we lost ourselves in a passionate kiss. My dick isn't inside of her but she ground her pussy so hard against me that she worked out another orgasm.

"Baby, I'm about to cum again," she squealed and a second later, her body tensed up and she called out my name, along with some other shit I didn't understand.

"Damn Haze! I ain't even gave you the dick yet and you 'bout to lose it." I smiled at her then nudged my face into her neck.

As she recovered, I decided to go ahead and slide up in her. I reached down and placed my dick at her opening, pushing it in just a little. She sucked in a breath as soon as she felt it.

"It's cool baby. I'll be gentle," I assured her.

"I know, it's just been a few months and your size is umm…"

"No worries baby." I kissed her again, mainly to distract her.

Gently and slowly, I began to push inside of her. She is so wet that I'm certain it wasn't painful. Her tightness had a nigga already about to bust.

"Haze baby! You tight as hell," I told her when my fullness was completely inside of her treasure.

She finally relaxed and wrapped her legs around my waist. That was my cue, letting me know that she is ready. I pushed my dick deep inside of her and pulled it almost all the way out. Looking down, I could see all of her juices on the condom. As I continued to stroke, going deep each time, Hazel began to match my match my movements and I promise I thought I had died and went to heaven.

I buried my mouth in her neck, to muffle my moans so I wouldn't sound like a bitch. I don't know if it's because I haven't had sex in months but pussy has never felt this good. I need Hazel to hurry up and cum because I'm not sure how long I can hold out.

As if she read my mind, she shrieked, "Bishop, I'm cummin'!" She began to grind her hips in a circular motion, while matching strokes.

"Fuck Haze, this pussy is so fuckin' good, I'm about to bust too! Shit baby! Argh!" I released my seeds into the condom.

All you could hear is our breathing for a good two minutes. I think Hazel had even dozed off. I pushed myself up and rolled over to her side.

"Baby you good?" I asked her.

She turned toward me, eyes lazy and smiled. "I'm more than good."

"Looks like I wore your little ass out." I kissed her forehead before I got up to flush the condom.

"Nope! Never that!" She laughed.

I walked back over to the bed and reached in my drawer to grab another condom. "Good, because he's ready for round two." I said stroking my dick with one hand and flapping the condom with the other.

"Bring him here then!" she demanded.

Oh yeah! I think I'm in love!

Chapter 41

Taylen

It's been almost a full two days and I'm still trying to catch up with Keith. He hasn't shown up at practice, I haven't seen him around campus, nor has he been to the dining hall. I've asked Trey if he knew his whereabouts and he claims to not have seen or heard from him. I thought that as time passed, I would calm down but I'm getting more and more pissed. Rizzy still has bruises and her neck is still sore but she's doing okay. I just can't let his ass get away with putting his hands on my girl.

Bishop and I are eating dinner, sitting with some of our teammates because the girls haven't made it to the dining hall yet. I swear their practices be forever some days. They damn near miss dinner every day.

"Aye Bishop, I'm starting to think Keith left town," I whispered.

"Well, I mean, so the fuck what if he did. I know you want to fuck him up but if he's gone, that's not a bad thing," he reasoned.

"Yeah, that's true. But I'm not lettin' this shit go until I beat his ass. I don't care how long it is before I see him. I'm fuckin' him up on sight."

"I feel you bruh! But, there go the girls." He nodded his head in their direction, standing and picking up his tray. I started to do the same.

"Damn, them bitches got ya'll whipped than a mufucka!" Eugene, one of our teammates said, laughing.

Bishop and I both dropped our trays and were in Eugene's face so damn quick. I grabbed the front of his t-shirt.

"Nigga, don't you ever in your life call them outta their names again," Bishop said between clenched teeth.

"I will fuck you up about mine," I said, letting his shirt go and pushing him in the chest.

"Damn, my bad, my bad!" Eugene said, putting his hands up, surrendering.

We grabbed our trays and went over to where the girls sat. I put my tray down next to Rizzy, kissing her forehead before sitting down.

"Eww, I'm all sweaty," Rizzy complained about me kissing her.

"I don't mind. Now give me those lips," I told her.

She turned toward me and pecked me on my lips that were puckered and waiting.

"What was that about over there?" Hazel asked Bishop.

"What?"

"You know what. Why was ya'll all in Eugene's face like that?" she asked again.

"Cause that nigga stupid," Bishop answered, leaving it at that.

We all finished our food while we got caught up on how each other's classes and practices were today. Once we put our trays away, we exited the dining hall. I put my arm around Rizzy's shoulder and kissed the side of her head as we walked out of the building.

"You must like the taste of dry sweat," she said, looking up at me.

"As long as it's yours," I replied, stealing a kiss from her lips.

"You nasty."

"Oh, you think that's nasty? When you gon' let me show you how nasty I can be?" I teased.

"Aye Tay," Bishop interrupted before Rizzy could answer me. "Look who came out of hiding." He looked across the way and I followed his gaze.

Keith walked, rather casually towards his dorm, talking to a girl. He's so engrossed in his conversation, he didn't notice Bishop and I walking towards him. Rizzy and Hazel followed behind us very cautiously.

"Aye nigga! I heard you like to put yo hands on women," I stated calmly.

Keith stopped walking and turned around, looking as if he had seen a ghost.

"What's wrong? You ain't got shit to say?" I asked, still very calm.

"Keith, what is he talking about?" The girl he was with pulled him by his arm, trying to turn him around to face her. He still didn't say shit.

“I’ve been lookin’ for you for a couple of days, man. You been hidin’ out?” I asked, still trying to get him to say something.

“Uhh, naw man. I, uhh, just been busy. Why you lookin’ for me?” Keith sputtered.

I’m now an arm’s length away from him. I just wanted him to admit what the fuck he did to Rizzy, not that I didn’t believe her. I just wanted to hear him say it.

“So you gon’ stand up here and act like you ain’t put yo hands on my girl.”

“Naw man, it wasn’t even---.” That’s all I needed to hear.

I swung on him landing a right hook on his jaw and he stumbled back, almost knocking down the girl that was standing behind him. He recovered quickly though and tried to come back with a right hook of his own but I blocked it and punched him in the stomach. He bent over, holding his stomach and I uppercut him in the face. I didn’t want it to be this easy. He was barely putting up a fight.

“I guess you only fight women huh! Punk ass bitch. Hit me like you hit my girl, bitch!” I spat. Out of the corner of my eyes, I could see that a crowd surrounded us.

Keith stood and I could see blood dripping out of his nose and one of his eyes starting to swell. Suddenly he lunged toward me, which caught me off guard, and I stumbled back a few steps. Once I gained my footing, I pushed him back against the building and beat the shit out of him. Game time is over. His face was damn near unrecognizable when Bishop pulled me away from him.

“That’s enough Tay, you gon’ kill ‘em!” Bishop yelled. I yanked away from him and got back in Keith’s face.

"Now this is what the fuck you gon' do if you don't want to end up in jail or dead. We got pictures of what the fuck you did to my girl. If you don't want her to give them to the police, you gon' pack yo shit up and get the fuck outta dodge nigga. I don't want to see your ass on this campus, ever again, or I'm fuckin' you up on sight and she's pressing charges. Lil bitch!" I kicked him for good measure before I walked away.

I found Rizzy in the crowd and pulled her into my arms, hugging her tightly, before we walked towards our building. Bishop and Hazel were right behind us. When we entered the building, I went to the stairs instead of the elevators and everyone followed. Once we got to our room, Rizzy sat on my bed and Hazel sat on Bishop's bed as he leaned against his desk. I paced back and forth trying to calm myself down.

"I could have killed that nigga!" I yelled, punching the palm of one hand with the other.

"Shit, nigga, you almost did. He's probably still on the ground over there." Bishop laughed.

"Baby calm down." Rizzy got up and stood in front of me so that I couldn't pace anymore.

"I am calm baby, I'm just pissed off," I told her.

"Well it's over. I'm sure he will leave and I won't have to worry about his ass."

"He would be crazy to stick around here," Hazel chimed in.

"Oh, he's as good as gone. I already talked to Coach and told him what happened, I even showed him the pics. He was gonna kick him off the team whenever he decided to show up to practice again. You know Coach don't want no controversy surrounding the team," I shared with them.

"Damn, I didn't know you did all that," Bishop said, surprised.

Keith putting his hands on Rizzy had me wanting to kill him and I can't do that. I had to do something to fuck up his world. Beating his ass made me feel a better for the moment but I knew I'd want to do that every time I saw him around campus. Not to mention, him walking around here after what he did to Rizzy, made her uncomfortable.

"I did what I had to do," I said.

"Even though I didn't want you to risk getting in trouble, I appreciate you having my back." She stood on her tippy-toes and planted a kiss on my lips.

"I always gotchu, Pretty Girl. Now go upstairs shower so you can come back and kiss my wounds."

"Nigga you ain't got no damn wounds. I don't think he landed one punch." Bishop laughed.

"Mind yo business bruh!" I told Bishop.

"Yeah okay. I guess that means I'll be up when Rizzy comes back," he told Hazel and pulled her up from the bed, kissing her lips.

I kissed Rizzy on her forehead and the girls left. I showered after practice but after handing out that ass whooping I decided to take another. Even though Keith didn't land a punch, my knuckles are sore and I'm tired. These past couple of days have been stressful as hell. I'm ready to lay up under my girl.

Chapter 42

Karizma

"Thanksgiving Break"

I'm kind of excited to go home for Thanksgiving break to see my mom, sister and my friends from high school. But I hate that I probably won't be able to spend much time, if any, with Taylen. We've been spending all of our free time together since we made it official and it'll be weird not seeing him daily.

Everything has been cool since Taylen beat Keith's ass. From what Taylen said, Keith packed up his shit and tried to tell the coach he had to go home because of a family emergency and he wasn't coming back. Coach told him that he knew about him attacking me and that if he tried to play on another team, he is gonna let those coaches know as well. I know that going to the police may have been the right thing to do, but I feel vindicated with the outcome of it all.

Marcus has even stopped trying to communicate with me. I've seen him around campus a couple of times with his soon-to-be baby mama. He just looks at me but doesn't try to approach. I'm glad his ass moved on.

The fact that Taylen could potentially be a father is bothering the hell out of me. He's still pretty adamant about Imani not being pregnant by him. He claims that when he asked her how far along she was, she kept beating around the bush and didn't give him an answer. That does seem kind of shady. He's gonna have to figure something out because he can't be in denial about the situation forever and he has to talk to her at some point.

I ain't gonna lie though, him seeing her has me worried. What if she is pregnant and it is his baby and all of his old feelings for her come back. Not to mention, we still haven't had sex.

A text from him took me out of my thoughts.

TayBaby: Hey Pretty Girl! Wassup?

Me: Nothin…what about you

TayBaby: About to come c u. Hazel down here w/Bishop.

Me: K

A few minutes later Taylen knocked on the door. When I opened it, he greeted me with a tongue kiss, wrapping his arms around my waist, backing me up and kicking the door closed. I put my arms around his neck and kissed him back.

"Dang babe, did you miss me?" I said, all outta breath, when we separated.

"I did miss you. I haven't seen you since last night," Taylen replied as he continued placing soft pecks on my lips.

"Aww, I missed you too. It's been a busy day. You got plans tonight?" I asked him as we sat on my bed and I gave him the remote to the T.V.

"Anything that includes you. I'm gonna miss you over break," he said while squeezing my thigh.

"I don't even wanna think about it," I told him.

"What's wrong?" he asked, hearing the sadness in my voice. "It's only a week. Honestly, if we wanna see each other, it's only a train ride away."

"I know. It's not that."

"What is it then?" He turned the TV on and began flipping through the channels.

"Are you planning to see Imani?" I asked.

"Yeah. I actually texted her the other day and told her to make a doctor's appointment for next week. I need to see what's up with this supposed pregnancy with my own eyes. Why?"

I didn't respond immediately and looked down at my hands. He lifted my head up by my chin and kissed my lips.

"Tell me wassup?" He kissed me again.

"How do you think you're going to feel when you see her?"

"What do you mean? I ain't gon' feel nothing?"

"You were with her for a good while Taylen. And she's supposedly carrying your child. Not to mention, she'll probably be throwing the pussy at you." I folded my arms across my chest.

"She can throw it all she wants. I don't want her ass."

"But---" I tried to say.

"There are no buts Rizzy. You have to trust me baby."

"I know."

"You act like a nigga ain't got no kind of self-control. I control myself around you all time."

"True." I decided to drop it and got up to look through some menus to see what we could order for dinner, while he flipped through the channels and stopped on some Martin reruns.

"What do you feel like eating?" I asked.

He got up, walked over to me and took the menus out of my hands. Then pulled me back towards my bed.

"Lay down," he demanded.

"Taylen, I'm hungry. Let's order some food," I whined.

"I'm hungry too. Now lay down."

Chapter 43

Taylen

Karizma sat on the bed and laid down. She looked so beautiful with her chocolate skin and deep dimples on display as she smiled up at me. I wanted so badly to make love to her but I didn't want to pressure her. I have been faithful to her since before we became official, unless you considered my hand cheating. A nigga is getting tired of beating my meat every day, shit, sometimes a couple times a day, if I'm being honest. Rizzy is worth the wait though, so I don't mind.

I walked over to lock the door and shot Bishop a text telling him to keep Hazel down there until he hears from me again. I want no interruptions while I show Rizzy that she is the only one for me. I've never eaten pussy before and I don't know if I'm good at it or not. But we are about to find out together.

I went back over to the bed and stood over Rizzy. I could see that she was nervous about what was about to happen because her breathing picked up. I took my shirt off and placed my body between her legs, laid on top of her, resting most of my weight on my elbows.

"You good Pretty Girl?" I asked her, before kissing her forehead, left cheek, right cheek, and finally pecking her lips.

"Yeah, I'm good," she whispered after kissing me back.

"You know you have my heart, right?" I asked her.

"If you say so."

"I say so."

I leaned down and kissed her hard on the lips. She allowed my tongue to enter her mouth. I've never in my life kissed a girl this way. Hell, Imani and I rarely kissed and if we did, most times it was a peck. Rizzy made me feel like I could do this for hours and be satisfied.

My mouth found its way to her ear, then moved down to her neck. As usual, Rizzy wasn't wearing a bra, which I was thankful for at the moment. But we will be having another conversation with her about that. I pushed her shirt up above her breasts and attacked them, giving each nipple some attention. She let out a moan so I know it felt good to her. I moved down to her stomach and started to slide her shorts down and she stopped me.

"Wait Taylen!"

"What's wrong baby?"

My chin rested on her stomach as I looked up at her waiting for her to answer.

"You trust me?" She nodded her head. "Then don't worry. I gotchu."

She relaxed and lifted up as I pulled her shorts down and off. Her pussy was bare and beautiful, like she had just shaved or gotten it waxed. My mouth watered as I prepared to devour her sweetness.

I slowly spread her legs and kissed her inner thighs. She released a soft moan and tried to push me away by the shoulders. I could smell her sweet scent as I stared at the moistness glistening from her pussy. I couldn't take my mouth being so close to her sweet spot anymore.

First, I took the tip of my nose and circled it around her pearl. She smelled so good that I couldn't wait another second to taste her. I took my tongue and licked her clit softly. The sounds that she made had a nigga ready to bust.

"Oh my God Taylen!" she whispered as my tongue worked its way up, down, and around, feasting on her juices.

Even though this is my first time eating pussy, I felt like a professional. The sounds she let out, made me go harder. I stuck my finger inside of her and continued assaulting her clit with my tongue.

"Ahhh Taylen, baby! Oh my God! Please!"

"Please what, baby?" I whispered between licks.

"Please don't stop!"

"You like that Pretty?"

"Ahhhh yes Tay baby!"

I never thought I would enjoy eating pussy but she had a nigga wishing I could taste her sweetness every day.

"Taylen, I think---oh my---I'm about to cum baby," Rizzy screamed just before I felt her walls contract on my finger and her juices splashed on my face.

I removed my finger and licked it until there were no remains of her juices left. She lay there, gasping for air, with my head resting on her stomach.

"You okay baby?" I asked her.

“Mmmm hmmm,” she replied, between breaths.

“Good! You're my first you know.”

She lifted her head up a little so I turned and looked up at her.

“What do you mean? Your first what?”

“I've never done that before. You taste so good baby, I think I’m hooked.”

I got up, helped her off the bed and she began getting her stuff together to take a shower, while I chilled on her bed watching Martin.

“Can you order some food? I'm starving?” She asked and I couldn't help but smirk.

“Well I just ate, so I'm good,” I said, winking at her.

“Oh my God, Taylen, you are so nasty.”

She threw her scarf at me and went in the bathroom. I heard the shower start as I looked through the menus.

“What do you want to eat?” I yelled as I peeked in the bathroom. I lost my breath for a moment as she stood before me naked. I looked her up and down until our eyes locked on each other's.

Chapter 44

Karizma

I don't know what came over me but I wanted him in the worst way. I turned the shower off and pushed him out of the doorway and towards my bed.

"I want you," I said softly.

He grabbed me by the back of my neck and kissed me and I could taste myself on his lips. I wrapped my arms around his neck and he lifted me by the hips and I wrapped my legs around his waist.

"Are you sure about this Pretty Girl?" he asked as we lay on the bed, with him on top of me.

I nodded my head yes and he gazed into my eyes.

"No, I need to hear you say it. Are you sure you're ready?"

"I'm ready."

He leaned down and kissed me again, then used his tongue to tease, lick and suck all of the pleasure points that were above my waist. I had no idea that all of those places on my body were so sensitive. He hasn't touched my pussy yet and I'm about to explode.

Taylen finally came up for air, stood up and stared at me as if he were looking into my soul. I could see the imprint of his dick through his basketball shorts. I knew he was big because I felt it a few times when we got carried away. The way he looked at me and the size of his dick made me nervous.

"You trust me baby?" My words were caught in my throat so again, I nodded.

"Tell me. I need to hear you say it."

"I trust you Taylen."

He stood up and took his shorts and boxers off and my eyes must have gotten huge. My heart began to beat faster and I was having second thoughts.

"It'll be fine baby. Don't be nervous," he assured me.

He kneeled between my legs and lined his face up with my pussy. He slowly let his tongue travel through the crevices of my vagina. I'm telling you he didn't miss a spot. He made love to my pussy with his mouth for the second time and I knew then that I had to see what his dick game was like.

When I reached my peak and my juices flowed onto his face, he came up for air with his face glistening. Again, he stared into my soul while I tried to catch my breath. Gently positioning his body on top of mine, his tongue invaded my mouth, allowing me to taste my juices that he seemed to thoroughly enjoy. I could feel his dick pressing against me and my body tensed up.

"Relax, I'm gonna take it slow. But you have to relax." I just nodded and tried to relax.

Kissing me again, he reached down and put the head of his dick at the entrance of my sacred place. I can't believe I'm finally about to lose my virginity, I thought. He rubbed the head up and down my clit, while he kissed me, sending electricity all through my body. I was getting so caught up in how good I was feeling that it caught me by surprise when he began to push inside of me.

"Owww, Taylen, it hurts."

"I know baby, it's gonna hurt some at first. Let me get it in."

"It's not in?" I began to panic.

"Shh. Hold on to my waist and when it hurts just squeeze. Okay?

"Okay."

"Kiss me."

We began kissing again and I could feel him pushing himself inside of me, very slowly. I moaned in pain and fear while we kissed and squeezed my fingers so deep into his back, I probably drew blood.

"Baby, I can stop if it hurts too bad. I want this to be a good for you."

"No. Keep going." I pulled his face back down to kiss me some more and relaxed my body as much as I could.

As he continued to slowly become one with me, it felt like my insides were being ripped apart. How much dick does this man have left, I thought, as tears rolled down the sides of my face.

"Ahhh shit, you're so tight baby, but I'm in. I'm gonna move slowly and it'll start to feel good to you," Taylen whispered.

Just as he said, his strokes were slow and gentle. After a little while, it did feel better.

Chapter 45

Taylen

Before Rizzy, I'd never had sex with a virgin or without a condom. This girl had me doing shit all out of my norm. I know she's been on birth control for about two months and she made me get myself checked about a month ago and I'm disease free. Even with that, the old Taylen still wouldn't have been going up in no bitch raw. But this is Rizzy, my pretty girl and future wife. I need to feel her, all of her, just this one time. After this time, I'll use rubbers.

I had finally worked my dick all the way inside of her walls and it took everything in my power to not beat this pussy up. The feeling is like no other that I've ever felt so I had to practice some self-control.

"Ahhh, shit, you're so tight baby, but I'm in. I'm gonna move slowly and it'll start to feel good to you." I whispered.

My strokes were slow and gentle, and with each stroke, she got wetter and wetter. I think it started to feel good to her because I could feel her body relax and she began to match my strokes.

"Taylen---Oh my God---Ahh---baby."

I need to focus if I don't want to be a two-minute brother but the sound of her voice in this moment had a nigga gone. I started thinking about the craziest shit to get my mind off this nut. Her pussy is so tight and wet, it felt like heaven. I could have shed a few tears because I swear I ain't never had pussy this good.

"Damn Pretty Girl, you feel so damn good baby."

"Taylen, I think I'm about to cum."

Thank God! "You think so? Don't hold it back." *Please hurry up and cum.*

"Oh---kay! Ah…Um...Hm!" she screamed as her juices drowned my dick. I was only a half a second behind her filling her up with my seeds.

We lay there, out of breath, for a few minutes before either of us said anything.

"That was amazing," she said, breaking the silence.

"Yeah, it was. Best I've ever had."

"I've had better!" she joked and I looked at her and she laughed.

"Don't play with me Rizzy. You know this is all mine now, right."

"Why do guys always say that?"

"How do you know what guys always say?"

"Well, I've read a lot of urban fiction books and the guys in the book always say stuff like that," she said, giggling.

"I don't know why anybody else says anything. I just know that this pussy right here, belongs to me. And I don't play about what's mine!" I said and gave her a quick kiss on the lips.

"Whatever! Since you claiming shit, I hope you know that this dick is all mine!"

"That's not a problem at all, Pretty Girl." I had yet to pull out of her and my dick got hard again. "It's all yours baby!" I been to stroke again slowly.

"It better be!"

"You know you're gonna be my wife, right?"

"If you say so, Taylen."

I don't think she took me seriously but little does she know, I'm serious as fuck.

Chapter 46

Hazel

Tomorrow my oldest brother and sister are coming down to pick me up. I'm excited to see my family over this Thanksgiving Break, although I'm not looking forward to this week away from Bishop while we are home for break. With me living in Peoria, there's no chance of us seeing each other. I must have been in deep thought because I didn't hear Bishop when he spoke to me.

"Huh? What'd you say?" I asked him.

"I said, what are you over there thinking about? I've been talking to you."

"Nothin' too much. Just how we won't be seeing each other for a full week and I'm going to miss you," I confessed.

"Yeah, that does suck but hopefully it'll go by fast. I'm gonna miss you too."

"I know you're excited to see your son. Is Keesha still trippin' about FaceTiming you?"

"Yep! But when my mom or sister have him, they've been calling so it's cool. I knew Keesha would trip so I'm not even surprised. I plan to have him for the whole week that I'm home so I hope her ass don't play with me."

"Have you talked to her at all since…"

"Not once. No calls, no emails, no texts."

We were on his bed, with him sitting with his back against the wall and me with my head in his lap. It was quiet for a few minutes as he played in my hair.

"Do you have any big plans over the break?" he asked.

"Not really. Just hanging with my family."

"You should come home with me." He looked down at me while he waited for me to answer.

"You're so sweet. But I can't. My family misses me and they would be devastated if I didn't come home."

"Maybe you can come to Chicago for half of the break?" he persisted.

"How would that work when Thanksgiving is on Thursday?" I sat up, straddled his lap and put my arms around his neck.

"My family knows all about you and you can sleep in the extra bedroom. I might have to sneak in there so I get some pussy but I would love it if you were there. Then you could meet BJ."

"Maybe for Christmas break I can come for a few days." I kissed his lips and he pulled my bottom lip into his mouth before releasing me.

Since the first time we had sex, I crave him. I thought I might regret giving up the goods so soon but if we broke up today, I would have no regrets at all.

Our kisses turned into a full blown make out session and I'm sure my pussy juices were leaking out of my running shorts. I reached down and pulled his shirt up and over his head and he did the same to mine. We looked at each intensely for a second before his mouth attacked my breasts. I pressed his face deeper into my bosom as I ran my fingers through his curls. Something about this moment feels different.

He somehow flipped me onto the bed so that he was now on top. His tongue pressed into my mouth with such passion that it was almost overwhelming. I tried to keep up with his pace and I was breathless doing so.

He reached underneath me and unhooked my bra to free my breasts. Going back and forth, licking each nipple like it was the best lollipop he's ever had. Making his way down to my stomach, he began to ease my shorts and panties down, as I lifted up to make it easier for him.

When I tell you that this man attacked my pussy with his mouth, I'm not even exaggerating. He put my legs on his shoulders and feasted on my love button until I was screaming in ecstasy. He lifted me up a little and licked from my asshole to my g-spot, stopping to suck on my clit along the way.

I'm not the most experienced person. Ricky was my first and only. I thought he was the be all, end all of lovers. But damn, was I wrong. Every time we had sex, Bishop blew my mind. He spent some time figuring out what I liked based on my reactions and paid a little extra attention in those areas. I couldn't take it anymore and finally released my juices all over his face. My orgasm didn't stop him though. This nigga had me backing up and pushing his head away.

"Don't run baby!" He managed to get out between licks.

"I can't take it Bishop! Oh my God, baby. That's enough."

He finally came up for air with my juices shining on his face. The smirk he wore was so damn sexy as he went to his drawer to grab a condom. I could see the head of his dick peeking out of the top of his basketball shorts and my mouth watered. As he pushed his shorts and boxers down, his dick sprang free. I only gave head to Ricky a few times. It wasn't something he ever wanted from me, probably because he was getting it on the regular from several others. But I'm about to suck the soul out of Bishop's dick.

Chapter 47

Bishop

I got up to grab a condom and took my shorts and boxers off. Just as I was about to open the condom, Hazel sat up and took it from my hands, tossing it on the bed. What she did next, shocked the hell out of me because it's not something that I was expecting. She grabbed my dick and licked around the head. It's been so long since I've had my dicked suck, I let out a moan.

After teasing the head with her tongue, she licked up and down my shaft, making sure it was good and wet before taking half of it in her mouth.

"Shit Haze!" I let out as she began to bob her head up and down, almost covering my entire dick with her mouth.

"Ah fuck baby, just like that!" I said, grabbing the back of her head, gently guiding her.

I must say, she was sucking this dick like a champ. I could tell that she wasn't extremely experienced in this area but she could hold her own. I could feel my nut about to rise and I didn't want her to feel pressured to swallow---this time. I pulled back and my dick slipped out of her mouth.

She looked up at me with worried hazel eyes probably think that I wasn't enjoying it, which was not the case at all.

"What's wrong?" she asked.

"Nothin'! I just want to be inside of you. Like right now!"

I grabbed the condom off the bed, opened it and slid it on. Hazel swung her legs around and laid back on the bed, giving me a full view of the heaven that I was about to enter. I balanced myself above her as I played with her pussy with the head of my dick.

With ease, I slowly pushed my way inside of her and she let out a small gasped. Once my full length was inside, I gently moved in and out. We've been sexing pretty regularly since the first time but each time, it's like it's the first.

"Shit!" I let slip because it felt so fucking good.

Continuing my soft assault on the pussy, she adjusted to my size and matched my strokes. Our tongues wrestled as we both tried to contain our moans. The more intense our kisses became, the deeper my strokes.

"Oh shit Bishop! Right there baby, that's my spot!" she screamed as she dug her fingers into my lower back. It must have been good to her because I know she's leaving scratches on me.

"Fuck Haze, yo pussy is the shit baby!" I expressed, hoping that she was about to cum. I was losing the battle of holding in this nut.

"Bishop, baby. You feel so good. Oh my Gaaaa.....I'm about to cuuu---mmmm baaabbbyy!"

"Cum on yo dick then Haze!"

"Aaahhhh fuck!" she yelled as she released all of her sweet nectar. I put in a few more pumps and I released my seeds into the condom.

"Damn baby! You got a brotha sprung!"

"That's the goal!"

"You got heaven between your legs."

"Whatever you say baby! It's always good for me too," she said, kissing my cheek and then my lips when I turned to face her.

Before I knew it, I was lost in her pussy once again.

Chapter 48

Karizma

So far, my time at home has been cool. I've been able to spend some quality time with my sister, Kayla. She's been giving my mother hell but hopefully my talks with her will help some.

My mom has been working but is off today, so that she can start cooking for Thanksgiving. Cooking is not my thing, so I'm not much help. I've just been hanging out in the kitchen sampling food and catching up.

"How are you and Hazel getting along? Do you like being roommates?" my mom questioned.

"Oh yeah! She's cool. I feel like I've known her longer than I've known some of my childhood friends. We get along well."

"That's good. Is Marcus still giving you a hard time?" I had told her all the crazy stuff he did when we broke up but it's been awhile since we'd talked about him.

"No actually. I've seen him around campus with his soon-to-be baby mama but he doesn't try to talk to me anymore, thank goodness," I shared.

"I thought Marcus was a good kid but clearly I was wrong about him. How are things with you and that Tyler guy you mentioned." She stopped cutting up onions, turned around and leaned on the counter.

"His name is Taylen mom," I laughed. "We've been kinda chillin'," I told her, not giving her a whole lot of details.

My mom had this way that she looked at you, with her head sideways and her mouth curled on the side, that let you know that she knows your ass ain't telling the truth.

"Is that right?" She gave me that look.

"Yeah, he's a good guy."

"Umm hmm. I guess that's good. How is track? Still going good?" Thank goodness she dropped it, busier herself with the food again.

"It's still hard but, I mean, I'm used to it now but every day is a struggle. The workouts haven't gotten easier."

"Well that's what you signed up for so you'll be just fine," she reassured me.

"Yeah, I know." It was quiet for a second. "Where's Wade? I haven't seen him much since I've been home?"

"You know things between us ain't been good. He's been in and outta here, saying he's staying with his mom. Little does he know, I'm filing for a divorce. I just let him do his thing until he gets served." I was shocked to hear that from her. She is usually a doormat when it comes to him, or any man that I've ever seen her involved with.

"Wow mom! Are you serious? You're divorcing him?" I probably shouldn't have been excited about them getting divorced but that was music to my ears.

"Hell yes! I'm not waiting around trying to work this out. I did that before and I refuse to go through that craziness again." She had turned around and put her hands on her hips.

"I certainly support you because you know my feelings towards him. You should have listened to me in the first place." I rolled my eyes and shook my head

"Oh shut up girl. You weren't grown enough then to be telling me what to do and you ain't grown enough now. Just learn from my mistakes." She turned back around and continued whatever she was doing.

"I sure am taking notes on what not to do!" *Shit! I didn't mean to say that out loud.* That was low. I could see the hurt in my mom's eyes when she turned around.

"I'm sorry ma, I didn't mean for it to come out like that," I apologized.

"Yes you did. But it's okay. Lord knows I've made enough mistakes for the both of us."

It was quiet in the kitchen, aside from the noise my mom made while she cooked. I felt bad because I'm sure what I said stung a little. We haven't had the greatest relationship but I still love and respect my mom. I just hope she finds happiness one day.

"Hey, Nadia and I are about to hang out at the mall for a bit. Do you need anything while I'm out?"

"No. I think I have everything. Tell her I said hello."

I grabbed my purse and slid on my boots so that I could meet her downstairs. We lived in the same apartment complex so I knew she would be here any minute.

"Okay mom! I'll be back later!" I yelled as I grab my coat and went out of the door.

Just as I walked out of the building, Nadia pulled up. We've been friends since our freshman year of high school. She goes to Northern Illinois University and we haven't seen each other since we left for school, although we communicate through text and social media a lot.

"Hey Rizzy!" she yelled as she reached across the armrest in her car and gave me a hug. "What's been up?"

"Nothin' too much. Been laying low since I've been home, trying to make sure I don't fall off on my workouts. What about you?" I replied as I closed the door and put on my seatbelt.

"Been workin' at my part-time job mostly. Tryin' to avoid Darren while I'm home. That nigga just won't let go!" Nadia exclaimed.

"Damn! That's crazy but I truly understand. Remember how I told you Marcus was trippin' when I broke up with him. Although he's calmed down since then, thank God. I think since I found out he was fucking with that Tanisha girl and got her pregnant, he figured he really didn't have a chance of getting me back."

"That damn Darren has been blowin' up my phone, FB, Instagram, and my damn email. I'm like, really dude. It's over!" She laughed. "But wait, did you just say Marcus and Tanisha are together and she's pregnant."

"Yup, I thought I told you."

"Wow…interesting," Nadia said, deep in thought.

"Shit! Speak of the damn devil. This nigga ain't texted me in months, now look at this shit!" I yelled then read the text aloud.

Unknown: Hey! How are you? This is Marcus. I was wondering if we could meet for dinner tonight?

"Oh damn! Is he serious? Wow! Does he think you're trying to deal with his crazy ass? Are you gonna go?" Nadia fired all of these questions to me.

"Hell naw! I'm not even gonna reply!"

Unknown: Just one dinner Rizzy. Pleeaasse! I swear I won't bother you anymore afterwards. I just want to apologize in person.

"This nigga!" I said disgustingly, as I showed Nadia the text message.

"Damn, he's really acting thirsty."

"I thought I was rid of his ass." I said in disgust.

"Just reply and tell him no, then block his number."

"How about I'm gonna just block his number!" I went to the text messages and blocked the number.

Nadia and I continued to catch up with each other as we rode to the mall. She had a new boo as well and he sounds like a nice guy. Her ex, Darren, was texting her while we were together and I began to wonder why she didn't take the advice she gave me and block his ass. But honestly, it doesn't surprise me that she hasn't because she loves any kind of attention. Knowing her, she's probably giving him false hope.

After a bit of shopping, we decided to head to the food court and grab a bite to eat. We found a table and put our bags down, and she went up to get something first, while I sat with the bags. When she came back, it was my turn to do the same. I figured I'd go to the bathroom before I got my food. As I walked down the long hallway where the restrooms were located, I got a text message from Taylen.

TayBaby: What are you up to Pretty Girl?

Me: Nothin'. At Gurnee Mills with Nadia. About to eat something.

TayBaby: How long will you be there?"

Before I could reply, my face ended up in someone's chest. When I looked up, I saw that it was the last person I wanted to see.

"Marcus! What are you doing here?" I yelled as I backed away from him.

"What do you mean? It's a mall Rizzy."

"I just find it an odd coincidence that we are here at the same time and running into each other."

"I don't think it's odd at all." He said, slowly walking towards me. With each step he took forward, I took one back and ended up against a wall. Marcus was in front of me, standing so close that I could feel his breath on my face.

"Did you get my text about dinner?" he asked.

"Uh no," I lied.

"So you're a liar now Rizzy?"

"I'm not lying Marcus. Just move so I can go please." I attempted to push him and tried to go around him.

"Naw, I can't do that Rizzy. Unless you plan on leaving with me." He pushed me back against the wall.

"What?! I'm not goin' anywhere with you. Move the fuck out of my way Marcus!" I yelled and looked around to see if there was anyone that could help me.

"I suggest you keep your voice down and don't make a scene," he spoke through clenched teeth. I felt something hard pressed against my side. I looked down and this nigga had a gun pointed at my side. *What the fuck?*

"Are you fuckin' serious right now Marcus? You're about to force me at gunpoint to leave with you? You got a whole baby on the way with someone else. Why can't you just move on?" I tried to push away from him and he jammed the gun into my side.

"I will, when I get what's owed to me. Let's go!" He pushed me in the direction opposite of the food court.

"Wait! Can I just use the bathroom? I really have to go." He looked at me for a few seconds before he said anything.

"Yeah! But give me your purse and phone and don't do no dumb shit."

I quickly gave him my purse and phone and ran into the bathroom before he changed his mind. I thought he would try to come into the bathroom with me but he just stood in front of the door.

I ran into a stall and used the bathroom because I did really have to go. What Marcus didn't know is that I used an old iPhone to hold all of my music and that I could still send iMessages when connected to Wifi. I connected to the mall's free WIFI and quickly sent Taylen a message.

Me: This rizzy need help Marcus has gun taking me from mall now his address is 4321 hollow st

"Hurry the fuck up Rizzy!" Marcus yelled.

"I'm coming! Don't fuckin' rush me asshole!" I finished and washed my hands, shaking my head at myself for ever getting involved this crazy ass bastard in the first place. I can't believe this nigga has been following me. I forgot that he worked here as a janitor part-time while we were in high school. He knew all kinds of secret hallways and exits.

Chapter 49

Taylen

Unknown: This rizzy need help Marcus has gun taking me from mall now his address is 4321 hollow st

"The fuck?" I said when I finished reading the text. This is unbelievable! I read the text again, hoping that I had misread it the first time. My heart began to race as I tried to figure out how the hell this is happening.

"What?" Bishop questioned from the driver's seat.

We were about forty-five minutes from Gurnee Mills. Rizzy told me yesterday that she planned to hang out there with one of her friends. I was fiending to see her and convinced Bishop and his brother Bryant roll out there. The plan was to surprise her.

"Man, speed the fuck up! Marcus bitch ass just forced her to leave the mall at gunpoint!"

"What the fuck? Are you serious?" Bishop yelled.

"What kinda bitch you done went and hooked up with? Bitches getting kidnapped at gunpoint?" Bryant said from the front passenger seat.

"First of all, she ain't no bitch. Her ex-boyfriend just can't seem to let go."

"Damn! Her pussy must be platinum! You hit that yet?"

"Yeah but her ex never did. She was a virgin. That nigga crazy as fuck. All of this because she broke up with his ass. That's some crazy shit!"

"Do you think he'll hurt her? Maybe we should call the police," Bishop chimed in.

"You know we don't fuck with the law," Bryant responded, giving Bishop a look. Bryant stayed into some illegal shit. I know he wasn't trying to call the police. His ass probably got a warrant.

"I don't know. This shit makes no sense," I responded. "What kinda fuck ass nigga kidnaps his ex-girl because she don't want his ass? She sent me his address."

I put the address that Rizzy had sent me into my GPS and it said thirty-five minutes but we broke all kinda speed limits on the way there.

Chapter 50

Karizma

"I bet you think that nigga loves you! He's probably laid up with a bitch that's giving up the pussy right now!" Marcus laughed.

"Fuck you Marcus!"

"Oh, you will, soon enough!"

He took me to the spare room in the basement at his house. His dad wasn't home as far as I could tell. He didn't have me tied up or anything but he still had the gun out.

"Are you hungry or thirsty?" I responded with an eye roll.

"Look, you're gonna be here for a while so you may as well relax. We have a lot of catching up to do since you've been ignoring me for months." I gave him another eye roll and a loud sigh.

"Okay, I'll go grab you a bottle of water and a few of your favorite snacks." *Is he serious?*

I still said nothing so he went upstairs, after locking the door from the outside, to get the water and snacks. I sat on the edge of the bed, determined to continue the silent treatment.

As soon as I heard the door lock, I took out my spare phone, which I had stuck inside of my boot. My phone automatically connected to the WIFI because I had connected to it several times before when I visited his house. I sent Taylen a text right away.

Me: we are at his house u comin

TayBaby: gps says 15 mins

Me: N spare room in basement there is a window but not sure if it opens he has gun

TayBaby: OK. Has he hurt u?

Me: no just hurry. he thinks he getting some pussy

I heard him coming down the stairs so I slipped the phone back in my boot. He unlocked the door and this fool came in with roses and a tray with what looked like a lot of my favorite fruits and snacks. As hungry as I am, I didn't give a fuck. I ain't drinking or eating shit that he gives me.

"So you still on that silent bullshit Rizzy?" he asked, sitting the tray on the dresser that's in the room. I still said nothing. I was just praying that Taylen got to me before his ass decided to take this craziness even further.

"You need to eat and drink this water. You're gonna need this energy for the night I have planned for us." He rubbed his hands together and nodded his head, with a crazy smile on his face. *Who the hell is he, Stevie J?*

I turned my head because I didn't even want to look at him. I wanted to punch him in the face but I'm sure that would escalate this situation a lot quicker than I wanted it to go.

"Fine Rizzy, since you don't want to eat, we may as well move on with our evening. I have a lot planned." He stood up and took off his shirt and shoes.

Shit! Taylen said he'd be here in 15 minutes. Maybe I'll slowly eat something just to kill time.

Without saying anything, I grabbed the bowl of strawberries and grapes and began to nibble. I refused to drink the water because the bottle is open and he probably put some shit in it to make me a more willing participant.

"Take your time, Rizzy. We have plenty of it. My dad is out of town and nobody knows you're here."

I can't believe that I dated him for as long as I did and didn't know that he was crazy as hell. I could do nothing but glare at him angrily as I continued to nibble on the fruit while he played on his phone looking for music. He found a station on Pandora and turned the Bluetooth speaker up louder than necessary, but not so loud that I couldn't hear the bullshit that he said.

"Are you ready to be mine again, Rizzy? I gave you some time and space but you've taken this too far. I've been so patient with you all these months and you took my patience for granted. You owe me!"

"How do I owe you Marcus? It's not like you were actually waiting for me? You were fuckin' other people. You got a whole damn baby mama!"

"It's your fault that I had to look elsewhere Rizzy. I was willing to wait a few months for the pussy but you took that shit too far," he replied as he paced back and forth along the side of the bed.

"Well I'm glad I didn't give your crazy ass my virginity. Would have been the worst mistake ever!" I spat.

"Well I'm glad I was fuckin' your friends and didn't wait for your ass. But it's cool, cause you're about to pay up!" He was in my face with spit flying out of his mouth as he spoke.

"Yeah right! None of my friends would stoop low enough to fuck you behind my back. I don't believe that shit!"

"You sure about that Rizzy. Because Nadia was down from day one," he confessed.

"What! That's all you can come up with. You expect me to believe that you were fuckin' one of my best friends. Whatever Marcus! Fuck you!" I yelled in his face.

"How do you think I knew you'd be at the mall today? It wasn't a coincidence. Nadia has never been your friend. Not a real one anyway," he said calmly.

"I don't believe that shit."

I moved back on the bed, against the wall, to the corner. He grabbed the bowl of fruit that was in my hands and threw the bowl against the wall above my head, then pulled me back towards the edge of the bed by my foot. Pushing me so that I was lying on my back, he laid the top half of his body on top of mine.

"Stop it Marcus! Get the fuck off of me!" I screamed and slapped him as hard as I could.

"Are you fuckin' crazy Rizzy?!" he yelled. "You owe me! I'm gettin' this pussy!"

He grabbed my hands and held them above my head and tried to kiss me. I moved my head from side-to-side, causing him to miss my mouth each time he tried. Since I couldn't use my hands, I spit in his face and kneed him in his nuts. He fell to the floor, holding himself and cursing. I don't know why these niggas think they can come for me and I'm not gonna fight back.

I hopped off the bed and grabbed the gun that he left on the dresser. I turned and pointed it at him. "I will shoot you Marcus! Just let me go and I won't tell anyone, not the police, not anyone."

He turned to face me and started laughing. "Go ahead, Rizzy. Pull the trigger!" He laughed even harder, "Do it! Pull the trigger. Shoot me!"

"Just let me go Marcus! Unlock the door!"

"Naw, I want you to shoot me!"

Of course, I don't want to shoot him but he's giving me no choice. Panicking, I point the gun towards the door, thinking I'd shoot off the locks instead. I closed my eyes, pulled the trigger, and nothing. The gun clicked but nothing happened.

Marcus slowly got up and walked towards me and I turned the gun on him and pulled the trigger again, and again, nothing happened. Shit!

"There are no bullets in the gun Rizzy, so you can stop!" He laughed this evil and sadistic laugh. Before I knew it, he grabbed the gun from me and backhanded me so hard that my body flew into the wall and I fell to the floor.

"I didn't plan to hurt you Rizzy! But you're giving me no choice." He picked me up off of the floor and slapped me again.

"This is all your fault!" he yelled and grabbed me by the neck and choked me. Just as he raised his hand to hit me again, I heard a loud bang against the door. He was so startled that he turned in the direction of the sound and let me fall to the floor.

Chapter 51

Taylen

"Rizzy!" I yelled, as the door crashed against the wall. Marcus, understandably caught off guard, didn't even have a chance to turn all the way around before I grabbed him and punched him repeatedly in his face.

"You crazy muthafucka!" I yelled as I held him down by his neck and continuously punched him in the face. He didn't hit back at first because he was trying to block my punches. He was able to grab my wrist and he quickly took a swing at me and landed a punch on my jaw. That pissed me off even more!

Somehow, as we tussled, Marcus got away from me and we ended up outside of the bedroom in what I guess was the living area of the basement. There were a few pieces of furniture and a pool table.

"Why the fuck can't you get it through your head nigga? You just can't move the fuck on!" I told him as I grabbed a pool stick from the table and hit him across his knees with it. He screamed and fell to the floor. I threw the pool stick to the side and kicked him in his face. Blood spewed out of his mouth, splashing on the wall nearby. I then kicked him over and over, wherever my foot landed. Suddenly, I felt hands on my shoulders, pulling me back.

"Tay, man, that's enough!" Bishop reasoned.

"Fuck you mean, that's enough. I'm about to kill this nigga!"

"Naw man, you can't do that. How the hell are you gonna explain that? Calm the fuck down and think!" Bishop continued, while still holding me by the shoulders. I thought about what he said for a second and he's right.

"Where's Rizzy? Is she okay?" I asked at the same time that I walked back towards the room.

"She was passed out on the floor and I put her on the bed. She's bruised up, but she's good," Bishop answered as he kept an eye on Marcus.

"That muthafucka! Let's get her and get the fuck outta here." I walked back to the room and picked Rizzy up, cradle-style, and carried her upstairs.

"We need to leave before I change my mind about killing this nigga right now!" I told Bishop and Bryant.

"What do you want to do with this bitch?" Bryant asked, pointing to a girl that was sitting at the kitchen table.

"Where did she come from?" I asked Bryant, just as Rizzy started to wake up.

"I, umm, I'm---" the girl stuttered.

"You can't talk?" Bryant yelled. Rizzy jerked awake and glanced around the room. When her eyes landed on the girl, she literally jumped out of my arms and charged the girl.

"You bitch!" Rizzy screamed, as she pounced on the girl. "I should kill your fuckin' ass!" she continued as she threw blow after blow to the girl's face. Bishop, Bryant and I just stood there watching. I figured she had a good reason to beat her ass, so I let them go at it for a minute.

"You set me up! He was gonna rape me you stupid bitch!" The girl was trying to fight back but she wasn't fairing too well.

"I'm sorry Rizzy!" the girl screamed as she used her arms to shield her face. "I didn't know! I didn't know Rizzy!"

I finally decided to pull Rizzy off the girl but Rizzy wouldn't calm her ass down.

"Rizzy calm down baby." I tried putting my body in between her and the girl. Rizzy was still swinging and her little ass fist caught me on the jaw.

"Aye now Rizzy! Calm yo ass down! Chill baby!" I moved her to the other side of the kitchen as Bishop helped the girl off the floor.

"Rizzy, I swear I didn't know what he was gonna do. He said he just wanted to get you alone so he could talk things through. I'm sorry Rizzy!" The girl cried, apologizing to Rizzy. Her busted lip was already swelling. She also had a two black eyes.

"Are you sorry for fucking him too, Nadia?"

I looked at Nadia and her face was full of guilt but she said nothing.

"Yeah, he told me all about that shit. You lucky I don't give a shit about that punk ass nigga or I'd beat your ass some more. I thought you were my friend. Ya'll deserve each other!" Rizzy spat as she walked towards and then out of the door.

"I don't think we need to worry about this bitch. Let's go!" I said as I followed Rizzy out of the door.

"I need my purse Taylen. Can you go find it?" Rizzy asked me when I stepped outside. She was still breathing hard and pacing back and forth.

"Naw, I'll go. If I let him back in there, we may have two dead bodies," Bishop volunteered.

"Hey Sugar Ray, I'm Bryant, Bishop's brother." Bryant introduced himself, giving her his hand to shake. His goofy ass always trying to be funny.

"Uhh, hi. I'm Karizma. Nice to meet you," she replied, shaking his hand.

"Is this it Rizzy?" Bishop asked, as he walked back outside, hold up a purse.

"Yeah, thanks!" She grabbed it and began searching through it.

"Rizzy," I said, pulling her close to me, "look at me baby." She looked up at me and her eyes began to gloss over. "Are you okay?"

She put her head into my chest and said, "Why can't he just leave me alone, Taylen?" Tears spilled down her cheek and that pissed me off all over again.

"I don't know Pretty Girl. He's crazy but don't worry about him right now. Look at me, let me see your face." She held her head up and her face is bruised up pretty badly. I had to mentally count to ten to calm myself down because I wanted to go back in that house and stomped a hole in that muthafucka.

"I'm sure it looks worse than it feels. I'm fine."

"Let's get you home."

Chapter 52

Hazel

Thanksgiving day with my family was great but I am missing Bishop like crazy. On Black Friday, I went shopping with my sisters and came back home to a beautiful flower arrangement that Bishop had delivered. The note inside said that he was counting down the minutes until he would see me again. One more day and I can show him how much I miss him.

We've been in constant contact with each other but it's still not enough. He told me what happened with Karizma and I couldn't believe that shit. I called her but she didn't feel like talking so I can't wait to see her and get the scoop. Bishop told me some of the details but I need to hear it from her.

"Hazel, someone is at the door for you." My sister Hayley stuck her head inside the room we shared.

"You don't know who it is?" I asked as I sat up from my comfortable lying position.

“Yup but go see for yourself,” she stated and walked away.

I let out a disgruntled breath and made my way to the front door. When I saw the person standing by the door, my heart skipped a beat. I haven’t seen him since before I left for school. Why is he here? Looking so damn good, I might add!

“Ricky, umm, wha--what are you doing here?” I stammered.

“I wanted to see you.” He walked towards me and pulled me into a hug.

I ain’t gon’ lie. It felt so damn good to be in his arms. So good that I didn’t push him away like I should have, not right away.

“Umm, how have you been?” I asked when I finally willed myself away from him and took a few steps back.

“Good. I miss you though. You been good?” He closed the space again, then grabbed and held my hands.

“I’ve been fine. How’s school? And basketball?” I nervously pulled my hands from his and took another step back.

“It’s all good. Today is the only day that I could come home. I gotta head back soon. I took a chance stopping by here. I needed to see you. Hazel I miss you so much. I’m so sorry about everything. I know I fucked up a lot and you didn’t deserve that baby. I’ve been wanting to talk to you to tell you how sorry I am but you kept blocking me. I just---I need you to know how sorry I am. Do you think we can try again?” Ricky poured out his heart.

He closed the space between us again. His closeness made me lightheaded and I couldn’t think. I’m trying to find the words to respond to him but nothing is coming to mind.

"Do you forgive me baby?" he asked with pleading eyes.

"Ricky I---" I began.

Before I could answer, the doorbell rang. I looked behind Ricky and I saw none other than Bishop standing on the other side of the screen door because the front door was open. *What the hell?* I quickly walked around Ricky to open the screen door.

"Bishop!" I exclaimed.

"Haze!" Bishop returned. He stepped inside and wrapped me in his arms so tight, burying his face into my neck and planting kisses there. I felt good in Ricky's arms, I'll admit. But this, being in Bishop's arms, this is what I've been missing and longing for.

"I've missed you baby," Bishop said. He cupped my face with his hands, kissed my lips and took a step back to look at me.

"What are doing here?" I asked, forgetting that Ricky was there.

"Tay's dad bought him a car, so we decided to leave today. Karizma is outside in the car too," he replied.

"Ah hem," Ricky cleared his throat, gaining our attention. Bishop looked in his direction and I turned around.

"Oh, uhh, Bishop, this is umm, Ricky. Ricky, this is my boyfriend, Bishop," I nervously introduced them.

"Ricky?" Bishop spoke as he looked back and for the between Ricky and I. "What the fuck are you doing here?" He took a few steps towards Ricky.

"It's really none of your business why I'm here. But um, Hazel, we can finish this another time," Ricky dismissed Bishop, stepped around him and walked towards the door.

"Naw ya'll ain't finishing shit at no time, so I hope you said all you need to say," Bishop said to Ricky's back as he reached for the door handle.

"Nigga, I was two seconds from having my girl back before you walked in. Don't get it twisted. A girl never forgets her first everything." Ricky winked at me and walked out of the door. No this nigga didn't!

Bishop frowned at me and went to the door and yelled after Ricky, "She does when her last is the best she's ever had. Don't you get it twisted nigga. The fuck outta here!"

He let the screen door close and turned back to me with a scowl on his face. He leaned up against the doorframe, then folded his arms across his chest.

"You ain't got shit so say Haze?" he asked after about thirty seconds of staring me down.

"Uhh not really. I didn't know he was coming over here just like I didn't know you were coming."

"But I'm your man Hazel. What the fuck did he want?"

"He was only here for five minutes before you came. All he did was apologize. If he wanted anything else, he didn't tell me," I lied.

Bishop looked at me with his mouth twisted up like he didn't believe me.

"Why are you looking at me like that? We were still standing by the door and he had his coat on. He had just got here Bishop." I told him again. When he didn't budge, I took the few steps it took to be standing in front of him and pecked his lips.

"His ass ain't come over here just to apologize. Don't even communicate with him no more." Bishop is jealous and it's so adorable. He put his hands around my waist. "Fucking up my surprise and shit." He gave me a lingering kiss.

"No he didn't. I'm so happy you're here. Go get Taylen and Rizzy so ya'll can meet some of my family. Everybody ain't here but you can meet whoever is here."

He went outside to get them and I checked my phone because I felt it buzz just as he left. It was a text from an unknown number.

Unknown: No matter what happens, I still love you. I'll wait for you. RS.

I'm not gonna even reply to Ricky's ass. Mighty funny he didn't give a damn about my feelings when I caught his ass with his dick in some bitches mouth but now he loves me and is willing to wait for me. Boy Bye! I deleted the text and put my phone in my back pocket.

Chapter 53

Karizma

Before I knew it, the first semester of college is over and it's time to go back home for Winter Break. I am pleased with how this semester ended. We had our first track meet last weekend at Illinois State and my team won the meet. I also won the 400-meter dash and my relay team won the mile relay. It felt good to finally compete after training for so long. My grades could have been better but I earned one A and four B's. Honestly, I'm cool with that.

After the crazy Thanksgiving Break, I don't want to go home at all. Marcus didn't come back to finish out the semester and I'm glad I didn't have to worry about him on campus. Hopefully the same goes for my time at home. Nadia's ass blew my damn phone up for several days after I beat her ass but I finally blocked her number and all of her social media pages. I'm done with that hoe.

I finished packing my two bags just as Hazel came out of the bathroom. Since Taylen has a car now, we are all riding home together. Hazel is going home with Bishop for a week or so. I'm taking my ass home because my mama ain't having it. We only get three weeks for break, instead of four like everyone else, because we have to come back early to train for a track meet. I'm gonna go back to Peoria when Hazel goes and we will head back to school from there when it's time.

"The guys are on their way up to get our bags. Are you ready?" Hazel asked, pulling me out of my thoughts.

"As ready as I'm gonna be. I'm mad my mom trippin' and I can't chill with Taylen for a few days at his house," I complained. I put my bag on the floor and laid on my bed.

"I know that sucks. I think my mom is going through some shit with my dad. She's never been real strict but I was surprised she was cool with it. They did hit it off when ya'll popped up at my house after Thanksgiving."

A knock on the door ended that conversation. Hazel let the guys in and as soon as Taylen saw me on the bed, he got right on top me and kissed all over my face.

"Taylen, you are too heavy!"

"You didn't say that last night!" he teased.

Yes, since we got back from Thanksgiving Break, which was only a couple of weeks ago, we can't keep our hands off of each other. It works out that Hazel and I are roommates who are dating roommates. I can't get enough of his ass and I'm still trying to figure out how I held on to my virginity as long as I did.

"Shut up and get off of me. We aren't alone."

"They ain't paying us no mind," he murmured into my neck. Sure enough, I look over to the other side of the room and Bishop had Hazel against her dresser tonguing her down. I focused my attention on Taylen until I felt his hard dick pressing against my center.

"Damn Pretty Girl, you feel what you did." He whispered in my ear.

"I didn't do nothing. You know we are about to leave so I don't know why you started and we can't finish," I whispered back.

"Like hell we can't!" He got up and his erection was on display through is sweats. Damn that thing looks like a third leg for real.

"Aye we'll be right back," Taylen told them and pulled me up from the bed and out of the room before I could protest.

"Baby, what happened to you wanting to leave at a certain time?" I asked as he dragged me down the hall to the stairwell.

"I need some of my good-good first. Now hurry up so we can hit the road!" he said and continued to pull me all the way to his room.

Chapter 54

Taylen

I know we are on a time schedule but fuck it. I need to slide up in my pretty girl before we hit the road. I never thought that I could feel so strongly about a girl, so quickly, especially at such a young age. I swear Karizma is it for me. I haven't said the words to her yet but I'm pretty sure I love her. When we got to my door, I quickly unlocked it, pulled her into the room, and immediately closed and locked door.

"Taylen, why you acting like you ain't never had none? Last night wasn't that long ago." She giggled as she leaned against my dresser.

"Cause with you, every time is like the first time," I grabbed the hem of my shirt and pulled it over my head, then tossed it on the floor. "C'mere." I reached my hand out to her. I was near my bed so there was some space between us.

Karizma stepped forward and removed her sweatshirt and was wearing a tank top underneath. As much as I fuss about it, she acts like bras aren't in her wardrobe. She pushed me back on the bed and I admired her beauty while she removed her shoes and pants. In the short amount of time that we've been having sex, I realized that my baby is a bit of a freak. She definitely has no issues taking what she wants. She stood there in her panties and tank top, with the look of seduction in her eyes.

As she straddled me, my dick began to throb. She leaned down and took my bottom lip between her teeth and gently pulled before sticking her tongue in my mouth. We kissed briefly, before I moved my mouth down to suck her neck, leaving marks.

I guess she couldn't take it anymore, so she kissed and licked her way down my chest until she made it to the waistband of my basketball shorts. Reaching inside, she grabbed my dick and pulled it out. She looked up at me as she gripped my rod with a questioning look in her eyes. She's never attempted to give me head and I have never pressured her to do so. Her pussy is A-1 so getting head is secondary.

What she did next shocked the hell outta me. She lowered her head down to my dick and licked the precum on the tip. I let out a quiet moan because it's been awhile since I've felt the softness of a tongue.

Karizma licked up and down my ten and a half inches a few times before spitting on the head and taking my full length in her mouth. Fuck! She been holding out. She bobbed her head up and down, unable to take in my full length without gagging. Regardless of her lack of experience, she had me about to bust. I stopped her before I filled her mouth up and she looked slightly disappointed. Ignoring her questioning eyes, I reached under the bed to grab a condom from the box I kept under there. I promised myself that I would wrap up after that first time and I've held myself to it. Neither of us could take the risk of her birth control failing.

I took my basketball shorts off and repositioned myself on the bed. I opened the condom and slid it on while Karizma removed her panties and tank top. She straddled me again and eased my dick inside of her. Karizma has the best pussy I've ever had and every time it's a struggle to not moan like a bitch.

"Ahhh, Taylen," she whispered. When I say every time is like the first time, I mean that shit. Her pussy is so tight and the fact that I'm the only one that's ever been with keeps my dick on rock.

"You like that shit huh?"

"Naw, I love this dick baby!" she whispered.

"I know you do. Ride this dick Pretty Girl!"

When I felt her walls tightening up, I flipped her over so that I was on top and put her legs on my shoulders. I was digging into her pussy so deep that I swear I was touching her tonsils.

"Taylen, oh baby, I'm finna cum!"

"Let that shit go!

"Ahh shit! Oh fuck, shit baby!" She tried not to yell but it was a lost cause.

"This my pussy Rizzy? Huh? Is this my pussy baby?"

"Yes, baby, it's yours. All yours! I'm finna cu---oh shit, I'm cummin'! Oh my Goooodddd!"

My dick pulsed and three more hard strokes and released my load inside the condom. Shit! Too bad we don't have time for a nap.

We laid there for about twenty minutes before either of us moved. Luckily, Karizma had a few pieces of clothing in one of my drawers. We showered before going back upstairs to let Hazel and Bishop know that we were ready to hit the road. When we got to her room, she knocked to make sure we didn't walk in on anything.

We heard the lock and Hazel swung the door open. "Ya'll horny asses ready," she teased.

"Don't try to act like ya'll wasn't in here doing the same thing," Karizma threw back at her.

Bishop and I smirked at each other and grabbed their bags. Ours were already in the car.

"You sure got everything Pretty Girl?" I asked.

"Yup, now let's go!" Everyone trailed out and Karizma locked the door.

*****

The ride home went quickly. It was much better than taking the train, that's for damn sure. We only stopped once to use the bathroom and are now within twenty minutes of Bishop's house.

"Hazel are you nervous about meeting Bishop's family?" Karizma asked.

"No, not really. I've met most of them on FaceTime so it should be cool," she replied as she looked out of the window.

"Well his brother Bryant is a piece of work. He'll have you crackin' up." Karizma laughed and Hazel agreed.

"Yeah, Bryant is stupid as –," I began to chime in but my phone rang through the car speakers.

It's Imani. I looked at Rizzy and she gave me the side-eye and told me to answer the phone.

"Wassup Imani?" I answered.

"This ain't Imani. You need to come to the hospital. Something is wrong with Imani and the baby," Amari, Imani's sister said.

Over the Thanksgiving Break, I found out that Imani is indeed pregnant. She's far enough along that the baby could be mine but my gut is telling me it's not. Being away at school, I haven't thought about it a lot and Imani and I only communicate if necessary and it really hasn't been.

"How the hell is she in labor? It's too early." I'm confused as hell. She is only about five and a half months, maybe six months.

"We don't know what's wrong. Just get here as soon as you can," Amari said.

"Well I just pulled up in the city. What hospital?"

"St. Bernard."

I changed my route and headed in that direction. This is about to be a fucked-up situation. I hope Karizma rides with a nigga until the wheels fall off.

To Be Continued

Thank you for reading and I hope you come back for Part 2 of this college love story. I appreciate your support and would love it if you could leave a review on Amazon. Please like my Facebook page Kay Shanee's Reading Korner, follow me on Instagram @AuthorKayShanee, and check out my website at www.AuthorKayShanee.com for updates and news.

Other books by Kay Shanee

Love Hate and Everything in Between